the
book o

This item was purchased for the Library
through the Zip Books for Rural Libraries
Project, supported in whole or in part by the
U.S. Institute of Museum and Library Services
under the provisions of the Library Services
and Technology Act
California by the

D0955008

book of luke

the
book of luke

jenny o'connell

POCKET BOOKS   MTV BOOKS
New York London Toronto Sydney

POCKET BOOKS, a division of Simon & Schuster, Inc.
1230 Avenue of the Americas, New York, NY 10020

ISBN-13: 978-1-4165-2040-5
ISBN-10:   1-4165-2040-6

This MTV Books/Pocket Books trade paperback edition April 2007

10   9   8   7   6   5   4   3   2   1

For my son, Tanner, who's
perfect just the way he is.

acknowledgments

Here's where I thank the people who challenge me to work extra hard: my editor, Jennifer Heddle, and my agent, Kristen Nelson. And the people who make sure I have fun when I'm not working: John, Carleigh, and Tanner.

the
book of luke

book of luke

prologue

My parents waited in the cab with TJ while Sean and I stood together on our front walk. It was the same front walk where we'd shared innumerable good-night kisses, held hands, and even taken a tumble in the bushes once after I jumped on him for a piggyback ride. So it wasn't like we'd never stood on the flagstone path before. But this time it was totally different. And not just because it was barely eight o'clock on a Saturday morning.

"I'm going to miss you," I told Sean, my chin tucked into my neck as I attempted to keep from freezing to death right there in the middle of our good-bye. It was maybe twenty degrees out and a few snowflakes were falling. I watched as the wet flecks landed on Sean's jacket and melted, leaving small dark brown spots on the khaki coat—a coat I had gotten him for Christmas, I might add. Actually, the color was called "saddle" in the L.L.Bean catalog, and it took me a week to decide whether Sean would look better in the light brown (to match his hair) or mallard blue (to match his eyes). I ended up going with the saddle field coat with the Primasoft liner (comfort rated to minus-25 below, something I thought would come in handy in Chicago)—size large.

"Me, too," Sean answered and then licked the last remaining smears of cream cheese off his fingers before digging his hands deep into his coat pockets. I'd made sure the toaster oven wasn't packed until this morning so I could make Sean one last sesame bagel with cream cheese. His favorite. "But it will be fine."

Fine? Was he kidding me? Moving right after Christmas was bad enough. That my father had decided at the last minute to stay behind in Chicago to "tie up some loose ends" made it even worse. Add in the fact that it was my senior year, and the situation truly sucked.

I glanced over at the idling cab, where my mom was tapping on the backseat window and pointing to her watch.

"I'd better go." I wiggled my toes and tried to get feeling back in my left foot. "If we miss the plane, my mom will kill me."

Sean dug his hands deeper into his Primasoft-lined pockets. "Sure."

Still, I didn't make a move. There was the small lingering matter of a conspicuous bulge in Sean's right coat pocket, a bulge that I was sure contained some sort of going-away present—nothing huge, just *something* he'd want to give me as a little reminder of him, a memento of our four months together.

"You know, Emily, I was thinking about it, and we should probably end this right here."

Great idea. I was all for ending the waiting. I practically held out my hands waiting for the little gift box that meant Sean was going to miss me as much as I was going to miss him. "Okay."

Sean moved his arm, pulling his hand out of his left pocket for the first time since he arrived to say good-bye. Only he wasn't holding a beautifully wrapped velvet box with satin ribbon, but a wad of Taco Bell napkins!

"It's better this way—it'd just be too hard to keep things going with you all the way in Boston," he continued, and all I could think was, *What is he talking about?*

"So you're okay with that?" Sean asked. "With breaking up?"

Wait. A. Minute. Breaking up? He was breaking up with me? On my front walk? With my parents and brother watching us from a yellow taxi? At eight o'clock on a Saturday morning—the very morning I was moving to Boston?

"You want to break up?" I repeated, but my words were drowned out by the honk of the cab's horn reminding me we had a plane to catch.

"I think you'd better go." Sean wiped a crusty smudge of leftover cream cheese from his cheek and stuffed the napkins back in his pocket.

He stepped aside so I could pass, and even though I wanted to drop to the frozen ground right there and cry, what could I do? Cling to his leg, begging him not to leave me? I may have just lost my boyfriend, but I still had my pride. There was no way I'd let Sean see me with frozen tears hanging from my lashes like icicles.

As I walked past Sean—brushing against the sleeve of the coat that *I* paid for with my own hard-earned money (okay, so working behind the desk of a public library wasn't exactly hard, but it was still earned)—I wanted to tell him he was making a mistake. I wanted to remind him that we'd been together for four months, four *amazing* months. I wanted to put him in his place, to tell him I was better off without him. I wanted to tell Sean to go fuck himself.

But when I turned back to face him, the words that escaped from my chapped lips weren't the ultimate put-down—they were the ultimate in humiliation.

"I love you," I told him, my breath creating puffs around the words in the cold morning air.

"I love you," for God's sake! *This* was when I chose to tell the guy I loved him? When he's breaking up with me and holding a wad of shredded paper napkins imploring him to "run for the border"?

What was wrong with me? Even when my boyfriend's breaking up with me I don't have what it takes to be mean, to say what I really think. It made me want to scream.

But I didn't scream. Instead, I crawled into the backseat of the cab next to my fourteen-year-old brother, who just happened to be wearing my Brown University sweatshirt, rubbing yet another failure in my face. Reminding me of yet another guy—this one with gold wire-rim glasses and a name badge that read RONALD PARKER, DIRECTOR OF ADMISSIONS—who lured me into a false sense of security only to crush me in less time than it took to read a letter that began: *On behalf of the admissions committee, I regret to inform you . . .*

"All set?" My dad looked over his shoulder into the backseat, the third guy in my triple play of devastation. My trifecta of mortification and disappointment. The Bermuda triangle that in the past two weeks had become my life.

"All set," I answered, and then sat back in the pine-scented cab and attempted to smile. Not because I was "all set." Or because I was thrilled with the idea of moving to Boston. Or because the scene on my now-former front walk of my now-former house was just dandy with me. Or because the damn letter from Director of Admissions Ronald Parker was a lovely piece of correspondence.

No, I smiled because that's what nice girls do. I smiled and fixed my eyes on the reflection in the rearview mirror, because the girl staring back at me really did look like she was "all set." Even though I knew that beneath the red nose and wind-burned cheeks, everything was all wrong.

chapter one

There are two problems with being the daughter of a best-selling etiquette guru. The first one is that everyone assumes you know how to do everything right. The second is that 99 percent of the time, you live with the fear you're doing everything wrong.

"You can't be serious!" I yelled when my parents broke the news to me. From the look on my mother's face, there was no doubt that yelling was the wrong thing to do in this situation. I did, however, resist the urge to fold my arms defiantly across my chest. It was one thing to stand my ground. It was another to look like a spoiled brat doing it. "There's no way I'm going."

My dad sat on the edge of my bed rubbing his knees while my mom waited for me to calm down so she could continue.

"We realize this isn't the best timing," she tried again, but I wasn't going for it.

"It's not just bad timing, it's halfway through my senior year. You can't expect me to leave my friends and everything right before graduation. I'm supposed to be the class valedictorian, for God's sake!"

Apparently my academic achievements weren't as important as the fact that my father's company was transferring him back to Boston, because my mother didn't even skip a beat. It almost made me wonder if she'd written a chapter on this in one of her books: Breaking Big News without Breaking a Sweat.

"I think you're making this out to be worse than it is," she went on, and then started rattling off all the wonderful, exciting things about moving "back to Boston." She kept saying "back to Boston" instead of "leaving Chicago," like somehow her choice of words would make it better. As if the fact that we used to live there made it easier.

"It's like going home," my mother insisted.

"No, it's like moving," I told her, and then added, "It's even worse than moving." At least if you moved somewhere new, you had an excuse for people not liking you—they didn't know you. But when you were moving back to the same town you lived in for most of your life, going back to the same school you once attended, the possibility that people you once liked, and who once liked *you*, might not want anything to do with you anymore, was slightly horrifying to say the least.

I glanced over at my dad, who was still sitting on my bed staring at his khaki-covered knees as if they were infinitely more fascinating than the conversation taking place around them.

"This isn't fair," I told him, and he looked up at me with an expression of total innocence. Like none of this was his fault, and yet, he was the reason we were having this conversation in the first place. He was the reason the rest of my senior year was going to suck.

"Can't you tell them you'll move in May after graduation?" I pleaded, and for the first time since he came into my room my dad decided to speak.

Only instead of telling me what I wanted to hear, he shook his head. "Can't do that, Em."

"Look, it's all decided. We'll move right after Christmas." My mom laid a hand on my shoulder and squeezed lightly. I'm sure it was supposed to reassure me, but it just made me even angrier. While my mother said all the right things as usual, my father just sat there like none of this was fault. But it was. All of it.

"Maybe I could stay with Jackie or Lauren until school's out," I suggested in an attempt to try and rectify what was left of my senior year. "It's just a few months."

"Absolutely not." My mom shook her head and didn't even bother looking to my dad for agreement. She was handling this because obviously Patricia Abbott knew the right way to handle every awful, unpleasant situation. "Come on," she chided, giving me a smile that I knew I was expected to reciprocate. "Everything's going to be fine. Promise."

She "promised," as if that was supposed to make me feel better. It didn't. And looking back on it, it just goes to show that even America's number one syndicated etiquette columnist isn't always right.

Six weeks later, our cab pulled up to the sidewalk in front of the United Airlines terminal. We probably looked totally normal, a family of four heading off on some warm tropical vacation right after Christmas. But even though four people exited the taxi, only three of us had our luggage. And the person who was responsible for ruining my senior year wasn't holding a plane ticket.

"Looks like that's everything," my dad told us as he placed two suitcases and TJ's Nike duffel bag on the sidewalk.

The cabdriver must have known this wasn't going to be a typical heartwarming family moment, and was smart enough to slip back into the driver's seat after closing the trunk.

" 'Bye, Dad." TJ was the first to say it, which figured. He seemed to be totally unscathed by all of this, completely oblivious to the fact that my father had single-handedly wrecked everything. My younger brother was always the problem child, so how did I end up being the difficult one in this situation? "I'll miss you."

While they shared a touching father-son moment, complete with hugs and manly pats on the back, I hung back by the sliding glass doors, grateful for the bursts of warm air that escaped every time a passenger entered.

There was no way my father would be getting a hug from me. And I wasn't about to tell him he was going to be missed.

When my dad told my mom he'd decided to stay behind in Chicago for a while, she actually thought he meant he'd decided we should *all* stay behind in Chicago for a while. Forget that we'd already sold our house, bought a new home in Branford, sent our transcripts back to Heywood Academy, and had a moving truck scheduled to haul all of our earthly possessions away in less than fifteen days. What bothered my mother the most about his news was that she'd already mailed the *We're Moving!* announcements to everyone on the Abbott family's Christmas card list. Apparently my dad had cleared it with his company and was going to stay in Chicago for a few months before making the transition. Too bad he hadn't cleared that with the rest of us.

"Emily?" My mom gave me a look that meant I was next in line for this Hallmark moment. I was expected to wrap my arms around my dad and act like all was forgiven. And I just couldn't do that. I couldn't pretend that the three of us were simply taking a trip instead of acknowledging what was really going on—my father was ditching us.

"It's cold, I'm ready to head inside," I told them and then grabbed the handle of my suitcase and picked it up before my dad could reach for a hug. My dad didn't deserve hugs and teary good-byes. " 'Bye, Dad."

Maybe he felt guilty about leaving us or maybe my mom had trained him well enough to avoid a scene in front of the skycaps, but whatever the reason my dad didn't force the issue. TJ, on the other hand, looked like he wanted to kill me. It had been that way ever since the second big announcement—TJ just didn't get it.

Finally my mom stepped forward and I waited for the explosion, the argument, or pointing of fingers that I knew was supposed to happen in a situation like this, but that, for some reason, never seemed to happen. Instead I watched two people have a conversation that seemed as civilized and rational as every other conversation they'd had over the past six weeks. And it annoyed me to no end. Was I the only one who wasn't willing to act like this was okay?

"Call me when you get in," my dad instructed us one last time before opening the cab's back door to get in. And then he looked directly at me. "Have a safe flight."

My mom, TJ, and I watched as my father pulled away and waved to us from the backseat of the cab. And because I'm nice, because I am my mother's daughter, instead of telling him what a shitty thing he was doing, I did the polite thing and waved back.

•   •   •

Our flight was delayed—of course. Was it too much to ask that at least one thing go right this morning? Wasn't it enough that I had to be frisked by a stranger wielding a beeping black wand after I set off the security alarm? Or that the female security officer waved the wand around my right boob so many times the line of passengers behind me must have thought she was casting a magic spell on my 34Bs? If I'd have known my underwire would be mistaken for a national security threat I would have worn a running bra and saved myself the humiliation.

"Want a mint?" my mom asked, holding out a roll of peppermint LifeSavers. My mother was strictly old school when it came to fresh breath. No tins of atomic Altoids for her.

She probably assumed the frown on my lips was due to a mild case of bad breath. Unfortunately, peppermint wasn't going to help my situation. Besides, with a lump in my throat, I wasn't sure I'd be able to swallow.

I shook my head slowly, fearing any vigorous movement would release the tears that were currently blurring my vision.

"I know this is hard on you, all of it, but we'll get through this," she assured me. Just like she did when our cat, Snickers, got hit by a car and we discovered her on our front steps whimpering and licking a broken leg. Or when TJ needed stitches after falling off his bike and I was convinced he was going to die (I was eight at the time and still relished my role as the big sister—I was over that by the time I was ten). Or even when I received the deferral letter from Brown and thought I might hyperventilate right there in the kitchen. My mom was always assuring me. Maybe that's a mother's job, but I had to wonder how, after all that had happened, she still managed to believe we'd get through this. Or maybe she didn't. Maybe she was trying to convince me as much as she was trying to convince herself.

"Come on, don't look so sad." My mom pushed my bangs off my forehead so she could look straight into my watery eyes. "You might actually discover you like being back in Boston."

I highly doubted it, but I didn't tell her that. I also didn't tell her about Sean.

One of the reasons I didn't tell my mother about Sean's driveway confession is that I knew what she'd say: "That boy needs to learn some manners." It was pretty much her cure-all for all societal unpleasantries, from people who tried to cut in front of her at the grocery store to children who cry in restaurants while their parents pretend they can't hear them. She truly believed that we'd all get along just fine if everyone knew the proper way to behave. So, while I knew she would have felt bad for me and offered a sympathetic hug after finding out about Sean, I also knew that she'd be planning to write about the correct way to break off a relationship for her next column, perhaps adding that a cotton hanky should be on hand (Polite Patty, as TJ and I once nicknamed her, hated paper tissues). It was just easier to let her believe that I was a mess because we were leaving Chicago.

My mother's nationally syndicated etiquette column runs in newspapers all over the country, which means no matter where I am, I can always get advice from my mom. I used to wish she wrote under a pseudonym instead of her real name, Patricia Abbott. That way, nobody would expect me to know the right way to eat an artichoke or ask me which fork to use for the endive salad (just for the record, you start with the utensil on the outside and work your way in). But, having a mother who knows exactly when you can wear white, who can teach you how to deposit a lemon pit discreetly in your napkin so nobody notices, and who gives you monogrammed stationery every year for your birthday (for thank-you cards, of course) does rub off on you. Which is why, instead of sobbing into a snot-soaked Dunkin Donuts napkin at gate B13, I used small puffs and folded it in half after each discreet blow.

The middle seat. In the last row. The row that doesn't recline, but does put you up close and intimate with every single flush taking place in the lavatory on the other side of the cardboard-thin wall. Not to mention the postlavatory smells emanating from passengers who sat in the gate area for two hours wolfing down bratwurst and burritos with a Cinnabon chaser while the woman behind the United Airlines desk announced yet another delay due to the snowstorm in Boston.

Yes, the middle seat in the last row was the perfect ending to a perfectly crappy morning. The fact that I was stuffed between TJ and a woman who had obviously never been taught to share the armrest, but *had* learned that chewing Big Red gum as loudly and rapidly as possible will reduce the effects of cabin pressure, was just the icing on the cake.

"Why do you insist on wearing that?" I asked TJ, my eyes not actually looking at him. You'd think that we would have become allies through this ordeal with my dad, but instead the opposite had happened. It almost seemed like the angrier I felt, the harder TJ tried to see my dad's side in all of this, almost protective of him. TJ didn't get it at all.

"What?" he asked.

I couldn't bring myself to say "my sweatshirt." But it was my sweatshirt, emblazoned with BROWN in capital letters across the front. Only now it should say FAILURE, or LOSER. Or maybe IDIOT, since I'd believed the guy in the admissions office when he'd told me I was a shoo-in (okay, those weren't his exact words, he'd actually said something like, "you'd make a wonderful addition to the class of 2011," but the implication was the same).

"You know what I'm talking about," I told him. "Don't tell me it's a coincidence that you've found a new favorite sweatshirt."

"What, this old thing?" TJ pointed to his chest. "It's just comfortable."

He wasn't fooling me. I knew the sweatshirt was his way of rubbing it in. It was no secret in my family—I was the good kid and TJ wasn't. Not that he was bad. TJ didn't hotwire cars or skip school or spray-paint gang signs on little old ladies' homes. My brother just wasn't like me. Nobody expected him to be perfect. And they certainly didn't expect him to get into Brown.

"Whatever." I flipped the page in the catalog on my lap, indicating our conversation had come to an end.

During a two-hour delay that seemed to last six days, I'd burned through the thirty dollars' worth of magazines I'd bought for the trip, and had even, in utter desperation, resorted to reading my mother's *Smithsonian* and the ingredients of my third Snickers bar. So when we finally boarded the plane and my seat front pocket offered 112 glossy pages of SkyMall glory, I grabbed it. And was thankful. Finally I had something to take my mind off what was happening—and what was happening to me.

But somewhere between the cat-friendly self-cleaning litter box and the digital camera/spy pen, my window seat neighbor decided that chewing gum at a rate ten times the speed of the jet engines outside her window wasn't enough. She wanted to carry on a conversation, as well.

"Is Boston your final destination?" she asked me, as if, after listening to gate announcements all morning, airport-speak had rubbed off on her.

I nodded, and waited for her to ask if my carry-ons were properly stowed in the overhead compartment.

"I was visiting my son in Chicago for Christmas," she told me. "And my new granddaughter. She's just one month old."

I smiled and told her what I figured she wanted to hear. After all, I was nothing if not well-mannered. "That sounds like fun."

She smiled back. "What about you? Did you have a nice holiday?"

I should have just said "fine" and stopped there. I should have just given her the standard answer everyone uses for seemingly innocuous questions like "how are you?" and "how's your day going?" I should have just said "good" and left it at that.

I knew that was the polite thing to do. But I was tired of being polite and I was sick of being nice.

Maybe it was that I'd had my fill of recirculated air or that I'd reached my tolerance for the constant rattling of the beverage cart, but more likely it was that I'd been up since six o'clock that morning and had already eaten my way through the top row of the candy counter in the Hudson newsstand. And so, even though I knew I was expected to say something courteous, I told her the truth.

"My holiday sucked."

"Oh." For the first time since we sat down, she took her elbow off the armrest. "I'm sorry."

She was sorry. Funny how a complete stranger can be sorry, yet a guy I'd known for two years and dated for four months didn't even think to apologize after he told me he didn't think we should see each other anymore. *It would just be too hard.* Who was Sean kidding? What he really meant was, *I'm a lazy shit who will forget you the moment your cab drives away.*

In psychology class we'd learned about the five stages of grief.

Of course, Sean wasn't dead (even though the idea was becoming more appealing by the minute), but those five stages also happened to fit my current situation perfectly. In the four hours between leaving Sean in my driveway and hearing the captain tell us we'd be traveling at thirty-seven thousand feet, I figured I'd gone through four of the five stages, and added a new one that Kübler-Ross forgot.

1. *Denial.* I kept telling myself that there was no way Sean just broke up with me. There was no way my boyfriend would dump me at eight o'clock on a Saturday morning in my very own driveway while my family watched from an idling cab. There was just no way. There had to be a mistake. Sean never was much of a morning person.

2. *Anger.* I hated him. More than I'd ever hated anybody in my entire life. Even more than I hated Curtis Ludlow after he told our entire sixth grade class I was the one who stepped in the dog crap and wiped it off on the front steps of the school.

3. Kübler-Ross called it *grief,* but I'm going to call it what it was—my heart breaking. Sitting there in gate B13, I swear I could feel my heart shriveling up inside my chest. I could feel everything Sean ever found lovable draining out of me onto the coffee-stained carpet. Even with hundreds of passengers swirling around me in the gate area, I felt completely and utterly alone.

4. *Bargaining.* Maybe if I let him think about it for a few days he'd realize he'd made a mistake. Maybe if I hadn't insisted he come over this morning to say good-bye, he'd still be at home in bed wishing he could give me one last kiss. Maybe if the plane suddenly plunged toward the

earth at mach speed and Sean came *thisclose* to losing me forever, he'd realize he couldn't live without me.

5. Kübler-Ross claimed the fifth stage was *acceptance*. Acceptance, my ass. The fifth stage is *Fury* (capital F), coupled with a seething desire to physically harm him, cause him emotional anguish, and make him regret the day he ever thought he could break up with me right after eating a sesame-seed bagel with cream cheese. The fifth stage was *wrath*. Rage. Resentment. That woman who cut off her husband's penis and tossed it out a car window? She was clearly in the fifth stage. And, now, so was I.

"Are you okay?" the woman on my right asked, and pointed to the wax-coated bag tucked in front of her own SkyMall. "You don't look so well."

"I'm fine," I assured her, even though I was the furthest thing from fine.

She didn't press the issue. "Well, it sounds like a change of scenery is exactly what you need."

"Change is exactly what I *don't* need," I told her. "What I really need is for everything to be the same."

chapter two

I don't know what I expected. It wasn't like I
thought there would be a WELCOME BACK, EMILY sign strung
across the front door of Heywood Academy, or a crowd of people
lined up to greet me—not that I was opposed to the idea.
But still. It was weird. Almost like walking into your bedroom
only to find someone's rearranged the furniture—it was still the
same place, but it wasn't exactly as I'd left it.

There was the new Astroturf soccer field courtesy of Josie's father, and an addition to the foreign language wing where the old
arts building used to be. The dull white hallways I remembered
were now painted shiny beige, and the maroon metal lockers that
I'd once carved my initials into were now navy blue with circular
holes where the built-in locks had been.

I glanced down the hall toward the library and wondered who

had my old locker now. Some ninth grader who had no idea I'd scrawled "E.A. + O.L." on the inside of the door using an unbent paper clip I took from the computer lab (I felt guilty afterward and tried to bend the clip back into shape and return it to the lab, but, of course, I couldn't come close to making it look like anything other than a mangled piece of metal and so I ended up burying it at the bottom of one of the small white plastic garbage receptacles they mounted on the walls of the girls bathroom stalls). A ninth grader who, even though there were barely three hundred students in the whole school, had no idea who "E.A." even was. Probably a ninth grader a lot like the guy staring at me right now, wondering, *Why the hell is that girl checking me out?*

I didn't recognize him, not that there was any reason I should. Although now he was wearing the upper school's standard navy blazer, maroon tie, and khaki pants, he would have been a sixth grader when I moved to Chicago. And I wasn't in the habit of getting to know the kids in the lower school beyond the mandatory Secret Santa chocolates we delivered to them before Christmas break. Besides, his locker would have been on the bottom level back then, safely tucked away from upper-school students and four-letter words that his innocent ears weren't supposed to hear.

But at that moment, he and three of his friends were watching me, sizing me up, trying to figure out if the new blond girl in the navy pleated skirt and blue oxford was someone they'd be interested in, or if she realized they were only freshmen.

As they examined me like some specimen in biology class, I attempted to look like I fit in. Which I once did. Three years ago I would never have stood in the hall outside the bathrooms wondering what to do next, where to go. I would have known where I belonged. But as I glanced down at my watch and pretended to be waiting for someone, *anyone,* I didn't feel like I belonged at all.

And I was starting to feel like I was spending way too much time in the vicinity of restrooms.

"Oh my God, Emily!" a voice called from the other end of the hallway, and I whipped around, knowing exactly who I'd find.

"I can't believe you're back." Josie rushed toward me and threw her arms around my shoulders, the small blond hairs on her arm highlighted against the tan she must have earned in the Bahamas over Christmas vacation. This wasn't some orange-y pseudo tan, like the kind we used to pour out of a bottle that inevitably gave us carrot-colored cuticles for a week because we forgot to use soap when we washed our hands. No, this was real. And the idea of Josie hanging out on some tropical island for Christmas break was completely *un*real. So unreal I felt my stomach clench, like that time I drank that bad eggnog.

"This is so great," Josie gushed, still holding on to me.

My first reaction was to return her hug like I'd done a million times before, but right away it was obvious that things were different—mainly that I was four inches taller and Josie was at least two cup sizes bigger. For a minute I thought maybe Josie had used her dad's recently acquired fortune to purchase a new set of boobs. But she would have called to tell me about any silicone enhancements, wouldn't she? Besides, Josie wasn't like that. Or at least she wasn't like that when I knew her.

My heart sank. Not because Josie was perfectly bronzed and so clearly superseded me in the chest department, but because it was exactly what I'd been afraid of—that we'd be different. That we'd changed. And the reality of Josie's chin barely reaching my shoulder was proof that, literally, Josie and I no longer saw eye to eye.

With my boyfriend gone, my valedictorian title left behind, and the recent news that I'd been practically rejected at Brown, Josie and Lucy were the only consolation I had for the next five months. They were the only things that made the idea of moving back to Branford even remotely bearable. And, now that I was staring at the side part in Josie's blond hair, and she was probably staring at the blackheads on my chin, even that consolation wasn't so consoling anymore.

Still, Josie pulled me in close, her sun-streaked hair falling across my face so that I had no choice but to inhale her long blond strands. And that's when, in a single sniff, I realized that there may be some hope after all. I may have grown up and she may have grown out, but Josie's hair still smelled like Pantene shampoo. Just like it used to.

I kept inhaling, taking comfort in the idea that maybe Josie hadn't changed that much.

"So, when did you get back?" Josie asked, pulling away. "Are you all unpacked? How's your new house? And why didn't you call me the minute you got in? Forget it, it doesn't matter, I'm just glad you're back."

Josie had a tendency to do that, to ask a question and then not bother waiting for an answer.

"I meant to call you," I told her, hoping she'd believe me. Josie used to say I was a horrible liar. I used to take that as a compliment, but now I wished I were more comfortable spouting intentional half-truths. Or no-truths. "We've just been so busy getting settled and all."

The whole-truth was, I hadn't called Josie in the forty-eight hours we'd been back because I was afraid. Afraid of getting on the phone and realizing we had nothing to talk about, or even that we didn't *want* to find anything to talk about anymore. Afraid that, if she knew that my relatively ideal life had taken a turn for the worse, that I'd gone from pretty much succeeding at everything I did to failing miserably, she'd realize I wasn't the same person she used to like.

"The moving truck got here two days ago, and my mom is still going through boxes," I told Josie, hoping that would be enough of an explanation. "Good thing I finally found a box of clothes, or I'd be wearing a Hefty bag."

Josie laughed. "You always did look good in green," she told me before taking my hand and leading me down the hall toward the seniors' lockers, and away from the no-man's-land I'd been standing in by the bathrooms.

"Lucy's been sick since New Year's Day, but she promised she'd be here today," Josie assured me.

And that's when the door to the stairwell flew open and Lucy's curly brown hair and red, chapped nose bounded toward us. "There you are," she exclaimed, her voice deep and nasal, like she was imitating those people on the NyQuil commercials. "Don't get too close, I don't want to make you sick," she warned, but that didn't stop her from hugging me.

"You look crappy," Josie told her, standing at arm's length.

"I feel even crappier," she assured us. "My mom wanted me to stay home but I told her *you* were coming today." Lucy nudged me just like she used to when she wanted to get my attention. Or anyone else's. Lucy was a nudger, an arm squeezer, a poker, and even an under-the-table kicker when necessary. She's also been the captain of the varsity soccer team since her sophomore year and the starting center on the lacrosse team, so it's not like any of these gestures was received without some degree of discomfort.

"So, what do you think?" Lucy asked me.

"About what?"

"About everything! The way the school's changed, how we've changed." She eyed Josie's chest but didn't poke her, even though I knew it was probably killing her not to. "Do we look different? I mean, you're taller, and your hair's longer, but otherwise you look exactly the same."

I smiled, not because my hair was longer or I was taller, but because they really didn't seem that different, either. "Besides the obvious, you guys look exactly the same, too."

"We don't have much time before first bell, so start talking," Josie instructed, taking a seat on the radiator lining the length of the hallway and pulling me down next to her. Lucy took my backpack and laid it on the floor before sitting down to my right.

I had about seven minutes to cover two-and-a-half years. There was no way I could tell them everything, explain who my friends were, or describe what it was like living in the Midwest. Did I start by telling them that everyone in Chicago called soda "pop," or that instead of applying to Williams and Wesleyan, my friends were applying to Northwestern and Notre Dame? Did I mention that my parents weren't living together and seemed on the verge of divorce? Did I begin by announcing that I wasn't accepted early decision at Brown? Or just come right out and tell them that Sean dumped me two days ago because he didn't think a long-distance relationship would ever work out?

But I couldn't tell them any of that. I knew who they were expecting. Nice Emily. Sweet Emily. Not bitching-about-everything-that's-wrong Emily. If you asked anyone at Heywood Academy what they remembered about Emily Abbott, nine out of ten people would say, "Emily Abbott, she was so nice!" The tenth person would probably remember I was the one who'd scraped dog crap on the school's front steps.

Even if Lucy and Josie were acting like no time at all had passed since we last saw one another, I wasn't convinced it was that easy. A lot had happened in two-and-a-half years. Josie had practically become an instant heiress thanks to some software program her dad invented, and Lucy was being wooed with scholarships and promises of greatness by every Division I school with a women's soccer team. And now I was supposed to jump-start our friendship with my own sucky life? No way. I'd give them the Emily they remembered.

"There's not enough time. You guys tell me what's been going on here," I demanded instead—in the nicest way, of course. The hallway was filling up with students and the sounds of locker doors slamming shut, and I only had a few minutes before Josie and Lucy would leave me and I'd be on my own. "And hurry up," I insisted, feeling our time together ticking away.

"Not much around here changes, unfortunately," Lucy answered. "A few other people have moved away, and a few new people started, but otherwise it's the same old faces you've known since sixth grade."

"Come on, there must be something? No cringe-worthy stories?" I asked, not bothering to hide my disappointment. I'd missed out on two whole years at Heywood, there had to be some piece of interesting news to tell me. "Any new guys?" I turned to Josie, remembering that the last time we spoke on the phone she had just gotten herself yet another new boyfriend. "What's going on with Luke?"

Josie's hands flew up between us as if attempting to deflect the question. "Don't even say his name."

"He cheated on her over Christmas vacation," Lucy explained.

"He didn't just cheat on me, I caught him making out with someone else at Owen's New Year's party."

"A sophomore from St. Michael's," Lucy added, knowing that added insult to injury.

For a second it occurred to me that a cheating boyfriend might be worse than a boyfriend who blindsided you with a breakup. Maybe my mom was right. Maybe things could be worse. At least Sean didn't break up with me because he wanted to be with someone else. He broke up with me because he just didn't want to go out with me anymore.

Okay. That didn't help at all.

"That had to suck," I empathized with Josie, attempting to put Sean out of my mind and focus on her cheating boyfriend instead.

I had a hard time picturing the Luke Preston I remembered cheating on anybody, no less Josie. When Josie and I would still talk on the phone our sophomore year, she'd mentioned Luke had changed over the summer, but I figured he'd just gotten his braces off, maybe lost a few pounds, and finally shaved the brown fuzz that seemed to hover over his upper lip like something more in need of a Swiffer than a razor. And even though Josie told me she and Luke had started going out in October, I still couldn't quite picture my Josie, the girl who totally had her act together, going out with Luke Preston, who was mediocre at best.

"He kept swearing he sent me a breakup e-mail right before I left for the Bahamas, like that made any difference. What kind of an asshole breaks up with someone in an e-mail?"

"And right before Christmas!" Lucy added in a show of support.

I figured it was the same kind of guy who thinks he won't get caught making out with a sophomore at Owen Lyle's New Year's party. Or the kind that tells his girlfriend he doesn't want to go out with her anymore while he's wearing the L.L.Bean field coat she gave him for Christmas and eating the sesame bagel she'd toasted for him.

"When I told Luke I bought him a present in the Bahamas, he told me to just keep it." Josie shook her head and frowned. "Then I called him a prick and he told me to get over it."

Get over it. As if catching your boyfriend with his tongue down someone else's throat is akin to twisting an ankle during a football game. It was like Sean telling me he didn't want to do the long-distance thing when I knew he had unlimited cell phone minutes. It was bullshit. I may have been gone from Heywood for almost three years, but it seemed like we were right back where we'd left off. So far we seemed to be having the same conversation we'd had the week before I moved to Chicago, when I'd nursed Lucy through three tubes of Toll House cookie dough after Matt LeFarge told the entire baseball team he'd popped her water bra with his watch band when he tried to feel her up. Add shitty guys next to Pantene on the list of things that just don't seem to change.

"I really can't picture Luke cheating on you," I admitted. "I can't picture him cheating on anybody."

"Oh God, you have no idea. He's nothing like the guy you remember. Totally different. 'I'm sure I sent it to you,' " Josie mimicked. 'Check your e-mail when you get home. Maybe it got put into your spam folder by mistake.' "

Lucy and I tried not to smile. Josie did a wicked imitation of her ex-boyfriend.

"Like it's AOL's fault he's a prick. I swear, I am so done with guys," Josie concluded. "The rest of the year, there's nobody."

"There's nobody left," Lucy pointed out. "You've gone out with everyone."

"Well, in a school this small, the pickings are slim."

As if on cue, a few of those slim pickings came walking toward us.

"Hey, Emily, what are you doing here?" Matt LeFarge asked.

"I moved back."

He nodded in agreement, as if I needed his approval of my explanation.

The water bra incident had happened almost three years ago, but still, I didn't know how Lucy would react to Matt. I waited to see if she would ignore him or make a sarcastic comment about the piece of toilet paper pasted under his chin where he'd obviously nicked himself shaving, but there was nothing. When I left, the water bra incident was huge, but obviously Lucy had gotten over it. That's why I couldn't figure out the look on Josie's face, a look of annoyance that verged on being completely and totally pissed. Maybe Josie still held a grudge against Matt out of loyalty to Lucy?

And that's when I saw him. Luke Preston. Except the guy coming toward us wasn't the Luke Preston I remembered from freshman year. And all of a sudden I understood why Josie was so pissed. Luke Preston didn't just get his braces off and buy a new electric razor. Luke Preston was gorgeous.

Josie hopped off the radiator. "We should get going," she told us, taking her books out of her locker and slamming the door shut so hard the lockers on either side flew open. "The bell's going to ring any minute."

I glanced down the row. "I haven't been assigned a locker yet."

"You can use mine until you get one," Josie offered, waving her arm in front of locker number 117. "Voilà. Your new home away from home."

"I'm right here," Lucy told me, pointing to number 115. "You can put your coat in mine for now."

How could I have doubted they'd be the same? How could I have even imagined we wouldn't be best friends again? I stuffed my coat in the locker before taking a notebook out of my backpack.

Even though I was facing Josie as she took my backpack and tucked it into her locker, I couldn't help glancing over her shoulder at the guy standing a few feet away. And I wasn't the only one. Down by the junior lockers a group of girls were watching as Luke Preston ran a hand through his floppy brown hair before telling a joke that had Matt LeFarge cracking up. He might be a prick, but that sophomore who snagged Luke Preston had to be one happy girl. She'd scored big-time.

"Come on, we'll walk you to your first class," Lucy offered, looking down at my class schedule.

If I'd been worried that things would be different between us, I wasn't worried anymore. Heywood Academy could change the wall color and remove the locks from the lockers and paint them blue, but some things would always be the same. I looked down the hall at the freshman watching me walk away, and I couldn't help smiling. I knew exactly what he was thinking. The new girl wasn't new at all. She was Josie Holden and Lucy Denton's best friend. And she was back.

The Guy's Guide Tip #9:
Your penis will not shrivel up and die if you admit you want an umbrella instead of standing in the rain acting like a little water never killed anyone. It's an umbrella, not a purse.

chapter three

Josie wasn't sporting a new Rolex or channeling Paris Hilton. Lucy wasn't fighting off recruiters or taping up offer letters in her locker (something a senior did a few years back when he was being courted by a few Ivies for their squash teams—it was completely obnoxious but it almost seemed cool at the time). All in all, as I followed Josie and Lucy down the stairwell toward the English classrooms, I was feeling a lot better about things. Lucy and Josie were on my side. And right now, that was the only thing I needed to get me through first period.

Or so I thought.

When we got to the lower level, Lucy pointed down the hallway. "Mrs. Blackwell's class is the second on the left."

"I'll see you in history," Josie told me before they both said good-bye, wished me luck, and headed off to French class.

As they walked away, their shoulders bumping into each other while Josie laughed at something Lucy had said, I felt on my own again.

I walked the ten feet to Mrs. Blackwell's room and reached for the doorknob. My fingers stayed wrapped around the smooth stainless steel while I watched Josie and Lucy disappear into the stairwell. They gave me one last wave before heading up the stairs, and I waved back like everything was fine. But instead of turning the knob and going in, I stepped away from the door, feeling like the monkey in the middle, wavering between being glad I was back and feeling like I just wanted to go home. To Chicago.

It was an hour earlier back in Chicago. While I was standing outside Mrs. Blackwell's classroom on the East Coast buying time before going in and facing a roomful of semistrangers, my two best friends for the past two years—the ones who knew that my boyfriend didn't want to see me anymore and that my chances of getting into Brown at this point were slim and none—were probably finishing up breakfast and getting ready to catch the bus. Today was like any other day for them, except I wasn't there. Lauren couldn't bum a pencil from me before math class, and Jackie would be bumped up to salutatorian now that Will Simmons was going to take my place at the head of the class. It was only an hour earlier in Chicago, but it already felt like it was a world away.

"Aren't you going in?" a voice asked, jolting me back to the glossy beige hallway. I looked up and saw Owen Lyle coming toward me.

"I guess I have to go in sooner or later," I answered, waiting for Owen to reach me.

"The bell's going to ring in about fifteen seconds, so it better be sooner."

I used to consider Owen my first real boyfriend, until I started going out with Sean. Once Sean and I were together, all the boyfriends who came before him paled by comparison. It was like believing you liked chocolate and then tasting Ben & Jerry's New York Super Fudge Chunk—up until that point you had no idea how amazing chocolate ice cream could really be. There was no way to even compare how I felt about Owen to how I feel—make that *felt*—about Sean. Owen and I held hands and kissed. Sean and I could spend all night on his couch making out, and our hands were doing way more than holding. For the past four months I'd thought of Sean as my real *first*. Not *the first* in the way most people think about it. We never had sex, even if, before I found out we were moving, I did think it was inevitable. That's probably why the thought of having sex with Sean consumed about eighty percent of my waking hours (the other twenty percent was evenly split between obsessing about my application to Brown and deciding what to get Sean for Christmas).

After a while I actually started to feel like I'd be better off just having sex with him so I could stop planning for it like some elaborate event that required orchestration and forethought, if not a party planner. First there was the question of *where* it would happen. There were so many options, including my favorite, the beach. I knew the reality of sand creeping into my private parts didn't sound all that comfortable, but it always looked so nice in music videos and romantic comedies. But being that it was almost December when I decided that Sean would be my first *in that sense,* the beach was pretty much out of the question. Then there was the *how*—a question that Jackie, Lauren, and I decided to answer by reading an old Kama Sutra Lauren found in her basement. After close examination and much discussion, we decided the *how* would definitely depend on the *where* due to potential space constraints and limited mobility. Admittedly, the illustrations also required a level of flexibility I had no hope of ever achieving, so it wasn't like I was in danger of performing the Yugmapada with my lotus-crossed feet any time soon. Of course, there was also the *when,* which almost created more questions than it answered. It got to the point where I'd put so much thought and planning into it that I almost felt like I should send Sean an invitation to the grand event—*please join me as I celebrate the loss of my virginity*—and the appropriate instructions to RSVP.

But even if we didn't end up sleeping together, Sean was the first in an entirely different way. Owen may have been the first, and at that point *the only,* guy to feel me up, but Sean was the first person I thought I truly loved.

Owen stopped in front of the classroom door. "I heard you were moving back. When did you get so tall?"

I stood on my tippy toes and attempted to look down on him. "When did you get so short?"

Actually, Owen wasn't short at all. He was the perfect height for things like kissing, resting your head on his shoulder during movies, and staring into his grayish green eyes. Owen was always cute. He was the guy everyone liked.

For a minute I wondered how easy it would be to get back together with Owen, even if it was just to get Sean out of my system. He could be the sprig of parsley that eliminated the bad taste of Sean from my mouth (parsley is a natural odor neutralizer, as pointed out in my mom's best-selling book *Everyday Etiquette for Everyone*). So what if I was on the rebound? Owen was still cute, still had that mellow walk that made it seem like he was in no rush to get anywhere. I used to love watching him come down the hall toward me after history class, how it almost looked like he was walking in slow motion. Or maybe I'd just been brainwashed by the Hollywood idea that special effects were supposed to substitute for love.

But, instead of being the least bit turned on by Owen, there was nothing. Not even a single spark for the first guy who'd successfully unhooked my bra. Sean had ruined it for me. Right now, the only sparks I wanted were the ones that could set Sean and his L.L.Bean field coat on fire.

"You remember Luke, don't you?" Owen asked, gesturing to his left where Luke now stood watching us.

Luke nodded at me. "Hey, Emily."

"Hi Luke," I answered cheerily, and then before I could stop myself added, "How're you doing?"

Damn!

If I could have smacked myself, I would have. This was the guy who'd dumped my best friend and here I was acting like I actually cared about how *he* was doing. Why should I care about Luke? It was Josie I cared about. What kind of friend was I, chatting up the guy who'd screwed over my best friend?

Luke smiled at me and I fought the instinct to smile back, which wasn't all that easy. After a lifetime of my mother ingraining pleasant and proper greetings in my brain, I wasn't sure how to kick the habit.

Even though I could hear my mom's voice telling me to say hello, maybe even extend a firm handshake and say it was nice to see him again, I didn't. If I was going to break the nice habit, now was a good time to start.

"Forget it," I quickly recovered, not bothering to hide my disgust as I looked Luke up and down. "I know how you've been. I already heard all about you, and it's more than I care to know."

At first, Luke seemed surprised by my reaction. In fact, he seemed almost confused.

I could guess what he was thinking—the Emily Abbott he knew would never be such a bitch. But then again, the Luke Preston I'd known wouldn't cheat on my best friend. And he wouldn't look like a model out of an Abercrombie catalog.

All of a sudden Luke smirked at me, and I knew he understood the situation. He knew he was too late. Josie had already gotten to me, and I was a loyal friend. I wouldn't just ignore what Luke did to her. I cared about Josie's feelings—I wasn't *a guy*.

"I'm sure you do," Luke muttered, and I shot him a look that said, in no uncertain terms, that he and I would not be friends.

Before I could lose my courage and dissolve into apologies for being so rude, I turned the doorknob and walked into the classroom just as the bell started to ring.

By lunchtime I almost felt like I was getting back into the swing of things. I had four classes under my belt and, thankfully, I wasn't completely lost. Not that it mattered much at this point. After hearing from Brown the day before Christmas—a lovely little Christmas Eve gift from the admissions committee who, come to think of it, should have just written "bah, humbug" on the envelope and called it a day—I'd sent in my applications to a bunch of other colleges, so the rest of this year was more about making it through in one piece, rather than attempting to graduate first in my class. I already knew that wasn't going to happen. Mr. Wesley, the headmaster, made it clear that no matter how well I did my last semester at Heywood, and no matter how well I'd done in Chicago before I left, I couldn't be valedictorian after returning midyear. My mom had actually thanked Mr. Wesley before hanging up the phone and telling me this news, and I'd wanted to tell her to call him back and say that wasn't fair. That I'd busted my ass for four years, and there was no way I was going to sit with the rest of the class at graduation and act like it was no big deal. It *was* a big deal. But ultimately, like everything else that had taken place in the last three weeks, I had no choice in the matter. Everyone else was making decisions for me and I was just being handed my life on a plate—and I was supposed to graciously accept it and say thank you. Even if it was a plate I didn't order and wanted to send back.

Besides, my mom told me, I should be thankful Heywood was willing to take me back at all, considering how late in the school year it was. But the only thing I was thankful for at that point was that I'd already be accepted at Brown by the time we moved back and it wouldn't matter. Goes to show what I know.

Lucy and Josie were waiting for me in the cafeteria after fourth period, just like they used to. They'd even saved me a seat, even though I was running late after having to go see Heywood's secretary about getting my own locker.

"How were the rest of your classes?" Lucy asked, scooting over to make room for me. "I heard you knew all the answers to Mrs. Blackwell's questions about *The House of Mirth*. What's up with that?"

I carefully laid my tray on the table, making sure not to spill my chili, and sat next to her. "Yeah, well, I read it last semester."

"Every time I open that book, my eyes glaze over. There's no way I'm going to do well on our test next week."

Josie peeled open her peanut-butter-and-jelly sandwich and scraped the purple goo off the bread with a plastic spoon. Josie's hated jelly ever since seventh grade, when she bit into her pb&j and a glob of grape jam fell into her lap. Josie claims jelly is disgusting, but I think part of the reason she still goes to all the trouble of scraping her sandwiches until they're jelly-free is that Curtis Ludlow told our entire class Josie had gotten her period and no matter how many times she insisted the reddish stain was Welch's grape jelly, everyone had liked Curtis's version of the story better.

I thought maybe Josie's mom would have finally given in and let Josie bring her lunch from home to avoid the daily scraping. But when meals are included in tuition, I guess it's hard to justify brown bagging it—at least that's what Josie's mom told her when she brought up the idea right after the Curtis incident.

"Oh, who are you kidding?" Josie asked. "The test hardly matters. You've got UNC and Duke battling it out for you."

Lucy rolled her eyes. "They're not 'battling it out.' "

"Then what would you call it?"

"They're 'actively interested,' " Lucy paraphrased, even though we all knew it pretty much meant the same thing.

"Hi, Emily, welcome back." Mandy Pinta put her tray down on the table and took a seat across from me. "Are you guys talking about what you're going to do for the time capsule?"

"They're still doing that?" I asked, kind of flattered that Mandy would automatically assume Lucy, Josie, and I would be doing something together for the time capsule even though I'd been back at Heywood for all of four hours.

"Of course," Mandy assured me. "It wouldn't be Heywood if we didn't have the time capsule, right?"

Ever since Heywood Academy's class of 1973 came up with the idea of creating time capsules before graduation, every single senior class has created one, throwing in stuff like a few magazines (mostly *Sports Illustrated*s from the guys, and *Seventeen*s or *Cosmo*s from the girls), some *Boston Globe*s, and music. It sounded cool in theory, but the truth is every time the capsules are opened nobody really cares. The most interesting thing that was ever uncovered was the roach clip the class of 1983 claimed to have used on a senior trip to a Police concert. When they opened the time capsule ten years later, the class of 1993 supposedly put the roach clip to the test, but I think that's just Heywood legend, like the year they claim a class opened the time capsule and discovered somebody's middle finger with a mood ring still on it.

Lucy shrugged. "We haven't even thought about what we're going to do. What about you?"

Mandy waited until she'd finished chewing her turkey sandwich. "Pam and Carolyn and I were thinking that maybe we'd do a scrapbook of our senior year."

Not exactly original, but then again, nothing in the time capsule ever was.

While Mandy continued to give us a rundown of the other mundane options they'd considered for the capsule—a video, a photo collage, or a collection of quotes from everyone in the senior class—I noticed something weird taking place over in the far corner of the cafeteria. It wasn't just weird. It was completely bizarre. A group of six girls, probably sophomores because I didn't recognize any of them, were walking in a line over to the table where Matt and Luke and Owen were seated. Only Luke didn't have any food in front of him. And the girl leading the line walking directly toward him was holding a lunch tray out in front of her like it was an offering she was preparing to lay at the foot of a god. Or, I was quickly realizing, at the foot of Luke Preston.

"What's up with that?" I asked Josie, and pointed my spoon toward the line of handmaidens now gathered around Luke's table.

"Luke's fan club."

"Don't tell me they do this every day."

Josie licked a glob of peanut butter falling out of her sandwich. "Okay, I won't."

"So they bring him his lunch? That's insane." I watched as Luke sent the girls away and dug into his own bowl of chili. "Don't those girls have any self-respect?"

"They're sophomores," Josie told me, as if that was enough of an excuse.

It was truly nauseating the way Luke just let the girls lay his tray on the table and walk away without so much as a thank you. I mean, letting a group of girls wait on you hand and foot is arrogant enough, but not even acting like you appreciate it is inexcusable. The whole scene was outrageous, and what made Luke's Lunch Legion even more annoying was that I couldn't help seeing a little of me in those girls. Because I could recall more than a few times when I'd brought Sean his lunch. I hadn't felt pathetic at the time, but seeing those girls look at Luke like he was perfection incarnate, I realized for the first time that I'd felt like that about Sean. I'd wanted to believe he was perfect, too.

"What a jerk," I mumbled into my chili.

"Oh, wait. The best is yet to come. When Luke's finished with his lunch he'll just walk away and the girls will clean up his crap so he doesn't have to."

I reached for my chocolate milk and held it up. "Guys suck."

Josie tipped her bottled water against the carton, toasting me. "Here, here."

"So, do you have any ideas, Emily?" Mandy asked me, and I managed to take my eyes off Luke before she could notice I'd been staring.

"Any ideas about what?"

"The senior class time capsule."

"We'll probably do the same as every other class—a few CDs, some newspaper clippings, maybe a lottery ticket." Lucy looked to Josie and me to see what we thought.

"Come on, we can come up with something better than that,

can't we?" I asked, attempting to balance a spoonful of chili without spilling it all over the table, but failing.

Lucy passed me a napkin. "We could try."

"How are you getting home this afternoon?" Josie asked me.

"My mom was going to pick me and TJ up. We're still figuring out what to do." Since Heywood students came from at least six towns in the area, we didn't have very many buses, just two or three for the towns with the most kids. The rest of us were either picked up by school vans, carpooled with other families, or, once we got our licenses, drove ourselves. When I left Heywood, none of us had our licenses yet, so it was bizarre to think that all the cars parked in the parking lot now belonged to the same classmates who couldn't ride a moped without causing bodily injury during our freshman class trip to Block Island. Even though Mr. Wesley had repeatedly warned us to be careful, half the class had ended up with gauze around their ankles after burning off several layers of skin on the mopeds' tailpipes. Josie still had a vague scar on her ankle, I think.

"Why don't you call your mom and tell her you're coming home with me and we can try to come up with something better than a copy of *People* magazine with Britney Spears on the cover?"

Wait out front with TJ for my mom to pick me up, or catch a ride with Josie. There was no contest. "Consider it done."

After last period I went to meet Lucy and Josie by their lockers, but only Lucy was there. She didn't see me at first, and I didn't call out her name or do anything so she'd notice I was walking toward her. Instead I stopped and watched her sort through her books as she obviously tried to decide which ones she needed to take home. Not that it mattered. It wasn't like Duke or UNC or any other school that was recruiting Lucy would turn her down because she didn't do well on a French quiz. Which was ironic, now that I thought about it. Here I was, the one who used to help Lucy conjugate French verbs—even though I took Spanish—and yet she was being wooed by schools while all I had was a wrinkled letter with a tear-smeared Brown University logo. Standing there watching Lucy spend so much time figuring out which books she needed, I felt something so unexpected, so urgent, I almost didn't know what it was. It was like how all of a sudden you're not hungry until someone mentions a cheeseburger and fries, and then it's all you can do to keep your stomach from growling. But what I was feeling weren't pangs of hunger. They were worse. They were pangs of jealousy.

I'd never envied Lucy before. Not when she'd be waiting at the finish line, barely out of breath, long before the rest of us completed our run around the soccer field. Not when she was asked to be on the varsity team when most freshmen were just hoping to sit on the JV bench in a uniform. And not even when she stood up at school assemblies and accepted yet another athletic award for "outstanding this" and "extraordinary that." It never bothered me because each of us seemed to have our place, our little niche where we fit. I was the good one, the nice girl who got good grades. Lucy was the amazing athlete. And Josie was the scholarship student who made decent grades and didn't stand out in any particular way except that she seemed to have a confidence that made her seem special, like how some stars seem to shine brighter or twinkle faster than others when you look at the sky, even though you can't quite figure out why. Which is why it was even more unbelievable that Luke Preston would ditch her for some random St. Michael's sophomore. Nobody ever ditched Josie. She was always the one who did the ditching.

"Hey, what are you doing?" Lucy asked, finally noticing me standing there watching her.

"Nothing." I went over to her. "I thought we were all meeting here after last class."

"Josie's finishing up in the art room; she's still got some pictures developing or something."

Josie is fanatical about her photographs. I'd say that more than half of all the yearbook pictures from our freshman year were taken by her, which is why there's only one candid picture of Josie and about a million of me and Lucy. And even in that one picture, Josie isn't alone. Lucy and I are standing right next to her, laughing as the shutter of the camera snapped closed.

"I don't know why she just doesn't do it at home," Lucy wondered aloud, moving aside so I could grab my coat out of her locker. "She has her own photo lab in the new house, you know."

No, I did not know. "Really? An entire photo lab?"

"Oh yeah. Wait until you see the Holdens' new place. You're not going to believe it."

Even more unbelievable than a house with a photography lab was the fact that Josie was actually one of the few scholarship students at Heywood before I left. Not that it made her any different from the rest of us, at least not in any real noticeable way. We all had to follow a dress code, so Josie didn't stand out from anyone else. I don't even know if anyone besides me and Lucy knew Josie received a scholarship to attend Heywood Academy; it was that much of a nonissue. There were only a few times when I can really remember thinking that Josie felt different from the rest of us, like when we took our freshman class trip to Block Island. The whole time we were there, everyone was buying souvenir T-shirts and baseball hats and little shot glasses with whales etched into the sides. But when we were all on the bus heading back to Branford,

I noticed that Josie was the only one who didn't have a plastic shopping bag stuffed with mementos of our trip. She only held a small keychain with a gray plastic whale dangling off it.

"She doesn't seem that different, though," I told Lucy, wondering if Josie still had the keychain.

"Oh, she's not, really. I mean, in the beginning when they started building the new 'estate,' as Josie's mother calls it, she was into it. But then she realized that her parents were *way* into it—or at least her mother was."

It was hard to picture Mrs. Holden, the woman who lived in a velour sweatsuit every day of the week, insisting on calling her house an estate. I don't think I've ever seen Mrs. Holden in anything but a running suit, although I'd never seen her actually run anywhere.

"Does her mom still wear those velour running outfits?"

"Oh yeah, only now they're Juicy Couture and she wears them to do yoga in her meditation room."

"A meditation room?"

"I told you. Wait until you see this place. You're not going to believe it." Lucy waited for me to grab my backpack out of Josie's locker. "Come on, Josie said to meet her at the car."

"I still can't believe she has her own car."

"Not just a car," Lucy assured me. "A shiny new BMW."

chapter four

"Are you ready for this?" Lucy asked over her shoulder as we slowed down and prepared to turn into Josie's driveway. At least, I thought it was a driveway, although it didn't look like any driveway I'd ever seen before. It looked more like some sort of cobblestone road.

"Wait until you see the stables," Josie told me. "My mom thinks I'm supposed to become some sort of equestrian just because she always loved reading *The Black Stallion*. I am now the proud owner of a pair of britches and a velvet riding helmet, if you can believe it."

"They have two horses, Ginger and Pinecone." Lucy lowered her voice. "Josie hates them."

"Only because they hate me."

"They don't hate you," Lucy insisted. "They just need to get used to you."

"Well, they had no problem getting used to Lucy. She was practically National Velvet out there, jumping over fences."

"Don't listen to her. I wasn't jumping over any fences."

The thing is, I wouldn't have been surprised if she was. Lucy was the kid who could ride a two-wheeler while the rest of us were still just thrilled to have pink streamers on our handlebars.

"Prepare yourself, we're here." Lucy tapped on the glass with her index finger, and instead of the silence I expected, there was a clicking noise as she rapped the passenger-side window. Lucy actually had fingernails! She's always been a nail biter, despite her mom's best efforts, including special gloves Lucy had to wear to bed at night, and even some toxic polish that was supposed make Lucy gag if she even put her fingers near her mouth. I never expected Lucy to ever stop biting her nails, but there they were. It wasn't like she had long red nails with rhinestones glued on the tips or anything, but, still, they weren't the nibbled-on fragments I was used to.

"Don't hold it against me," Josie said before flipping on her blinker. "I had nothing to do with this."

I didn't know what she was talking about until we pulled into the driveway and were face-to-face with two stone pillars flanking a wrought-iron gate with a huge script *H* in the center.

"The *H* is for Holden, obviously, but I think it's for horrifying. It's obnoxious, I know," Josie apologized, pointing to the gate. "Not to mention that it sucks when you're in a rush." Josie pushed a code into the number pad tucked inside the stone column and the black iron gate slowly opened.

Lucy pointed toward the end of the long driveway. "You think this is good, wait until you see the house."

Calling what was waiting for us at the end of the driveway a house was like calling the ten acres of rolling lawns a yard. I mean, there was a stone turret, for God's sake! I almost expected knights on horseback to be jousting on the front lawn, like the time Mandy Pinta had her eleventh birthday party at Medieval Times.

"What, no moat?" I joked.

"Oh, my parents would have tried, but the town probably wouldn't have given them a permit," Josie answered, and I couldn't tell if she was joking or not. "So we have some CIA-endorsed security system instead. I swear, I'm lucky they didn't go for the attack dogs. That was an option for a while." In addition to horses, Josie is afraid of dogs.

The massive stone mansion wasn't anything like the house I used to go to for sleepovers, Crystal Light, and an endless supply of Pop-Tarts. It had to be five times the size of Josie's old house.

"Welcome to my world," Josie announced, pulling around the circular drive before coming to a stop in front of two huge front doors with monstrous bronze door knockers that appeared to be staring at us.

"Are those lions' heads?" I asked, climbing out of the backseat.

"Oh yeah," Josie confirmed, shaking her head as if she couldn't believe it herself. "Wait until you see the hippopotamus statues out back by the pool. It's like freaking Wild Kingdom around here."

As Josie led us through the front door and down the cavernous marble hallways that twisted and turned around impeccably decorated rooms, I felt totally out of place. It was like visiting a museum, not somebody's house. And definitely not *Josie's* house. How could she possibly be comfortable surrounded by chandeliers and fluted columns and intricate oil paintings? And that was just in the powder room we passed on the way to her room. It almost made me wonder if this was how Josie used to feel around Heywood before she traded in her scholarship money for a field named after her dad.

"Incredible, huh?" Lucy asked, grabbing my hand and pulling me around a corner before I could bump into a bubbling fountain of water in the center of the hall. "Come on, Josie's room is this way."

It was surreal. Here we were sitting on Josie's bed just like we used to, only the bed had been upgraded from a twin to a queen, and instead of a hodgepodge of pictures Scotch taped to the wall, Josie's black-and-white photographs were artfully displayed in frames like something out of a Pottery Barn catalog. I would have killed for a room like this when I was younger, but it was slightly overkill for a seventeen-year-old. I mean, there was a sheer white canopy covering the bed and a huge quilted headboard with a billion little pink rosebuds. It looked like something out of a feminine hygiene commercial. The only thing missing was the gentle breeze and the billowing curtains—and the voiceover of a woman talking about feeling fresh as a daisy.

No, this wasn't the bedroom I remembered. In fact, Josie didn't even have a bedroom anymore. She had what most people, like my mother, would refer to as a "suite." There was the sleeping area, where we were sprawled out on the bed, and the sitting area, with a love seat and ottoman that looked as if they'd never been used. And then there were the panels of mirrors creating some sort of fun-house effect outside a walk-in closet that could have housed a family of four. Very comfortably.

"It's called the '*dressing area*,' " Josie explained, without me having to ask. "It's ridiculous, I know. But not nearly as ridiculous as the ass fountain in the bathroom."

"She means the bidet," Lucy told me.

Josie sighed. "The interior designer insisted."

An interior designer, now that made sense. I knew there was no way Josie's mom was responsible for the perfectly matched fabrics, impeccably placed furniture, and tastefully arranged throw pillows. Maybe if they'd been velour.

"So, give us your take on Heywood." Lucy propped up a throw pillow behind her back, grabbed a catalog from the stack of magazines on Josie's night table, and sat cross-legged while she waited for me to provide commentary on our school from an outsider's perspective. Or, at least the perspective of a former insider coming back.

I gave them a preliminary rundown—Mandy Pinta looked way better than she used to even though I couldn't figure out why, our headmaster had lost about forty pounds, and the new gym teacher reminded me a lot of our nurse. I intentionally left out any commentary on Luke, although he was probably the person who had changed the most.

They filled me in on a few details that made my observations make more sense—Mandy got a nose job last year for her birthday, Mr. Wesley joined Weight Watchers after he realized he could no longer button his headmaster blazer with the Heywood Academy crest, and the new gym teacher was Nurse Kelly's brother.

I waited for them to go on, to continue talking about the people in our class, but instead they both sat there waiting for me to say something. Only I didn't know what else they expected me to say.

And that's when it happened. The awkward silence. The moment we ran out of things to talk about because, apart from sharing the same school, we really hadn't shared anything else in way too long.

I knew it had been too easy.

My eyes darted around the room looking for something to comment on, something to talk about. All I could hear was the second hand on the grandfather clock in the corner of the room counting how long it would take for us to find something, *anything*, to say to one another. But, unless I wanted to bring up the pleated trim on the love seat in the sitting area, I couldn't come up with anything.

Just as I was approaching a level of desperation so dire I almost considered asking to see the bidet, Josie finally broke the silence. "So, is Chicago as windy as they say?"

I explained how the Windy City actually referred to the long-winded politicians and not the weather. "Even though it can get pretty cold by Lake Michigan," I conceded, beginning to get depressed by our conversation—or lack thereof.

Really, the weather? Was this what we'd been reduced to? Was it my turn now? Was I supposed to ask them about the average accumulated snowfall for the month of December? This entire scene reminded me of an exercise my mom would give her clients for a seminar on the art of small talk.

Lucy shifted uncomfortably and punched her throw pillow twice, like she was trying to buy time before having to come up with another topic and an insufficiently plump pillow was part of the problem. "We don't want to inundate you with a bunch of questions, but there's so much we don't know. Like who your best friends were or even where you're applying to college. Isn't that crazy?"

"Yeah, it is," I admitted, slightly relieved that she felt like I did. "But ask away, I'll tell you anything you want to know. Where do you want me to start?"

"How about with your friends?"

So that's what I did. I told them about Jackie and Lauren. "Jackie and Lauren? *J* and *L*? Do you see any sort of coincidence there?" Josie asked, and I realized for the first time that my best friends in Chicago and Boston shared the same first initials. I gave them the abridged version of my school in Evanston, including a brief description of the city and how we could go to the beach and still see the top of the Hancock Building in downtown Chicago. I told them about Sean, and how we'd broken up before I left for Boston, but I left out the part about it not being a mutual decision, and made it sound like a rational agreement between two people instead of an arbitrary decision by one. Instead of repeating the scene, instead of going through the gory details, I told Lucy and Josie the same thing Sean told me: *It wasn't like we'd be able to see each other anymore, so it just made sense.*

Then I told them I was applying to Amherst, Swarthmore, Northwestern, Smith, and Bowdoin, but I didn't tell them I'd been deferred at Brown. I just wasn't ready to go there yet. I knew it was ridiculous. It wasn't like I needed to impress them, but in a way I wanted to. Maybe not *impress* them exactly, but at least give them the Emily they remembered instead of the reality, which wasn't a pretty picture. I didn't want them to take a second look at me and realize I wasn't the same person who'd moved away or that I wasn't someone they still wanted to hang out with. My mom would call it "focusing on the positive." I'd call it leaving out the mortifying details.

"I thought you always wanted to go to Brown," Lucy commented, noticing I'd left it off my list. I didn't know if it should make me feel good that she remembered, or make me feel even worse for not telling them in the first place. "Remember how, in sixth grade, you told Mrs. Fitch she couldn't give you an A minus on your King Tut diorama because you had to get into Brown?"

Josie laughed. "You were obsessed."

"Well, it was one kick-ass diorama, if you remember. I deserved better than an A minus."

"Sure, but don't you think asking for a second opinion was a little out of line?" Lucy asked.

"Maybe," I admitted.

"Maybe?" Josie repeated. "You wanted her to call the freaking curator at the Museum of Fine Arts!"

I debated whether or not to tell them the truth about Brown, and decided to take the chance. It was either that or spend the next five months pretending that everything was rosy and fabulous. And I just didn't have it in me anymore.

"I applied early and got deferred," I finally admitted.

Lucy nodded as if she understood, but then I caught her giving Josie a look. I recognized those raised eyebrows and the flat, knowing smile. It meant there was something else Lucy wanted to say. But she didn't. Instead she reached for a Victoria's Secret catalog—as if she'd ever trade in her boy shorts for a sequined thong.

And then the room fell silent again as Josie and Lucy pretended to be busy reading catalogs.

I had a hard time believing that pages filled with striped cotton pajamas were that exciting. So that meant one thing—I shouldn't have told them the truth. "What's wrong?"

"You could have just told us about Brown," Lucy answered. "It's not like we'd think you were a loser or anything."

"I know," I agreed, even though I wasn't sure I did. "It's just that I don't really want to talk about it with anyone."

"We're not just anyone." Lucy put down the catalog and looked right at me. "We're your friends."

"Or, at least, we used to be," Josie added, looking more hurt than mad.

They were right. They were my friends, years ago. And if they were going to be my friends again I couldn't be afraid to come clean, swallow my pride, and admit the truth. I wanted Josie and Lucy to think of me as the girl who had the perfect life. The girl who would never get dumped by her boyfriend as soon as the moving truck pulled up in front of her house. Someone who was smart enough to get into Brown early decision. I wanted to be the same girl who was voted Most Likely to Be Nice in eighth grade.

I took a deep breath and then let it out. "I didn't break up with Sean. He broke up with me."

"Why? When? I just talked to you a few months ago and everything was fine." Josie sat up and waited for my answer.

"When I asked him to come over to my house and say good-bye one last time."

"The night before you left?"

"Actually, the morning. While the cab was parked in our driveway waiting to take us to the airport."

Josie let out a painful moan. "Ugh. I bet you wanted to smack him. *I'd* want to smack him."

"Smack him, have the taxi run him over, let an icicle fall from the gutter and spear him through the chest. Any one of those would have done just fine." I tried to laugh as if I was joking, but instead it came out sounding like I had something caught in my throat.

"So go on," Josie encouraged. "That can't be the whole story. There has to be more to it than that."

"Well," I began, but then stopped, realizing how pathetic I was about to sound.

"Keep going," Lucy encouraged, reaching over and squeezing my knee. "We're listening."

And so I told them everything. I repeated every mortifying

minute in detail, and when I finished the story both Josie and Lucy groaned.

"Oh my God, that's just too cliché," Josie exclaimed. "It's like something from a made-for-TV movie."

"Really? Who would play me?" I asked, even though I knew it was slightly off-topic. I wanted to hear what they'd say.

"Maybe Sarah Michelle Gellar from her Buffy days?" Lucy suggested, and I loved her for it. And I loved the idea that I could slay Sean like an evil demon. It seemed highly appropriate, given the circumstances.

"That is such bullshit." Josie turned to me, then reached out and touched my arm. "Not that Sarah could play you, of course, but that Sean would pull such a dick move right before you're supposed to leave."

"Total bullshit," Lucy agreed.

"The least he could have done is brought you going-away flowers or something."

"I'm really sorry." Lucy reached over and squeezed my hand. "But, hey, look at it this way: You're here and he's there, and while he's probably sitting around talking to his idiot friends about who's going to win the Super Bowl, you're here with us."

"Were you sleeping together? Do you have a picture of him we could see? Did you love him?" Josie asked.

I shook my head, but didn't bother answering any question specifically.

"So, that's everything," I told them, even though there was still the small matter of my parents' separation. But I didn't bring it up, maybe because I was hoping my dad would still show up on our doorstep and say it was all a mistake. Or maybe because I still wasn't ready to think about what would happen if he didn't.

Josie gave me a reassuring smile, one that said they still loved me, screwed-up life and all. "See, aren't you glad you told us? Don't you feel better?"

I wouldn't say I was all that psyched about having even more people know about how messed up my life was, but I did feel a little better. Maybe even slightly relieved that I didn't have to hold it all in anymore.

Lucy suddenly clapped her hands against her thigh like she always did before she ran onto the soccer field. "Okay, no more talk of *him*. We hate him."

Josie pretended to wipe her hands clean of the subject. "As far as we're concerned, the boyfriend-formerly-known-as-Sean no longer exists." She tossed the Abercrombie catalog on the floor. "Thank God I didn't sleep with Luke."

"You didn't?" I didn't bother hiding the surprise in my voice. For some reason I guess I'd assumed Josie slept with Luke, probably because I couldn't imagine she'd be *that* angry to discover Luke cheating on her. Josie had gone out with cute guys before, and, even though they weren't as hot as Luke, when things went bad she'd just moved on and never looked back. Josie went through boyfriends like my mother goes through antibacterial hand wipes. I couldn't think of a single guy who actually mattered to Josie the way Sean had mattered to me. I guess I figured sex had to be the one thing that made this time different for her.

"She was planning to surprise him on New Year's Eve after she got home from the Bahamas," Lucy explained. "But then she walked in on the sophomore."

"At least he didn't know what I had planned." Josie pulled her legs up to her chin and hugged her knees. "That would have sucked even worse."

"Forget about them," Lucy suggested. "We have to talk about the time capsule."

I frowned. "I can't even believe they're still doing the time capsule."

"Believe it. Every senior class talks about how stupid it is, but we all do it."

"Can't we come up with anything better than a few CDs and an Abercrombie catalog?" I asked. "Isn't there something more useful? Something the class of 2017 would really be glad to find?"

Lucy shrugged. "Who even knows what the class of 2017 will be like?"

"One thing I can guarantee," Josie declared. "The guys in the class of 2017 will be pulling the same crap the guys in the class of 2007 have pulled on us."

Boy, was that the truth.

Lucy nodded. "It's too bad the girls can't learn from our experiences. They'd be so much better off."

"Maybe they can," I ventured. "Maybe we can help them out so they have it easier."

"What, you want to give them our old exams?" Lucy asked.

I shook my head. "No, something even better."

"The essays we're using for college applications?" Lucy tried again.

"I mean something that they can really use."

"Like what?"

"I don't know, like a handbook for guys." The minute I said it, I knew a handbook was exactly what we had to do. It was perfect. "Something that could spare a future generation of Heywood girls from all the garbage we've had to put up with, like an instruction manual that teaches guys how to treat girls, something that they can use as a reference guide to avoid all the glaring 'guy don'ts' the guys in our class seem to have mastered."

Josie made a little *hmm* sound, rubbing her chin as she considered my idea. "And does this manual of yours have a title?" she wanted to know.

I thought for a minute. "The Guy's Guide to Girls—A Handbook for the Clueless."

Josie and Lucy stared at me silently, their eyes wide and unbelieving.

"You hate it?"

"Hate it?" Josie cried. "We love it!"

Lucy agreed. "We have *got* to do it. It's perfect."

Josie hopped up onto her knees and leaned forward. "I mean, really, how do they learn about girls? From one another. It's the blind leading the blind. They have no idea what to do, and the cycle keeps repeating itself. They have no clue about relationships, no less relationships with girls. We're looking at guys who have no problem pulling their dicks out in front each other at a urinal, but they don't even know their best friends' birthdays."

"Or their middle names," Lucy added. The middle name thing was always a sore subject for Lucy, whose own middle name was Agnes-Georgina after her two grandmothers.

"The fact is, they don't know any better," Josie rationalized. "And that's where we come in. We can teach them. It's just like what your mom does in her articles and books, right?"

Josie was right. It was pretty much exactly what my mom does. Only my mom gets paid for it, and she's always nice. Too nice. "Wait a minute, this can't be some watered-down 'gee, it would be great if you acted like this' guide," I said. "It has to call guys out on all the crappy things they do. We're not here to coddle their ego. We're here to straighten them out, not play Miss Manners."

Josie looked at Lucy and they both seemed a little shocked by my response. I don't think they expected me to be the one to suggest we shouldn't be anything other than kind.

"I'm not doing this to be nice," I continued. "I'm tired of being nice. Now it's their turn."

Lucy nodded. "We couldn't agree with you more."

"Do you think Mr. Wesley will go for the idea?" I asked.

"He doesn't have to go for it, as long as we adhere to the guidelines—no sexually explicit content, nothing valued at more than one hundred dollars, and no drug paraphernalia—they added that after the roach clip thing. So as long as we're not offering sex tips, which, granted, a lot of guys could use, we should be fine."

Sounded good to me. "So how do we start?"

Josie leapt up and went over to her desk, returning with three pencils and a pad of paper. "Here," she said and tore off three sheets. "Start writing down everything that ever drove you crazy about a guy. We need to catalog all of their annoying habits and the stupid things they do."

Lucy waved her sheet of paper in the air. "One page? I could fill an entire notebook with this stuff."

"That's exactly what we're going to do," Josie told her. "But first I think we should begin by taking an informal survey of senior girls to find out what bothers them the most. To prioritize our grievances and make sure we tackle the worst things first."

"I don't think anyone but the three of us should know what we're planning to do," I told them. "We'll ask the girls questions, but it has to be done in a way that doesn't give away that it's for the guide."

"I've got it!" Josie cried out, startling Lucy and me.

"What do you have?"

"I have the first 'guy don't.'" Josie scribbled something on her sheet and then read it aloud to us. "Don't lay your hand on the top of a girl's head and pretend to stroke her hair in a not-so-subtle attempt to push her facedown into your lap—you're not fooling us."

Lucy and I smiled. That was a Guy Don't we could all identify with.

While Lucy worked on the questions for the survey, Josie and I started our Guy Don't lists.

"We should probably swear off any guys for the rest of the year," I decided, as if, given my current situation, that might actually be a problem.

"Already done," Josie told us. "I'm through with guys until they get their shit together."

"When do you think that happens?"

"I don't know. Maybe when they're older? Like twenty?"

"Twenty!" Lucy repeated. "I'm not swearing off guys until I'm twenty."

If anybody was going to object to our ban on guys, I thought it would be Josie. She wasn't one to sit around and lament an ex-boyfriend. She was more likely to call out "next!" But Lucy? What did she care? Guys were way less interesting to Lucy than the win/loss record of Heywood's soccer team. Or at least they used to be.

"Okay, then let's just promise that we're done with guys until we finish the guide. We can't very well be objective if we're dating someone."

I didn't think there was much danger in that. Sean had pretty much cured me of any interest in the opposite sex.

"A future generation of Heywood girls will thank us for this some day," Josie declared, already on her sixth Guy Don't: Don't say you're going to call unless you really plan to pick up the phone, dial my number, and talk to me. Which dovetailed nicely into Guy Don't #7: Don't call me and then sit there expecting that I'll carry on the conversation by myself.

"That's a good one," I told her, remembering some brutal phone conversations I had with Owen our freshman year. He'd call me and then sit there with the TV on in the background. "Do not call a girl unless you actually have something to say and plan on carrying on a conversation—and playing with your Xbox while I tell you about my cat is not a conversation," I added, motioning for Josie to write down my contribution to her Don't list. "Neither is phone sex."

Lucy and Josie laughed at me. "You're really serious about this not being nice thing, aren't you?"

"You bet I am."

They both grinned and seemed almost proud. "Then this should be interesting."

"Not just interesting," I told them. "This is going to be fun."

In ninth grade we may have been bonded together by our complete and absolute devotion to Josh Hartnett and Neutrogena self-tanning cream, but now we had something even better. Something stronger. Josie, Lucy, and I were taking matters into our own hands and taking back control. Misery might love company, but we loved something else. It's called getting even.

And that's exactly what we were going to do.

Even if it wasn't nice.

chapter five

Around five o'clock, Josie said she'd drive me home and I took her up on the offer, not even getting depressed about going home to a house that was filled with brown cardboard boxes, but absent one father. For the first time in days, I felt like I had something to look forward to—and I knew that Lucy, Josie, and I were on to something fabulous. Every time I thought about it I couldn't help smiling. It was truly amazing how much could change in three days. Now I had hope. I had purpose. I had control over something. Finally.

I don't think Josie and Lucy expected me to be so into the idea of picking apart the guys in our class. Every time I came up with a new Don't, they kind of looked at me like they were trying to figure out if I was serious or not, like they were wondering if just below the surface of the Emily they thought they knew, this less-nice Emily had been lurking, waiting for the right time to come out. Well, I was out. Big-time.

Gone was the girl who used to listen to her mom's advice that if you have nothing nice to say, don't say anything at all. Now I just wasn't going to say it, I was going to write it down and let future generations know that Emily Abbott was tired of being the good girl.

"Hang your next right," I instructed Josie, trying to get my bearings straight in the dark. I'd only been to the new house in the daytime. "Then it's the third house on the left."

When I moved to Chicago, none of us could drive, no less tool around in our own black BMW 3 series still reeking of new car smell. I never in a million years would have predicted this. Josie used to hope she was going to get to drive her dad's old Jeep with the duct tape keeping the torn plastic top from flapping in the wind, and now here we were getting our butts toasted on heated leather seats.

"Don't forget, tomorrow we begin our research for the guide," Josie reminded me as I opened my car door and started to get out.

"How could I forget?" I asked. "Tomorrow is the beginning of the end for the guys in our class."

"You know, I wouldn't have thought you had it in you, but I almost think you're going to enjoy writing this guide." Lucy shook her head at me. "Makes me glad I never did anything to piss you off."

I narrowed my eyes and attempted to sound menacing. "Let's keep it that way."

She laughed at me and they sped away.

Even though it was only five o'clock, it was already pitch-black outside. And, because I'd lived in my new house for all of two days and nobody had bothered to shovel the front walk, I had to make my way through almost a foot of snow to get to the front door. If my dad were here, he would have been outside shoveling the walk before we were even up this morning. But, of course, he wasn't here. And all of a sudden I envisioned the front walk piling up with snow all winter, and how the job of shoveling would naturally fall to me. Not because I especially relished the idea of laboring with a shovel, but because I knew I should offer. And I knew TJ never would.

I left my boots and coat in the front hall and made my way into the living room, which was beginning to resemble some form of order, even if discarded bubble wrap and packing tape still littered the hallway. As tempting as the bubbles looked, I resisted the urge to step on them. My mother would definitely not approve, which is why, when we were packing up our house back in Illinois, she forbade TJ to go near the bubble wrap. While my brother and I both knew better than to pop all the little air pockets, my mom knew us well enough to know that TJ wouldn't follow the rules. And I would.

"So, how was it?" my mom asked, stepping out from behind a stack of cardboard boxes, her hair held back by a red bandanna, looking vaguely like her idol, Jacqueline Kennedy Onassis, only without the dark sunglasses and presidential seal of approval.

"It was okay," I answered, almost surprised by how *okay* my first day back at Heywood had been. "It actually wasn't as bad as I thought it would be."

"It never is," she singsonged, picking up a matching pair of candlesticks and walking them over to the fireplace mantel. "I knew you'd be fine all along."

Of course, my mom would never admit otherwise. She's eternally optimistic. It's an occupational hazard.

"I'll be upstairs," I told her, even though I knew I should offer to help her unpack. I had my own unpacking to do.

"Your dad already called to see how it went today," she told me. "You can call him on his cell phone."

My dad. The man who's lived with Polite Patty for twenty years and yet still managed to handle the past two weeks all wrong—which, come to think of it, didn't bode well for our ability to change the way Heywood's guys treat girls.

I stopped next to the pile of bubble wrap. "Do I have to call him now?"

My mom looked over at me and frowned. "It would be nice."

Of course it would. "Maybe later," I told her, turning to go upstairs. And then I stopped. And instead of walking away on the hardwood floors, I stepped to the right and let my foot land on a sheet of bubble wrap, setting off a series of little pops that sounded a lot like firecrackers.

"Emily." My mom gave me her best disappointed look, which included a furrowed brow and a slight shaking of her head.

But instead of apologizing I found myself smiling. Yeah, I knew better. But the new Emily didn't care. And she certainly wasn't returning her father's phone call.

"Don't forget to call your dad," my mom called after me as I headed upstairs, as if oblivious to the fact that she was reminding me to call a man who had decided he was better off nine hundred miles and an entire time zone away from us.

But I wasn't oblivious to that piece of information, and there was no way I'd be picking up the phone to call him. He'd made his choice, and now I was making mine.

chapter six

The next day Lucy, Josie, and I went to work. We'd decided that the most efficient thing to do was split up the girls in our class and find a way to bring up a topic that would get us the information we wanted. We had to be subtle, so we wouldn't give away our time capsule idea, but we needed to get honest answers.

Before lunch I took a walk by the library and peeked in, looking for a few seniors I could start with. And I found exactly what I was looking for. Pam Stoddard and Carolyn Mills were hunched over a table, flipping through what looked like art history books.

I couldn't just walk over and start playing twenty questions. I needed a reason to sit down and start a conversation.

I pulled open the library door and walked in, grabbed a *National*

Geographic from the shelf, and sat down across from Carolyn and Pam.

Art history. There had to be an opening there somewhere. I tried to remember everything I learned from class field trips to the Art Institute of Chicago. Statues of perfectly chiseled men who seemed to be superhumanly endowed? While it may give me a chance to bring up anatomical preferences, it wasn't exactly the right direction. Maybe tormented artists with super-sized egos? That was a little closer to what we were after. Didn't Van Gogh cut off his ear to impress a girl?

I laid my magazine on the table and opened to a random page. "Is that for art history?" I asked, glancing up at them.

Carolyn nodded. "Yeah. We have to pick an artist for our term paper."

"Who are you looking at?" I asked nonchalantly, pretending to be interested in an article on mating rituals of Madagascan aye-ayes.

"Pretty much the regulars: Jackson Pollock, Mary Cassatt, Monet, Van Gogh."

Bingo!

I looked up from the aye-ayes and prepared to get the ball rolling. It was the moment of truth. Could I, the person who'd been raised to believe that honesty is the best policy, get Carolyn and Pam to give me the information I wanted without coming right out and asking for it?

"Hey, is it true that Vincent van Gogh cut off his ear and gave it to his girlfriend?"

"That's what they say," Pam told me. "Why? You think we should do Van Gogh?"

Carolyn shrugged, like that wasn't such a bad idea. "There is a ton written about him."

"I was just thinking how a guy today would never do something like that," I started, hoping that Pam and Carolyn would take my lead and run with it.

Luckily, Pam took the bait. "Yeah. Or if he did he'd show his friends first, just so they knew how tough he was. And they'd probably think he was, even if the rest of us knew he was an idiot who'd be hard of hearing the rest of his life."

"Or, he wouldn't even show his friends," Carolyn said, "because God forbid he actually acts like he really likes her. Instead he'd walk around with a bloody bandage strapped to his ear pretending like nothing happened. And his friends wouldn't even ask."

"Of course they wouldn't. Why ask a personal question when you can rehash the Red Sox World Series for the billionth time."

That was all it took. Pam and Carolyn were off and running. I pushed aside the *National Geographic,* tipped my notebook against the edge of the table, and pretended to write about the aye-aye's diet of insect larvae. It was time to take notes. And fast.

- That gargling noise guys make in the back of their throats before they hock a loogie six feet (the farther the better, for some reason).
- How they can remember every single word to a movie that's twelve years old, but they can't remember what we told them fifteen minutes ago.
- The way a guy scratches his crotch or adjusts his junk in public, rummaging around like he's looking for something he misplaced.

It was amazing. I could barely write fast enough to capture the stream of intolerable traits flying across the table at me. And, although their answers were exactly what I was looking for, it wasn't the quality of the material that kept a smile on my face as I scribbled down gripe after gripe. It was that I felt like I was part of some covert operation only Lucy, Josie, and I knew about. I'd never belonged to a secret club where you picked a code name like Penelope or Leticia and made up some secret handshake (secrets are rude, after all). But that's exactly how I felt right then, sitting across from Carolyn and Pam as they gave me exactly what I was after without even realizing it. Like I was going undercover. Like I should be wearing dark sunglasses and a trench coat. Okay, maybe that was too much. In any case, I didn't have time to plan out an appropriate wardrobe for my mission. I was having a hard enough time keeping up with Carolyn and Pam as it was.

It was like they'd saved up every single annoying, obnoxious, irritating action of every single annoying, obnoxious, irritating guy they've ever known. By the time I was on the third sheet of paper, my fingers were cramping and I was writing so fast my hand was smeared with black ink from dragging along the page. They'd given me more than enough material to start with.

"So, what do you think?" Carolyn asked. "Which artist should we do?"

"Mary Cassatt," I told them, collecting my notebook and standing up.

"Really? Why her? I thought you said we should do Van Gogh."

"I think the guys have gotten enough attention already. It's time us girls got a little airtime, too."

"Hey, don't you need your magazine?" Pam called after me as I made my way toward the door.

"That's okay," I answered. "I've got everything I need."

This wasn't going to be so hard after all. In fact, I almost wondered why someone hadn't done this sooner.

•   •   •

As I passed a guy in the hall or sat next to one in class, I started to look at all of them differently. I studied their every move, dissected every word they spoke. Out of the corner of my eye I caught some junior basketball player cupping his crotch, rearranging himself like it was the most normal thing in the world—almost something to be proud of—while a group of freshman girls diverted their gaze, embarrassed. I watched two sophomore guys sit with their eyes glued to a pair of boobs as they bounced down the hallway toward earth science class, and then break into big grins before making snide comments filled with innuendo.

And, once I started looking at them as specimens to be scrutinized and examined before we cut them up into pieces, they almost became more interesting than annoying. Almost.

Luke still bugged the crap out of me. I may have been on my way to looking at Matt LeFarge, Curtis Ludlow, and Ricky Barnett with a sort of detached scientific curiosity, but I couldn't help but get irritated every time I saw Luke. Not that he had much to say to me; in fact, ever since our encounter outside Mrs. Blackwell's class, he seemed to look right through me, instead focusing his attention on the adoring little twits who were dumb enough to get snagged in his web of floppy hair, perfect teeth, and an ass that begged to be wrapped in a pair of faded Levi's. And it grated on me. Not just because his adoring posse of girls seemed incapable of seeing him for the asshole he was, or because, for the first time *ever*, I didn't care if someone didn't like me—because that part I loved. It felt great. I didn't care if Luke thought I was a raging bitch. Let him. In the end we'd expose him, and the rest of the guys, for what they were. No, what bothered me was that I couldn't for the life of me figure out how the Luke Preston I remembered could become just like the rest of them. Make that the *worst* of them.

And it was obvious Luke knew how I felt. There was just no way he *accidently* bumped me while passing in the hall. And, yes, I am genetically programmed to utter polite phrases regardless of the situation, so I did mutter "excuse me" the first time—but the second time I knew better. And the third. And the fourth.

Luke wasn't just annoying, apparently he was persistent, as well.

I still had a hard time reconciling everything Josie and Lucy said with the person who was Owen's best friend. I could see it if they were talking about Ricky Barnett. He'd always been the kind of guy who went out of his way to be annoying, like the time he found a loose bolt behind my chair in algebra class and turned to me and asked, "Wanna screw?" But Luke Preston was nothing like Ricky. Until now.

It didn't seem possible that Luke could change that much. That I could move away for a few years and return to find an entirely different person. Because the person I remember was nothing like the Luke that Josie and Lucy described or the guy I watched walk down the hallway like he owned Heywood and the rest of us were just lucky to be visiting.

In sixth grade I came home from school one day and noticed something strange in our mailbox. And, from the curved red cardboard keeping the mailbox door from closing, and the imitation lace etched along its edge, I knew exactly what it had to be. It was five days before Valentine's Day, after all, and Carl Mattingly and I had been talking on the phone every night for weeks, even if he just sat there watching ESPN the whole time. I grabbed the candy-filled heart and the rest of the mail, as well (because, even in my state of utter ecstasy, I knew it was the right thing to do), and ran inside the house. I dropped everything on the kitchen table and tore open the heart-shaped box's cellophane wrapping, revealing sixteen perfectly plump chocolates. It was so obvious Carl loved me!

"Aren't you going to open the card?" my mother asked, frowning at me. You *never* opened a gift before the card, and I knew that.

So I slipped my finger inside the pale pink envelope that had been taped to the top and pulled out its contents. But when I opened the card it wasn't Carl's scratchy block writing professing his undying devotion. It was Luke's name scrawled across the bottom, directly under a picture of Snoopy declaring "Dog gone it, I like you!". There was no "Love Always" or "Yours Truly" before his name. Not even a "from." Just Luke's first name and last initial: Luke P. My first thought was, *Luke?*

My mom had watched me open the box of chocolates, so there was no hiding it. And there was no getting around what I knew was coming next.

"Aren't you going to call him and say thank you?" she asked, watching me pick out the pieces I wanted to keep (caramels, dark chocolates, truffles), and then offering her the ones I didn't want (coffee liqueurs, white chocolates, and peanut clusters).

"I don't know his number," I'd told her, hoping she'd take my excuse and let it drop; of course, she didn't.

"Look in the Heywood directory," she told me and grabbed the book out of her desk drawer. "It's got to be in there."

There were times when the school directory came in handy, like when Lucy and I wanted to call Carl and see if Brian Conroy wanted to go to the movies with us. But now it was no help at all. Now it just meant I'd have to call Luke and act like I was actually appreciative of his chocolates—which I was, I love chocolate. I just didn't love them from Luke Preston.

With my mother standing there watching me stuff two caramels into my mouth, there was no getting around dialing his number. She handed me the cordless phone. And I dialed.

The thing is, when he answered and I told him it was me, Luke didn't say anything. Not one single word. There was complete and total silence on his end of the line. What could I do? Sit there and listen to him breathe? I said thank you for the chocolates and waited—for something, a "you're welcome," or a "hope you enjoyed them." But all I got was a single-word response. "Okay."

And that was it. I never mentioned the Valentine's chocolates to him again, and he never mentioned them to me. For a few days afterward I almost convinced myself he'd sent them to me by mistake, that his silence upon learning it was me on the phone wasn't due to an inability to speak, but a result of his complete mortification that he'd sent chocolates to the wrong girl. But in a class of fifty students, I was the only Emily. And he wasn't that dumb.

I never told Josie or Lucy about my Valentine's surprise. It was more of a nonevent than anything else. Besides, I still liked Carl Mattingly, and the last thing I needed was Lucy and Josie reading all sorts of meaning into the cardboard heart and Snoopy card, or, worse, asking Luke the question I kept asking myself. Why?

Three years later, when I let Owen feel me up, I assumed Luke knew about it. I mean, they were best friends, after all. But Luke still never mentioned the candy or made a snide remark or made me feel like a slut. He was still just nice—of course, in a different way than I was. Luke didn't say "please" and "thank you" and "excuse me" and know every chapter and verse in Polite Patty's books by heart. He was nice in the way that someone who always seemed to know how you were feeling or what you were thinking is nice. He was nice enough that you always knew he'd say hi to you and carry on a conversation if you wanted to, but he wasn't someone you were aware of unless you went out of your way to notice him.

But now it was impossible *not* to notice Luke, and there he was, acting like he was oblivious to me. No matter how close I stood to him or how long I'd stare at him as he came down the hall, he barely met my gaze. It was like he was purposely trying to drive me crazy just to prove that he could. And he did. By the end of the day I felt like I *had* to make him look at me.

Luke and Owen and Matt were standing in front of the boys' locker room door talking, and I was on my way into the gym. But instead of pushing the gym door open, I stopped and turned to face them. I focused my unblinking eyes on Luke, narrowing them until they sent the message I wanted, which was: *Don't screw with me.*

I sent mental daggers in his direction, willing him to feel my gaze boring into his head. He'd have to be blind not to see me.

"Em, is something wrong?" Owen finally asked.

I shook my head no.

"You sure? The nurse's office is that way, remember?" Owen pointed in the opposite direction. "Maybe Nurse Kelly can give you something for that."

I didn't know if Owen meant my unattractively flaring nostrils or the tic that I'd suddenly developed in my left eye.

Still, Luke wouldn't even acknowledge my presence. So I headed to gym class with the beginning of a wicked headache emanating from my left eye.

Luke was testing me while I was testing him, and we were both waiting to see who'd break down first. And all day I made sure it wasn't me. Except one time, when three junior girls were clustered around Luke vying for attention. He glanced over at me, caught me watching, and almost seemed to smirk. Like he'd won. Which he hadn't, but I hated that he thought he beat me. And it was even easier to hate him after that.

So is it any wonder I found it practically impossible to reconcile the guy flirting with a group of junior girls with the breathing on the other end of that phone and the messy little signature under Snoopy's Valentine wishes?

When I passed Lucy in the hall on my way to history class, she tipped her head and signaled for me to meet her by the water fountain. I discreetly turned around and followed her. We both knew it was ridiculous, but for some reason the idea of keeping our plan a secret made it more fun.

"How's it going?" Lucy asked.

"I've got tons of stuff. What about you?"

"Are you kidding me? It's as if all the girls in our class were just storing up their complaints waiting for me to ask them. It's crazy."

"We should get together after school and start going through everything," I suggested.

"Want to go to your house?" Lucy asked.

Lucy and Josie still didn't know about my dad, and I wasn't ready for them to find out.

"TJ will probably be around. Why don't we just go to Josie's again. We'll have more privacy."

Lucy gave me a knowing nod and turned to leave. I almost expected her to say "ten-four, good buddy," or "over and out." Thank God, she didn't.

"There's even more stuff here than I thought there would be." Lucy flipped through my pages of notes, astounded I could get such good dirt in such a short amount of time. "How are we ever going to come up with a way to explain all of this."

"I think we need to start by putting them into groups." I took the notes from Lucy and ran my finger down the lists. "Maybe by annoyance factor or something?"

"Annoyance factor? They're *all* annoying." Josie glanced down at her own lists piled on her lap. "Listen to this: Eileen says a guy shouldn't hang his arm around your neck so his hand just happens to hang right over your boob—by accident, of course."

"Mandy hates it when guys start playing the air guitar when it's obvious they have no idea what the hell they're doing," Lucy added. "You never see a girl rip into an impromptu air solo just because she likes a song. And then there are the guys who expect you to kiss them even if they haven't shaved in days, like it's no big deal if we end up looking like we've exfoliated our chins with sandpaper. They're too lazy to scrape a razor across eight square inches of facial hair, but we're supposed to feel like we're turning into raging lesbians if we forego shaving our legs one morning."

"Okay," I conceded. "So the annoyance factor won't help. How else can we do this?"

"Maybe categorize them in some way?" Lucy suggested. "Like how your mom breaks up her books into things like table manners and correspondence and stuff like that."

"Let's try that," Josie agreed, numbering a blank sheet of paper as she waited to hear what categories made sense. In the end we came up with four sections that addressed various areas of concern: personal habits, communication, things you do in public, and relationships.

"You know what I've been thinking?" Lucy glanced up at us. "It's too bad the class of 2016 gets to benefit from our dismal experiences when there are so many guys who need our help today."

"Well, we can't show anyone now. The guys would probably

just find a way to remove it from the capsule or something. Remember, they think they're just fine the way they are."

"Josie's right," I added. "If any of them find out we're doing this, it will ruin the whole thing."

Josie frowned. "Although if anyone needs to change, it's Luke. He's a walking handbook *don't.*"

"Last year he devised the jiggle scale." Lucy pointed to Josie's boobs. "You know, so the guys could rate the breast size of Heywood's female population."

"Classy guy, right?" Josie shook her head . "I cannot even believe I went out with him."

"Are guys really so clueless?" Lucy wanted to know. Obviously it was a rhetorical question. Of course they were. "Do they just not know how to act like rational, normal human beings? Are we really expected to put up with their crap?"

Again, rhetorical, but Josie pondered Lucy's questions. "You know, maybe it's not enough to just give them a handbook. I mean, look what happened when that class put a Rubik's Cube in the capsule with instructions. Their directions totally didn't work at all. Nobody ever figured out how to get all the same colors on one side."

"So, what? We have to prove the handbook works?"

"Or at least prove that you can change a guy, that there is some hope of getting him to act at least remotely the way you want him to."

"How are we going to do that if we can't tell anybody about the handbook in the first place?"

"We have to try it out. We have to follow it page by page and see if we can teach some unsuspecting guy to change his ways," Josie explained. "And it should be the worst offender of all."

Lucy and I looked at each other and knew exactly who she was talking about. Luke.

But Lucy wasn't convinced. "How are we going to do that? He knows you hate him."

"Oh, I wasn't thinking that I should do it." Josie grinned and turned to me. "I was thinking it should be Emily."

My mouth dropped open, which must have been quite unattractive considering it was stuffed full of Pop-Tart. "Me? Why me?"

"Because he'd never suspect you. First of all, you've been gone so you have no idea what he's been like since sophomore year."

I shook my head. "Oh no, two days is more than enough to see what he's like. And he already knows I can't stand him."

"It's only been two days, Emily. He probably just thinks you're PMSing or something."

"So what you're telling me is that you want me to perform some sort of experiment on Luke Preston?" I repeated, just to make sure I understood. "You want me, *personally*, all by myself, to rehabilitate him?"

"Exactly. Luke loves attention and he'll never suspect you have an ulterior motive behind your sudden interest. He'll just think you find him as irresistible as every other girl—another conquest to add to his long list. But while he's thinking you're into him, you'll really be way too smart to actually fall for his crap," Josie concluded. "It's perfect."

Lucy agreed. "She's right, you know."

"But I haven't said one single nice thing to him since I've been back," I protested. "There's no way he'd believe I was interested in him."

"Maybe Emily has a point." Lucy pushed the lists we'd made aside. "Besides, it is kind of wrong, pretending to like him and then writing an entire book about what a dick he is."

"Wrong? Do I have to repeat what he did to me?" Josie pointed to my chest. "Would you like to know where you score on the jiggle scale?"

I immediately stopped licking Pop-Tart icing off my fingers. "You know where I score on the jiggle scale?"

Josie threw her hands in the air, exasperated by both of us. "No! That's not the point."

I went back to licking my fingers, even though there was a tissue about three feet away on the night table and wiping them off would have been the more proper thing to do. I even considered wiping them on my pants as a sort of emancipation proclamation, but then decided that declaring my freedom from other people's expectations was one thing—looking like a slob with icing on her thighs was another. "Look, I can't do it. First of all, he knows I'm your best friend."

"True." Josie tapped a pen on her knee as she tried to figure out how to finesse that small crimp in her plan. "Well, you can tell Luke I'm over him."

Over him. Josie was probably over the reality of being Luke's girlfriend, but she certainly wasn't over the idea that Luke could be over her. "You can't even stand being in the same room as him," I pointed out.

"Then I'll just have to try harder," she decided. "It's worth it. I know you can do it, just pretend he's Sean. Take out your revenge on Luke."

"So, I'd get to be a total bitch to him?"

"No!" Lucy cried. "You can't be a bitch. You have to be nice."

Figures. Just when I'm ready to finally stop being nice, I still had to pretend to be nice to be mean. Couldn't I ever catch a break?

"And what if I don't feel like it?"

"You *have* to feel like it, it's the only way this will work. Besides, you'd only be pretending to be nice. If you're going to try to teach him all the lessons in the handbook and make sure they work, then he has to actually believe you like him—and he has to like *you*."

"Think of Luke as your senior project. And you want to get an A, right?" Josie teased, knowing me all too well. "Then, once the guide's been tested, we can make any modifications before we actually have to put it in the capsule."

"Come on, you have until the middle of April to work up to it. If we can do this for Luke, the rest is a piece of cake."

"What kind?" I wanted to know.

Lucy didn't even hesitate. "Devil's food with buttercream icing and chocolate sprinkles."

She knew that was my favorite.

"If anyone can reform Luke, it's you. Besides," Josie added, "just think what Sean would do if he knew you succeeded in getting the hottest guy at Heywood to fall for you."

Josie had hit a nerve and she knew it. Here was my chance to show Sean. Here was my chance to really get even. "Okay," I agreed. "I'll do it."

"That's awesome. Wait, I bought us a little present." Josie got off the bed and removed something from a shopping bag she'd had on her dresser. "Here, you'll be needing this," she said, handing me a plain brown spiral notebook.

"What's this?" I asked, taking the empty notebook and turning it over. A label read: Made from 100% recycled material.

"That is our new guide."

"I sort of pictured the guide as some leather-bound journal with a satin ribbon to keep our place," I told them. "You know, something that looks official."

"I thought of that, but we don't want to draw attention to it. This way you can carry it around and nobody will ever suspect anything." Josie crumpled up the bag and tossed it toward her garbage can. She missed. "It's where we'll write down everything we've learned and where you can take notes about how you got Luke to change. And now that you have the guide, you need a strategy."

Lucy picked up the bag, came back to the bed, and made her own attempt at scoring a basket. This time it landed exactly where it was supposed to. "Yeah, you can't just start telling him how he should act and what he should do. You need to ease into it. Make him realize the right way to act. Think of it like you're training a dog."

"Exactly!" Josie exclaimed. "It's our version of obedience school. You're training Luke to change."

Lucy and Josie immediately started giving me a crash course on Luke. If the only way to lure him into this was to play nice, then we needed a plan. A three-step plan, to be exact.

Step one: Gain Luke's trust. As probably all dog trainers would agree, this was just common sense. You don't approach a dog and start calling out orders, you offer him your hand, let him sniff around and feel comfortable, and then go to work.

Step two: Guide Luke in the right direction. It's the whole "you get more bees with honey than vinegar" theory—a theory my mother subscribed to, by the way. Pointing out everything Luke is doing wrong wouldn't help him change, and it sure wouldn't make him like me. But giving him a little nudge in the right direction could get us where we wanted to go.

Step three: Reward Luke's changes. When he did something right, I was supposed to let him know, tell him how great he is, give him a little pat on the back. Praise and acknowledgment would be my Milk-Bone.

"What happens when it's over and we have what we need for the time capsule?" I asked, assuming I'd be able to do what I was charged with. "I mean, once we've proven the guide works and a guy can change, what am I supposed to do then?"

"You dump him, of course," Josie answered.

Dumping Luke Preston. Doing to him what he did to Josie. And what Sean did to me. Just thinking about it made me smile. I couldn't get closure with Sean nine hundred miles away, but Luke could be my surrogate, my chance to get even right here in Branford.

I didn't have control over moving, or my dad staying in Chicago, or getting deferred at Brown. I didn't even have any control over the fact that my boyfriend broke up with me. Now there was something I could do to take back control. Only it turned out that something wasn't a something at all, but a some*one*. And that someone was Luke Preston.

chapter seven

That night, I was supposed to be lying on my
bed finishing up chapter twelve of *The House of Mirth*. At least,
that's what I told my mom I was doing. In actuality, I was lying
on my bed reading the same sentence over and over again because
the only thing I could think about was the assignment Josie and
Lucy had given me.

Imagine it. Me, daughter of Patricia Abbott, etiquette guru and
minister of all things mannerly, taking on Luke Preston in a
scheme that was so deceitful, so deceptive, he'd never see what hit
him. I'd get to be a bitch without acting like one. I was going to
fool the biggest player around and enjoy every minute of the fact
that he was the one getting played. Even though my job was going
to be a million times harder than my mom's, who just had to teach
eight-year-olds proper dinner manners (in her seminar Elbows Off

the Table: Manners for Munchkins) or tell brides the appropriate seating arrangement for wedding guests (in her seminar I Do, Don't I?: 101 Etiquette Tips for Brides-to-Be), I was sure I could do it. And I wanted to.

I was still imagining Luke's face when I told him it was over, that he'd been nothing more than an experiment, when my cell phone rang. Again. For the fourth time in the last hour. I watched the silver case vibrate slightly on my desk each time the phone played its Asian-inspired ringer (the least obtrusive of my ringer options, of course), the red light blinking to tell me I had a call. But, just like the last three times, I didn't get up to answer it. I figured it had to be my dad, and I just wasn't ready to talk to him yet. He'd called last night and talked to TJ, but I got in the shower before my brother could pass me the phone and force me to say something. Avoiding my dad had become a daily test and so far I'd been passing with flying colors. TJ, on the other hand, didn't seem to give a rat's ass that my dad had conveniently bailed out on us. For the life of me, I couldn't understand how TJ could talk to him and act like nothing out of the ordinary was going on, like it was normal to talk to your father on the phone every night instead of sitting at the dinner table asking him to pass the peas (you always pass to your right, by the way, just in case you were wondering).

Every time TJ hung up the phone he told me how Dad asked for me, and then Mom would give me a look of disappointment, like I should feel bad for hurting my father's feelings. But I wasn't about to let her guilt trip get to me. What about *my* feelings? What about how *I* felt? He certainly wasn't taking that into account when he drove away in the backseat of a cab like he was just dropping off visiting relatives for their flight.

Avoiding a few phone calls paled by comparison. Let him leave a message.

When the phone finally stopped ringing, I stared at it, trying to decide what to do. I'd never seen the one-bedroom apartment on Ohio Street where my dad was currently living, but I figured it wasn't nearly as nice as our new four-bedroom Colonial house. Or at least I hoped it wasn't. I secretly hoped that the tiny apartment in some corporate housing complex was about as homey as a public restroom. See, I was already getting into the persona of the new un-nice Emily. And it wasn't that difficult, at least not when I had such unpleasant circumstances to draw upon.

But as I attempted to read each page of my paperback book, it was becoming increasingly difficult to ignore the red flashing light that pleaded for my attention. Every little red burst seemed to send a subliminal message to me—selfish . . . ungrateful . . . cruel . . . rude. . . . There was only so much a girl could take, even a girl who had pretty much convinced herself that, in the last two days, she'd grown a thicker skin (or maybe that was just the result of the dry, cold air and the fact that I'd run out of moisturizer). So, against my better judgment, I finally got up and went over to the desk to listen to my voicemail. Only when I flipped open the phone and looked at the last number I'd missed, it wasn't my dad's. Instantly, I felt a wave of relief rush through me, and I quickly scrolled through my programmed numbers, passing by Sean's along the way, until I came to the seven digits I wanted.

"Hey, it's me," I told Lauren as soon as she answered.

"Jackie's here," she informed me. "I'm going to put you on speaker."

"Hey, why haven't you called to tell us how it's going?" Jackie asked a second later, her voice echoing a little over the speaker. I figured they had to be in Lauren's bedroom. "Did you forget about us already?"

She didn't sound mad, exactly, but I got the point. They'd been expecting me to call last night, and now they were calling to check up on me and make me feel appropriately bad for blowing them off.

I explained that I'd been busy unpacking and everything, and they seemed all too willing to forgive me. As I knew they would.

"Tell us all about it," Jackie instructed and I could almost see them both sitting on Lauren's pale blue carpet, waiting for me to give them my exciting news. Only I really didn't have any. After a few minutes telling them about my classes and Lucy and Josie, I'd pretty much summed up the last four days—as long as you didn't count the guide. And I didn't. For some reason, I wanted to keep it a secret, to separate who I used to be in Chicago from who I wanted to be now, and that was someone capable of pulling off the greatest deception ever. Someone who could get the hottest guy in school to fall for her so she could get back at her ex-boyfriend.

I knew Jackie and Lauren were expecting me to ask about him eventually. The ex-boyfriend. I just hated myself for even bringing him up so soon. "So, have you seen Sean?" I asked, knowing that there was no way they hadn't seen Sean. They went to school with him every day. Jackie even sat next to him in homeroom.

"Yeah," Lauren told me and then hesitated slightly before adding, "he's acting like nothing's changed."

"He sucks," Jackie declared, even though I knew she was only saying it for my benefit.

"He isn't acting like anything's different?" I repeated, cringing at the sound of my own voice. Can you say needy? Whiney? Desperate?

Jackie paused. "Uh-uh."

How was it possible that Sean could just wake up and go to school and not even acknowledge what happened? I don't know what I'd been expecting, that he'd be moping around or seem repentant or something—anything to demonstrate some level of remorse for being such an asshole to me.

I knew I should let it drop. I knew I should forget about it and move on. But Sean was like a scab I couldn't stop picking.

"Do you think I did something wrong?" I asked, even though, when I'd called Lauren from the airport, she'd insisted I wasn't the one to blame.

"God no," Lauren instantly shot back, just like she had when I'd asked her the 837 times before. "You were probably the nicest girlfriend ever."

If this is what being the nicest girlfriend ever gets you, I'd take being a bitch any day.

"Should we tell him we talked to you or anything?" Jackie offered.

I shook my head, even though they weren't there to see me. "No, don't say a word. I don't want Sean to think I care."

I went over to my bed and crawled under the covers. "I don't want to talk about him. Tell me what else is going on back there."

Fifteen minutes later, Jackie and Lauren had me laughing as they told me stories about people I wasn't sure I'd ever see again. They even almost had me forgetting about Sean. I had Jackie and Lauren and Josie and Lucy. Who needed a guy?

"Are you sure there isn't anything you'd like us to tell Sean?" Jackie offered again, right before we hung up. "Like that you're already dating the hottest guy in school or something?"

I would have told them they were crazy, if it wasn't so close to the truth. "Not yet, but tomorrow I'm going to start working on it."

Heywood Academy doesn't have a prom. The school is so small we also don't have a homecoming or homecoming parade, and the closest thing we have to a marching band is four guys walking to the parking lot listening to their iPods. But we do have a Valentine's Day dance. Although nobody knows the real reason why Heywood throws a dance for a Hallmark holiday that caters to couples, everyone's always speculated that our headmaster read an article that said the majority of kids lost their virginity on Valentine's Day, or something equally ridiculous. We assumed he thought that we'd be less likely to have sex in a gymnasium decorated with little pot-bellied cupids shooting arrows all over the place.

So with the Valentine's Day dance coming up, Lucy and Josie thought it was the perfect opportunity to put Operation Luke into action. After working on it for weeks, we'd finally completed the guide, which came in at a whopping fifty-one pages of tips, don'ts, and miscellaneous advice to be followed. Now it was my turn to take over where the guide left off. Only, by the time I had to actually *do* it, the idea of asking Luke to the dance wasn't exactly as appealing as when Josie first came up with the idea. It wasn't just that he was horrible, or that seniors never went to the dance and I'd look pretty lame for even asking him. It was that, faced with actually asking Luke to the dance, the bravado I worked up at home in my bedroom and in front of Lucy and Josie just wasn't nearly as convincing when I was face-to-face with him. Besides, I still had to undo the damage I'd done my first few days back at Heywood. And that required swallowing my pride and sucking up to Luke. Not exactly something I looked forward to.

My lame attempts included:

- A garbled "hi" on my way to history class, while I had a mouthful of M&M's and gobs of melted chocolate probably caked in the corners of my lips.
- An ever-so-casual "mm, bad cramps" as I laid my hands against my stomach in the vicinity of where I figured my uterus must be positioned, in hopes that Luke would attribute my prior attitude to a dire need for Midol.
- Nonchalantly dropping a copy of a *Psychology Today* article on courtroom strategies onto the library table where Luke was studying. I figured temporary insanity was more easily forgivable than plain old bitchiness.

If Luke was suspicious of my sudden change of heart, he didn't act like it. In fact, he didn't act like anything. And Josie and Lucy were getting restless waiting for me to make the ultimate move—asking Luke to the Valentine's Day dance.

It had been easy enough to declare that the old Emily Abbott was gone, but it was one thing to sit in Josie's bedroom talking a good game, and an entirely different thing to pull it off in real life. I think they were giving me the benefit of the doubt, but they were starting to lose patience.

Maybe a part of me was hoping someone else would get to him first, that I'd be spared the first step in our plan. But let's face it. Chivalry may be dead and asking a guy to a dance may be perfectly acceptable, but when that guy is incredibly hot and has his pick of girls, who wants to risk the ultimate in humiliation? Certainly not a freshman or sophomore who's still naïve enough to harbor thoughts of Luke Preston walking up to her in the hall and proclaiming his love for her in front of a group of friends. And not a junior who'd like to think she's past caring if Luke asks her or not, even if she isn't. And not a senior, who would just look desperate.

So if anyone was going to ask Luke to the dance, it was going to have to be me.

"You have to ask Luke to the dance," Lucy finally reminded me on Monday. "It's only a week away."

It was actually more than a week away—twelve days, to be exact. But I got her point. I had to make my first move on Luke if we were going to really do this.

"What if he says no?" I asked, looking for some positive reinforcement.

"Who cares if he says no, it's not like you're really asking him. If he turns you down, we just have to come up with another plan. We need to persevere."

"Besides, Luke's never turned down an interested girl, so I can't imagine he'll start now."

If that was supposed to make me feel better, it didn't. Luke wasn't choosy, so if I couldn't do this I'd really look like a complete idiot.

"Okay, I'll ask him soon," I conceded.

"Get on it today." Lucy used her soccer captain's voice and I almost expected her to tell me to drop and do twenty. "We're all depending on you."

"You can do it," Josie encouraged. "Maybe the old Emily Abbott couldn't fool someone so badly, but the new Emily can. Right?"

I could. All I had to do was think of Sean and remember how it felt to be standing there in the freezing cold, wiggling my toes to make sure I didn't lose feeling in my feet, even as it felt like my heart was being ripped out.

Lucy patted me on the back. "Of course she can do it."

"I feel like I'm going off to war," I told them.

"You are," Lucy confirmed. "This is the battle of the sexes and we can't afford to lose."

But, even if I was prepared to do what I had to do, I still wasn't that thrilled with the idea of asking Luke to the dance. I couldn't help but think Luke would see me as the desperate new girl, like I moved back and now I was rushing to ask Luke to the dance because I wanted to be with the hottest guy in school. I couldn't help thinking he'd see me as one of his adoring lunch legion. And I was done being adoring. And I wasn't about to carry his lunch trays no matter how much I wanted to show Lucy and Josie I could pull this off. I had my limit.

Even if I didn't ask him today, I'd do it tomorrow. And the more I thought about it, tomorrow was looking better every minute.

But then during calculus I had to go to the bathroom. There were less than ten minutes left in the class, but I couldn't wait, courtesy of two cartons of chocolate milk and a bowl of chicken noodle soup for lunch.

And when I walked out of the girls' room there was Luke, bending over the water fountain. He didn't even notice me, but the way he was slurping down water I wasn't very surprised. If I wanted to, I could have slipped past him, turned the corner, and not done a thing. But I didn't. I held my ground and waited for him to stand up and look at me. And that's when I got my courage up to look fear straight in the eye.

"What?" he mumbled, using the back of his hand to wipe away a few drops of water that were still clinging to his chin.

And my stellar response? My answer that was supposed to indicate I was interested in him and on the verge of getting him to fall madly in love with me? "Hey."

"Just finished shooting hoops for gym," he told me, as if he had to explain why he'd been slurping up water. It also explained the slight pink flush to his cheeks (note to self: Thinking about Luke's flushed cheeks and the chiseled cheekbones above them, was not the best way to go about hating him).

He could have walked away, and, quite honestly, that's what I expected him to do. But instead he stood there waiting for me to say something back to him. And there it was. My opportunity.

I could ease myself into it, mention that Valentine's Day was coming up, or ask if he was planning to go to the dance. I could pad our conversation with all sorts of niceities and pretend that this was just two old friends talking, two people who once shared a box of chocolates and a Snoopy card. But I didn't. I couldn't think of Luke as the guy I used to know—the person I used to know. I couldn't let myself think of him as a person at all. He was an experiment. A project. And when I thought of my task that way, it helped. A lot.

"Do you want to go to the dance with me next Friday?" I blurted out.

Luke didn't say anything and I wondered if maybe I'd just asked him in my head. Was that possible?

"Do you want to go to the dance with me next Friday?" I repeated, this time making sure I said the words out loud.

"I heard you the first time," he told me, still not bothering to answer my question.

The hallway was silent and I wondered if Luke could hear my heart pounding in my chest. The waiting was excruciating. I didn't know if he was deciding how to tell me no or if he was trying to figure out why the girl who dissed him three weeks ago was now inviting him to a dance.

"Well?" My voice rose more than I'd intended, making me not only sound impatient, but vaguely on edge. It did not sound like the voice of someone in control of the situation.

"I wasn't planning to go," Luke finally answered. "I don't know if you remember this or not, but mostly just freshman and sophomores go to the dance."

Of course I remembered, but I was on a mission. I had to think fast or I was going to lose round one to Luke. He hadn't crushed me, but it would definitely be a technical knockout in his favor.

"I heard a few seniors were going to go this year," I lied, leaving out the part about the few seniors being his ex-girlfriend and her two best friends. "I just thought if you were there, we could meet up or something."

Talk about wimping out. I was supposed to ask Luke to go to the dance with me *as my date*, and here I was defaulting to meeting up with him. Not exactly a fabulous display of cunning on my part.

"Yeah, we could do that," he agreed, although not as enthusiastically as I would have liked.

All of a sudden I thought of the chocolates Luke had sent to me in sixth grade. "It will be just like old times," I joked, attempting to ingratiate myself with someone I found quite loathsome, no matter how cute he looked in a pair of gym shorts.

Luke looked thoroughly confused.

"You know, sixth grade, how you sent me the Valentine chocolates," I explained, trying to jog his memory.

It didn't work. Luke gave me a smile like he almost felt sorry for me, and left me standing there wondering if he was really worth all this effort. And I kind of got the feeling Luke was wondering the same thing about me.

After last class I went to find Josie and Lucy and tell them that I'd put the plan into action. When I passed the library, I spotted Lucy through the plate glass window. She was hunched over a table intently reading a textbook. I waited for her to notice me staring at her, but she didn't. And I didn't walk in. For the first time I noticed that Lucy didn't look exactly the same as I'd remembered. Under the fluorescent lights her hair looked like it had light brown highlights woven through it, and if I didn't know better—if I didn't know that Lucy was the last person on earth who cared about her hair, much less went to the trouble of getting highlights—I would have thought she'd gone to some high-end salon instead of her usual Super Cuts.

I pushed the door open. "I did it. I asked Luke to the dance."

Lucy looked up from her book. "And?"

"And he said he'd meet me there."

Lucy snapped the book shut. "That's so great. See, we knew you could do it."

"Do you think Josie is going to freak out?"

"No, I wouldn't worry about it too much." She attempted to wave away any concern I had. "I mean, they only went out for a few months, right?"

I only went out with Sean for a few months and I certainly wouldn't like watching someone attempt to get him to fall for her. Then again, I wasn't Josie. Maybe Josie was really more into the idea of being with the hottest guy around than actually being with Luke. Knowing Josie's history with guys, I wouldn't doubt it.

"Where is she?" I asked, looking down the aisles to see if Josie was somewhere nearby. "We should tell her about my date."

"She's in the photo lab developing some pictures."

I pulled out a chair and sat down.

"Why doesn't she do that at home?" I asked. "She has her own lab."

Lucy shrugged. "She says she'd rather do it here. I guess she's just more used to it."

"So, was it weird when Josie's dad made all that money?"

"Sort of. All of a sudden her mom wanted her to start doing all these things they couldn't do before, like the whole horseback-riding thing."

Here we were talking about Josie's dad and Lucy had no idea that my dad was still in Chicago. A part of me wanted to tell Lucy that things weren't exactly perfect at my house, either. But there was no way I could tell Lucy and not tell Josie. And so I didn't. Not because I didn't want Josie to know, but because I guess I was still hoping that it was just a temporary situation, and if I actually said anything out loud, it would only make it seem more permanent.

"Should we go get Josie?" Lucy asked.

I nodded and handed Lucy her backpack. "Did you do something to your hair? It looks different."

Lucy held out a strand and examined it before tucking the piece behind her ear. "Does it?"

"Yeah, it looks lighter than it used to be."

"I started getting highlights last year. I totally forgot you didn't know." She shook her head so her hair fell around her shoulders. Whatever happened to Lucy's ever-present ponytail? "It's called 'toasted caramel,' do you like it?"

It was hard to imagine Lucy sitting in a salon with foils stuck to her head. In eighth grade she barely had the patience to brush her hair, period. "I do. It looks good."

"Hey, do you think Owen will go to the dance if Luke is there?" Lucy asked me, collecting her books and heading toward the library door.

"I don't know. Maybe. Probably."

Lucy stopped in the doorway and considered my answer. "I hope so."

She hoped so? I was hoping Lucy would elaborate, but she just pushed the door open and continued into the hall. And I was left wondering if, in addition to highlights, Lucy was interested in a lot of things I never thought she'd want. Including Owen.

The Guy's Guide Tip #22:
Just because I haven't shoved every single
french fry in my mouth doesn't mean I don't plan on
eating them all. And it doesn't give you permission to
reach over and take as many as you want. Ask me
first. I'll probably say yes, but I'd at least
like the opportunity to say no.

chapter eight

The day of the dance I was a basket case. I couldn't concentrate in class (which meant I raised my hand but prayed I wouldn't actually be called on for once), at lunch I could barely eat anything (even though it was my favorite, cheeseburgers and fries—okay, I had a few fries, but I didn't really enjoy them), and by the time there were five minutes left before the last bell, I was seriously doubting whether or not I could go through with our plan. Or if I could really get Luke to like me.

Here I'd spent my whole life making sure people liked me and up until now it hadn't been a problem—unless you counted Stephanie Potter, which I didn't. They say there's always an exception that proves the rule, and I'd decided that Stephanie Potter was my exception. She transferred to Heywood in eighth grade, and, having spent years watching my mother welcome new neighbors with baskets of muffins and suggestions for plumbers, I took it upon myself to be a one-person welcome wagon. Only instead of muffins and references for handymen, I'd brought a pack of Starbursts and directions to Friendly's. Armed with candy and a map to my favorite ice cream place, I'd gone right up to Stephanie Potter and introduced myself. At lunch, I invited her to eat at our table and kept the seat next to me open even though I really wanted to sit next to Josie or Lucy. During study hall I offered to take Stephanie to the library and go through the previous year's yearbook and put names with faces, even though I had homework I could have finished. But even though I made every effort to be Stephanie's friend, even though I waited for her outside classes and after school for the entire first week of school, she had no interest in me whatsoever. Instead she always gave me some lame excuse (I mean, really, she doesn't want to go to the library because she had a bad experience with the Dewey decimal system? Come on, who was she kidding?). By the second week of school, I even had the feeling Stephanie was going out of her way to avoid me (it was probably more than a feeling because every time she saw me wave, Stephanie would turn around and walk the other way as fast as she could, her head down like she was concentrating on something terribly important). At lunch she started avoiding my table like the plague, taking the long way around the perimeter of the cafeteria until she reached Carolyn Mills's table. And then she'd sit with her back to me, just in case I didn't quite get the hint.

"What's her problem?" I asked Josie and Lucy.

They just shrugged.

"Doesn't she realize I'm trying to be friendly?" I asked them. "Maybe she doesn't get it."

"Maybe she doesn't want to be your friend," Lucy ventured, stating the obvious.

Josie agreed. "Why don't you just forget about her, she's fine with Carolyn."

Stephanie may have been fine with Carolyn, but I wasn't fine without Stephanie. There was absolutely no reason why she shouldn't have liked me. I did everything right—I was nice and helpful and friendly. I followed every single rule in my mother's books and Stephanie still didn't want to be my gym partner. And that only made me more determined. There was no way I'd fail, and no reason I *should* fail. For the first three months of school, I poured it on, until one day Stephanie just came right up to me and said, "It's not working."

"Excuse me?"

"The whole going-out-of-your-way-to-be-my-buddy thing—it's not working," she clarified. "You can stop."

"But I'm just trying to be nice," I explained. After all, who would actually turn down someone's attempt to be nice?

"Well, don't," she told me.

"Did I do something wrong?"

Stephanie shook her head. "Enough already. I get it."

"Get what?"

"You want to be my friend. Only I don't really want to be yours. You try way too hard." With that, Stephanie turned around and left me standing in front of the science lab, like some experiment gone awry. And I never got an explanation from Stephanie, and she never cared to elaborate further.

As much as it annoyed me, I decided that something must be wrong with Stephanie, not me. Despite her claim, she *didn't* get it. She didn't get it at all.

I should have learned my lesson then, but I didn't. Like an idiot, I still believed if you followed the rules and did the right things, you'd succeed. I believed it up until the day the letter from the admissions committee at Brown arrived. Up until the morning Sean broke up with me. Even up until my dad dropped us off at the airport. And I should have known better, because I did everything right with Stephanie Potter and it never paid off. She ended up transferring back to public school for freshman year, so I never had a chance to change her mind (and, no, I don't think that she transferred to get away from me, even though TJ once implied that it was awfully coincidental). Just thinking about it still bugged me.

So if I couldn't get Stephanie Potter to like me, there was always the possibility that I wouldn't be able to make Luke like me, either. Even if the circumstances were radically different. Even if I was only pretending to like him. Whether it was my guilty conscience nagging at me about fooling Luke, or my growing lack of confidence in my ability to pull it off, there was a niggling feeling in my head that something wasn't right (I'd decided to call it Stephanie Potter syndrome). The only thing was, I didn't know what would make it go away—deciding not to change Luke, or proving that I could.

When I left school on Friday afternoon, I waited for Luke outside the front entrance, hoping to confirm our date.

"So, I'll see you tonight?" I asked, confirming our plans in the most nonconfirmational way. I didn't want to put too much pressure on him. I didn't have a pack of Starbursts or a coupon for a free cone at Friendly's, but I already had a feeling he was seeing me as quite desperate.

"Yeah, sure." Luke gave me something that looked like a half wave-half swat and headed to the parking lot. It wasn't a resounding answer from someone who was supposed to fall head over heels for me in time to put our guide in the time capsule, but it was a start. And, at that point, I'd take whatever I could get.

Damn Stephanie Potter.

I glanced down at my watch: 3:07. I had four hours to get ready, a mere four hours to make myself into someone that Luke Preston would go crazy over, to become someone he'd like. And I wasn't fooling myself. I'd need every single minute.

But before going back to my locker to collect all my stuff, I stood there and watched Luke walk the entire way toward his car—even if I had to keep reminding myself not to notice his ass.

"You look awfully nice for a Valentine's dance that even TJ doesn't think is worth going to." My mom stood in the bathroom doorway and watched me paint another coat of mascara on my lashes. I was never very good at mascara, something that had to do with reading about Helen Keller in fifth grade and an irrational fear of going blind, but I thought that I needed to pull out all the stops for Luke if this was going to work. My phobia of losing my vision to a brush coated in black dye would have to take a backseat to my fear of being rejected by a guy I couldn't stand.

"Yeah, well, I'm meeting someone there," I explained, although, with my mouth open in an O so my eyes were wide enough to keep from stabbing my corneas, it sounded like, "Ell, I eating um-one air."

"Someone?" my mom repeated, coming into the room and putting down the toilet seat so she could sit. I expected a reminder that proper bathroom etiquette required replacing the seat to its closed position after each use, but either she knew it was TJ's fault, which it was, or she was more interested in finding out about my "someone."

"Luke Preston."

"Luke Preston? Wasn't he the boy who sent you that box of chocolates one year?"

I nodded and wound up dabbing a nice black streak of waterproof mascara under my left eye. Luckily, my vision was still intact, even if my flawlessly prepared face wasn't.

Mom reached into the vanity and took out a Q-tip and some baby oil. After soaking the small cotton tip with the oil, she handed it over to me. "So, does Sean know you're meeting someone at the dance?"

I took the Q-tip and only succeeded in turning a small streak into a smudge that ran from the corner of my nose to my ear. If this was a Halloween dance, I'd be all set.

"I doubt he cares."

"Of course he cares, Emily. He's your boyfriend."

"Not anymore." I watched myself in the mirror as I prepared to say the words out loud. "He broke up with me." Even though the words still felt like a knife stabbing me in the chest, the reflection in the mirror was surprisingly blood free.

My mom made a sympathetic *tsk* sound with her tongue. "I'm sorry, Emily. Why didn't you tell me?"

"I didn't want to talk about it." I moved the mascara wand to my right eye and concentrated. "He told me the morning we left for Boston."

"Well, that's too bad, and I have to admit I'm a little surprised. I thought you'd be the one to break up with him."

"Me?" I blinked and gave myself matching black eyes. "Why would I break up with Sean?"

"Well, you were the one moving, and I figured you'd want to be able to date someone here if you wanted to."

"Why would I want to date someone here?"

"Obviously you do, you're going to the dance with Luke, right?"

I couldn't tell my mother the real reason I was meeting Luke at the dance, so all I could do was agree with her. No matter how much I didn't. "Right."

"I told the guys I'd meet them at Phil's at six," TJ told us, appearing in the bathroom doorway. "Hey, nice makeup job."

I didn't thank him.

My mom stood up. "Do you need a ride to the dance, Emily?"

I shook my head and reached for more baby oil. "No thanks," I told her, trying to remove the last remaining mascara smudge. "Josie and Lucy are picking me up."

"Hot date, huh?" TJ laughed at me. "Don't do anything I wouldn't do."

I ignored him, but couldn't help thinking that what I was about to do was exactly the sort of thing TJ would enjoy.

"I can't believe it's working!" Lucy gushed, practically levitating as she held open the gymnasium doors for us.

"I knew it would," Josie replied, letting me walk through first. I was the evening's entertainment, after all. "You are the last person in the world Luke would suspect of doing something like this."

By "like this" I assumed Josie meant something so completely calculated and devious. Contrary to everything I'd grown up believing, I actually took it as a compliment.

The dance committee did their best to turn the gym into something resembling a Valentine's Day paradise, but there's only so much you can do with crepe paper and balloons. The place looked like a Hallmark store gone bad. The bleachers were pushed together so only the first row provided any seating, and the basketball nets were hiked toward the ceiling with pulleys, but even with red-and-white balloon clusters framing the doorway in the shape of a heart, and music coming out of the PA system instead of basketball scores, it was still no place for a senior to be on a Friday night.

"I don't think he's here yet," Lucy observed, glancing around the gym in search of Luke.

I didn't see him anywhere in sight, but I did see plenty of freshman and sophomore girls dressed in so much red and white they looked like poster girls for *trying too hard*. Because we knew better, Lucy, Josie, and I just wore the same things we'd wear on any other Friday night, but our jeans and sweaters almost seemed to make us stand out even more compared to the groups of walking candy canes milling around the basketball court.

The last time I went to this dance I was going out with Owen. And I was about to get felt up for the first time. Josie and Lucy and I had discussed the situation at length for weeks before the dance, considering every single scenario that would put me and Owen alone in some dark corner behind the bleachers or in the little alcove leading to the guys' locker room. Owen and I had been seeing each other for well over two months at that point, and I figured this was the night he'd try to go up my shirt. I'd thought about it for weeks, even though now I'm sure the only thing Owen put any thought into was whether my bra hooked in the front or the back.

All guys seem to think that girls are so lovestruck by Valentine's Day that they'll go for anything after getting a bouquet of wilted daisies or some white stuffed teddy bear holding a plastic heart with the words "be mine" in the center. And I'll admit that I expected Owen to put in some level of effort before reaching for my Victoria's Secret Angels bra.

I'd had my mom take me out special, claiming I needed new underwear. I mean, what mother is going to deny her child new underwear? Then, once we got there, I asked if I could get the matching bra. Did I feel guilty that my mom was using her Visa to buy an undergarment my boyfriend was only going to attempt to remove? Of course! I kept waiting for her to put two and two together and realize that my urgent underwear request happened to fall on the day before the dance.

But my mom never suspected a thing, and Owen didn't give me a wilted bouquet or cheesy stuffed animal. He gave me a five-dollar gift card to Starbucks. And, while it might not sound like the most romantic gesture in the world, I thought it was perfect. The first time we went anywhere together it was freezing cold in December and he took me to Starbucks for a hot chocolate. So that night at the Valentine's dance, Owen scored some serious points for the gift certificate and also landed the honor of copping a feel of my new satin bra (color: coral peach).

Luke hadn't been at that dance, although at the time I didn't really care where Luke was. Luke Preston wasn't somebody you noticed back then. It wasn't like he was an outcast or anything like that, more like he just didn't stand out. Sure, he played sports, but he wasn't exactly a jock. He did well enough in classes, but his name never appeared in the framed list of honor students that hung in the front hall (my name was always first, mostly because the list was alphabetical and Abbott was pretty much guaranteed to land me first in any alphabetical listing). Luke was the type of guy who seemed to always be in the background, one level removed from what was going on. Owen and I were going out, Matt LeFarge and Carolyn Mills were dating, but Luke never seemed interested in any of the girls in our class, and, with his braces and an odd little cowlick on the back of his head, it wasn't like Luke was much to look at, although, now that I thought about it, and as time has proven, both of those things were easily remedied. All he had to do was remove the silver brackets from his teeth, grow his hair a little longer, and shoot up a few inches. He also used to be one of those guys you'd call "husky," but it seemed that everything had equalized in the three short summer months between freshman and sophomore year. And here it was taking me two years to grow out my bangs. Go figure.

Now Owen and Luke were best friends, and all I could think about was that Owen had probably told Luke about feeling me up. That, when it came to the jiggle scale, Owen had firsthand experience—literally. Maybe that's why Luke said he'd meet me at the dance. Maybe he thought he'd be able to cop an easy feel.

I kept telling myself that I was immune to anything Luke could try. I was practically Teflon-coated, I was so impervious to what limited charm Luke might lay on me. I was no sophomore. I was a senior who knew what she was doing. And what I was doing was teaching Luke Preston a lesson.

"Where can Luke be?" Lucy asked after an hour had passed and we were still sitting on the bleachers, waiting for him to walk through the door. Even TJ had come and gone, bored with the whole scene. He never actually came over and said hello to me or anything, just sort of nodded in my direction and acknowledged my presence. Or maybe he was merely making sure I noticed him so I'd vouch that he'd put in his forty minutes and then he could leave without feeling like he'd lied to our mother about where he was going to be. Even my younger brother thought he was too cool for the dance, yet here I was sitting on the bleachers like I had nothing better to do. I mean, I didn't, but that wasn't the point. The point was I got the feeling that we were being stared at by everyone in the gym, like they were trying to figure out what the hell we were doing here.

"Do you get the feeling people are looking at us?" I finally asked.

Lucy nodded. "Yeah, I do. Mandy Pinta's little sister was even pointing at us before."

"I saw that," Josie exclaimed. "She pointed right at us and then whispered something to her friend."

That was definitely not normal. When I was a freshman, I would never have whispered about a senior. There was always a sort of unspoken reverence for the senior girls, and there was no way we'd talk about them. At least not while they were right there to see what we were saying. Even though my mom had drilled into me that I shouldn't talk about people, sometimes I just couldn't resist. Like the time I heard a rumor that Stacy Voland, a senior who wouldn't give a freshman girl the time of day, was pregnant and had to go to Connecticut to have an abortion. But I wasn't the only one talking about it. Everyone knew, so somehow that made me not feel so bad about repeating it.

But none of us was pregnant or the source of anything else remotely scandalous, so what the hell were all the looks for? "Is there something going on that we don't know about?"

Josie shook her head. "No, I just think they're wondering why three seniors are here."

"I'm beginning to wonder the same thing myself," I muttered.

Lucy patted my knee, trying to make me feel better. "Maybe Luke had some family thing he had to do at the last minute. Or he could have gotten sick. I heard something was going around, you know."

"Maybe his car got stuck in the snow," Josie offered, but we all knew the truth. Luke wasn't stuck in the snow. He wasn't at home with his family or in bed with some debilitating disease. There was nothing wrong with him. But there had to be something wrong with me. Because, even though none of us said it out loud, we all knew why he wasn't there.

Luke Preston was blowing me off.

I'd been stood up. And even though I shouldn't have cared, even though I should have let it roll off my back as yet another example of how badly Luke needed our guide, all I could think was that it was just another example of how my life was circling the toilet bowl.

"We should just get out of here," I told them, gathering up my coat and standing. "He's not coming."

"Maybe we should give it another half hour?" Josie suggested, but all that would do was give me another thirty minutes to watch groups of freshman girls dance together while I thought about what a loser I looked like, sitting there waiting for Luke to show up.

I shook my head and headed for the balloon-covered door, where Mr. Wesley wore a set of little feather wings and pretended to shoot me with his arrows of love. Getting broken up with on moving day was bad, but now I'd hit a new low. Stood up on Valentine's Day while Cupid watched. "Let's get out of here."

On the way to Josie's car I couldn't help but think about Sean. There were so many reasons to think about him at that moment, not to mention that less than two months after he broke up with me I was getting blown off by another guy. So what if I didn't really like the guy blowing me off? That wasn't the point. The point was, here I was supposed to lure Luke into a date, to get the hottest guy in school to fall for me so I could show Sean that he'd blown it, and I couldn't even get the guy to show up.

"You can sit in the front seat," Lucy offered, as if my consolation for an evening of rejection was a warm ass courtesy of the heated leather passenger seat. But I didn't offer to sit in the back, in the dark, where I could avoid having to talk about what just happened. It was February, after all, and even though I'd just been humiliated in front of my two best friends, I wasn't about to turn down a heated seat.

Lucy leaned forward from the backseat, her hands holding on to the headrests as she talked to me. "Look, it was just our first shot, we still have time."

"She's right," Josie quickly agreed. "If anything, this just goes to prove how badly our guide is needed."

I understood what she was trying to say, but I also realized that the reason Luke didn't show wasn't because he didn't know better. He didn't show because he didn't really give a crap about seeing me.

"This should motivate you even more, not bum you out."

Lucy nodded. "Yeah, use this to your advantage. Don't get mad, get even. Get him to change."

How was I supposed to get motivated to change a guy who was so obviously beyond help? And that's when it hit me. The ugly truth. What if it wasn't Luke who had the problem? What if the person beyond help was me?

"What a prick," I mumbled, throwing my coat against the bench in the laundry room.

"Who's a prick?" The light in the kitchen flicked on and TJ was standing there waiting for my answer.

"Nobody."

"It wasn't nobody," he corrected me, pouring himself a glass of orange juice. "I know who you're talking about."

"How would you know who I'm talking about?"

"Two words: Luke Preston."

"And why would I be talking about Luke Preston?" I wanted to know, even though I already knew damn well.

"Because you were supposed to meet him at the dance tonight."

I froze, my hand in midair as I reached to take the carton of orange juice from TJ. "How do you know about that?"

"It's a small school, Emily. Everyone knows everything. Especially if it involves Luke."

"When you say everyone, you mean . . ."

TJ wasn't one to sugarcoat the situation. He told me exactly like it was. "I mean *everyone.*"

He had to be kidding. "So tonight, when we were at the dance?"

"Everyone knew you were waiting for Luke."

Oh. My. God. Mandy Pinta's little sister wasn't pointing at us—she was pointing at me! And we weren't getting stared at because we were the only seniors at the dance, *I* was getting stared at because I was the pathetic girl waiting for a guy who was never going to show up!

Now I was pissed. This was even worse than getting blown off. This was getting blown off and publicly humiliated at the same time. And there was no way I was letting Luke Preston get away with that. He wasn't going to win this battle. I was. This wasn't just about the guide anymore or helping the girls in the class of 2017. This was personal.

"The Celtics were playing the Lakers tonight," TJ informed me, as if I should have studied the NBA schedule before making any plans. "There's no way Luke was ever going to show up. Everyone knew that."

Everyone, apparently, but the three idiots sitting on the bleachers.

I grabbed a glass out of the cabinet and poured my own glass of juice. "And how did everyone know that?" I demanded.

"Like I said, it's a small school. Everyone knows everything."

Not everything, I thought. Not everybody knew I was going to change Luke Preston. Or kill myself trying.

chapter nine

wanted to tell Luke that he was a dick. That he had no right standing me up or making me look like a complete idiot in front of my friends and the entire school. My God, there was a forty-five-year-old headmaster donning feather wings and shooting imaginary arrows around the gym, and yet everyone was looking at me like *I* was the loser! But, even though I should have called Luke out for not meeting me at the dance, I didn't. Not because I was incapable of being cruel like Luke (although, at this point, Polite Patty's daughter had yet to prove she was capable of acting less than considerate—I was working on it), but because treating Luke the way he treated me wouldn't help prove the guide worked. It would only prove I was capable of being nasty, too. Which was what I wanted to prove, what I wanted to *do,* but in an entirely different way.

So confusing.

I had to forego my short-term gain, and the personal satisfaction I'd get from bitching out Luke, for the long-term goal. Permanent change. And ultimate humiliation.

So, instead of saying what I wanted to say, I stuck to the plan. Only now it was my plan. Luke wasn't just going to like me, he was going to fall big-ego, bloated-head over heels for me. He was going to want me more than he'd ever wanted anyone before—and definitely more than he wanted some sophomore from St. Michael's. And then I was going to dump him on his perfect little ass. Hard. And everyone was going to know about it. I swear, in the end, everyone was going to know that Luke Preston didn't get the best of me. And they'd know that I was the one who got the best of him.

On Monday, right before lunch, there he was, standing at his locker while an adoring group of eighth graders giggled as they walked by. Yes, they actually giggled. I knew Luke wouldn't say anything to them—they were eighth graders, for God's sake. But just as the girls peered over their shoulders for one more look at Almighty Luke Preston, he did something that shocked the hell out of me. He winked. And in that instant, Luke gained the admiration of an entire generation of young giggly girls who would never forget that moment for as long as they lived. I knew this for a fact. And it made me want to throw up.

When we were in eighth grade there was a senior, Billy Stratton, who everyone—and I mean *everyone*—was gaga over. The thing was, he had no idea. I don't think he dated a single girl his entire time at Heywood. That's why I never felt bad when he didn't notice me smiling at him or how I'd circle the hallway outside his classes even if it meant I was late for mine (okay, by now you know I'd never be late for class, but I came awfully close, thanks to Billy Stratton). I always chalked Billy's lack of interest in me up to the fact that he never seemed to notice anyone, rather than the reality that I was a five-foot-tall, thirteen-year-old with pink rubber bands on her braces and hair in a perpetual state of static cling (a situation I have cured with ample amounts of styling product).

Luke was definitely as cute as Billy Stratton, but he also enjoyed it way too much. Billy seemed oblivious to his effect on the girls in our school—Luke Preston reveled in it. Luke was the type of guy who had girls sidle up to him at movie theaters and introduce themselves. He was the kind of guy who had strange girls pass him notes with their names and phone numbers written in big bubbly writing, their i's dotted with little hearts. And it made me hate him even more. Which was probably just as well. I found my disgust highly motivating.

I waited until the posse of adoring girls disappeared down the hall, then I took a deep breath, put on my best Polite Patty smile, channeled my mother's finest cocktail party banter, and went to work.

"Hey, I missed you on Friday night." Asshole.

Luke looked over at me and shrugged. "Yeah, I didn't go."

Obviously.

"Well, I missed seeing you there," I said softly, biting my lip to keep from telling him he made me look like a total fool.

He gave another halfhearted shrug and offered a very unconvincing, "Sorry."

Yeah, right.

"Hey, no problem." I mustered up a laugh that I hoped didn't sound as fake as it felt. And then I charged on. "It was pretty funny, going back and remembering what it was like to be a freshman and all excited for a dance." I flashed Luke my most sparkly smile, exposing two years' worth of braces, rubber bands, headgear, and retainers and six months' worth of Crest Whitestrips.

Luke turned back to face his locker, completely dismissing me. "I don't think I've ever been excited for a dance."

My pearly whites and twelve thousand dollars' worth of orthodontia were lost on Luke. Could this guy get any more annoying? Did he not notice I was attempting to flirt with him?

Apparently not, because whatever he was looking for in his locker was about a billion times more interesting than the excruciating conversation he was having with me. And, honestly, I couldn't really blame him. I sucked at this.

I swallowed hard and gave Luke another smile that was supposed to appear coy, but probably just made me look constipated. "Maybe you just never danced with the right person," I told him. Jesus, after this I'd be able to write my mom's next chapter on how to grovel at the feet of the most annoying guy in the world.

Luke stopped pulling books from his locker and stood up. "Really? You think so?" he asked, an amused grin spreading across his lips. It was a grin that so obviously meant, *If you're trying to flirt with me, you're doing a crappy job.*

"And why is that?" he asked.

"Well, I just meant that maybe if the right person was waiting at the dance for you, you'd actually be excited," I answered, pretty much just paraphrasing what I'd already said. So much for my witty repartee.

"So, did you actually have fun at the dance?" Luke leaned against his locker and waited for my answer.

"Not so much. I guess I was just waiting for the right person to show up."

Luke tipped his head to the side and squinted at me as if all of a sudden he realized who he was talking to. It was like a light-bulb went on. Literally. His face seemed to turn on as if he'd flipped a switch. All of a sudden he wasn't looking at me like I was the girl who'd given him nasty looks before English class. Instead, I was the next conquest, someone who would bask in the glow of his usual charm—although if this was his attempt at *charm,* he could use a few lessons. On second thought, that's what I was here for.

"Are you doing anything for lunch?" Luke asked.

I shook my head and gave him a vague, and what I thought was a slightly teasing, "No real plans."

Luke grabbed his coat and slammed the locker door shut. "I was going to go to Sam's and get something to eat. Want to come?"

I knew Lucy and Josie were already waiting for me downstairs in the cafeteria, but they'd kill me if I didn't take Luke up on his offer.

"Sure. Sounds great."

"Grab your coat and I'll go get my car. I'll pick you up out front."

What, he couldn't wait three seconds while I got my coat? Boy, I was really letting him off easy. Polite Patty would have insisted he wait for me and then come around to open my car door.

But instead of pointing this out, I just smiled and gazed at Luke like he was the greatest thing since concealer. It was sickening. And it was working. "Great. I'll be right there."

Sam's is a little general store that's about five minutes from Heywood. Only seniors are allowed to leave school premises during the day, and mostly they just go to Sam's. Not that there's anything to do there except buy food—they have amazing potato logs, these huge french fry wedges that you can get loaded with sour cream and cheese and just about anything else in the deli—but at any rate, it's somewhere to go. Usually there's at least a few Heywood seniors sitting in their cars in the parking lot killing time before they have to make it back for the next class. But when we pulled into the gravel parking lot, it was empty.

"I used to wonder what went on here," I told Luke, glancing around the vacant lot. "Apparently I wasn't missing much."

"That's funny. I used to picture all the seniors huddled over a bong in Billy Stratton's car feeding their munchies with potato logs."

Was Luke talking about *my* Billy Stratton? The Billy Stratton I used to imagine coming over to my house one afternoon and proclaiming his love for me? "Billy Stratton used to carry a bong around in his car?"

"I don't know if he actually carried it around in his car, but he was always stoned, so it had to be somewhere."

"Are you sure? How do you know all this?"

"Everyone knew; it's a small school, Emily. What, did you think he walked around with his head down because he found the pattern on the linoleum floor fascinating?"

"I just thought he was shy and aloof."

"No, Emily, he was baked out of his mind most of the time."

And, just like that, my fantasy of shy, perfect Billy Stratton with the faraway eyes evaporated in a puff of pot smoke.

Luke must have noticed I was spending way too much time thinking about this news, because he waved his hand in front of my eyes in an attempt to get my attention. "Not you, too."

"Me, too, what?"

"You were hot for Billy Stratton."

"I was not," I protested, although I don't know why. It's not like I was the only one.

"You don't have to deny it. We knew all the girls were hot for him."

"And how did you know that?"

Luke squinted at me and tapped his head with an index finger. "I watch things," he told me, his voice soft, like he was telling me a secret.

"Like what things?" I wanted to know.

Luke leaned across the seats and got so close I swear I could smell the fabric softener on his collar. "Like how you were standing outside Mrs. Blackwell's class waiting for me."

"What?" I pulled away too fast and smacked my head on the passenger window.

"I saw you there talking with Owen, how you wouldn't go in until you knew I'd seen you," Luke explained, still hovering awfully close.

God, the ego on this guy. What next, I moved back to Branford just to be near him? "I was not waiting for you," I insisted.

"You weren't?" He sat back and toyed with the buckle on his seat belt. "Then what were you doing out there?"

I almost told him that I was preparing myself to go into the classroom, that I was thinking about everything I'd left behind in Chicago, when I remembered that I wasn't supposed to be trying to convince Luke that I wasn't interested in him. I was supposed to be convincing him I *was*. Step one was earning Luke's trust, and I was about to try and do that.

"Okay, you're right," I admitted, trying to sound like he'd found me out. "I was waiting for you."

Luke smiled and leaned toward me again. "See, I thought so."

I avoided looking at him, and instead stared at the windshield, which, with all our conversation going on inside, and the frigid temperatures outside, had fogged up.

This was probably how Luke approached all the girls he thought he could make out with. He lured them into his car, parked in a deserted parking lot, and then moved in. Maybe this was even how he confirmed the accuracy of his jiggle scale.

I stared straight ahead and braced myself for what I was sure would be a kiss somewhere in the vicinity of my lips. But instead of making a move on me, Luke opened his car door, letting in a cold gust that wasn't nearly as warm as the kiss I'd been expecting. "Come on, I'm starving."

Luke ordered Sam's famous potato logs and I asked for a turkey sandwich, something I figured wouldn't make a mess in Luke's car. Not that I should have been all that concerned about messing up his upholstery, but I couldn't help it. I'd been brought up to believe that cleanliness was next to godliness, and that godliness extended to the interior of automobiles.

Once we were back in the car, Luke really did seem more interested in his potato logs than the girl in his passenger seat. Mainly, me. The very same girl who was supposed to be taking care of step one.

"Thanks for inviting me to have lunch with you," I said, and then couldn't resist adding, "I mean, sacrificing your tableside service and all."

Luke laughed and suddenly seemed awfully intent on the Styrofoam container in his lap. "Yeah, well . . ." Luke avoided looking up at me and, if I didn't know better, I'd say he almost looked embarrassed.

"When you asked me to come to Sam's, I almost thought you'd expect me to carry your lunch to the car," I went on, enjoying his discomfort a little too much.

"They're sophomores," he told me, tearing open a couple of packets of ketchup and squirting a pool of it next to his potato logs. "What can I say?"

There was a lot he could say. He could say it was disgusting to expect a bunch of girls to serve him lunch every day. He could admit that it verged on degrading every single girl who stood next to his table asking if he needed a straw for his drink. He could even tell me that tomorrow he'd ask them to stop.

But I didn't point that out. Instead I took a bite of my turkey sandwich. "I guess it beats waiting in line for sloppy joe's, right?" It wasn't like I expected Luke to offer an excuse, or even an explanation, for the lunch legion, but that's exactly what he did.

"Look, I don't *ask* them to bring me lunch. I don't force them. They offer. Besides, they like it."

The sad thing was, Luke was possibly right. Bringing Luke his lunch was probably the highlight of their day. As sad as that was. I know if Billy Stratton had given me a chance to bring him his lunch, I would have donned an apron and hopped to it. Amazing how four years and a little perspective can change things.

"I guess," I told him, covering my mouth with a napkin so I didn't spit shredded lettuce all over his dashboard. "And to think I remember the good old days in middle school, when you had to actually wait in line with everyone else."

"Is that what they were? The good old days?"

"Why, are you saying they weren't?"

"I'm just saying maybe you and I remember things differently." Luke dipped a log in the pool of ketchup. "So, are you glad you're back? Did you miss Branford?"

I didn't really feel like talking about myself with Luke, but I couldn't ignore the lesson learned from all those cop shows where the detective creates a rapport with his suspect by talking about himself. If I had to offer Luke a few personal tidbits to earn his trust, then that's what I'd do.

"I don't know if 'glad' is the right word, but things haven't changed as much as I was afraid they would." I glanced over at Luke and watched him take a bite of his potato log. "Well, most things, I mean."

"It must have been tough, moving in the middle of senior year."

"It was," I told him, and it occurred to me that Luke was the first person to acknowledge how hard it was. My parents always acted like it was no big deal because we were just moving back to Branford. TJ didn't have any problem leaving his old friends and taking up right where he left off in seventh grade. Even Lucy and Josie never acted like they thought it was any big deal, they were just glad I was back.

"I bet you were wondering what we'd all think of you," Luke went on, like he'd been reading some self-help book on all the things that go through your head when you move.

"Maybe," I hedged.

"But I guess you aren't wondering anymore. Everyone seems to be glad you're back."

"Yeah, I guess so."

I must have sounded like I was trying to be modest or something, because Luke went on. "You guess so? Come on, who are you kidding? Everyone always liked you." He dipped another potato log in ketchup. "Well, unless you count Stephanie Potter."

For a minute I thought Luke was making fun of me, but then he laughed. "I'm just kidding."

"How do you know Stephanie Potter didn't like me?" I asked.

"I watch things, remember?" Again, he tapped the side of his head with his index finger.

"That's right. I forgot."

I went back to eating my sandwich, but it sort of bothered me that Luke knew about me and Stephanie Potter.

"It bugs you, doesn't it? You wanted her to like you."

"No it doesn't." I shook my head and a piece of lettuce flung across the car and landed against Luke's driver's side window.

"If it helps any, I never really liked Stephanie that much." Luke reached for the lettuce and flicked it off the window.

"You didn't?"

"Nope. Didn't like her at all."

I didn't know why, but for some reason that did help.

For the first time since we got to Sam's, I looked at Luke instead of keeping a safe distance between us, afraid he would try to kiss me or something. There was no way he was kissing me with a mouth full of potato and ketchup. And as I watched him eat his lunch it dawned on me that, as much as I wanted to hate Luke, maybe he wasn't *all* bad.

"So, maybe you want to do something Saturday night?" Luke asked. At least I think he did. I mean, really, does asking somebody if they *maybe* want to do something count as actually asking anything at all?

Not that it mattered. I couldn't do something *maybe* anyway. I'd promised my mom's friends I'd babysit Saturday night so they could go out to dinner. And, while most girls would probably ditch a babysitting job in two seconds flat for a date with Luke Preston, I wasn't one of them. My mom had written an entire chapter in one of her books on babysitting etiquette and lesson number one was that you don't cancel on a family once you've made a commitment unless life or limb is at stake. A date with a guy didn't exactly count as either. Even if it was Luke.

"I can't. I'm babysitting for some family friends."

"Too bad, Curtis is having a party this weekend. His parents are going out of town." Luke reached for the radio dial and flipped the station. "Maybe I'll stop by and see you, say hi."

Babysitting etiquette number two: no guests allowed.

"That's not a good idea. I don't think the Brocks would like it if I had any visitors." I pointed to his chin. "You have some ketchup there."

Luke dabbed his finger against his cheek. "Where, here?"

I shook my head.

"Here?" He wiped his sleeve along the other cheek.

I shook my head again.

"Wouldn't this just be easier if you took that napkin you have folded on your lap and wiped away the ketchup yourself?" Luke suggested.

"But it's more fun watching you try to find it."

"Oh yeah? Let's see." Luke dipped a potato log into the pool of ketchup and dabbed it on my nose. "Um, you've got a little ketchup there," he mimicked, not sounding anything like me.

I reached for a potato log and swiped it in the dollop of red on my nose. "That's actually quite good. And convenient."

Luke took his half-eaten log and dabbed it against my nose. "You're right. This is very convenient. Maybe the next time the cafeteria has french fries for lunch I'll suggest you walk around and offer up your nose."

"Maybe when they have fish sticks I can serve tarter sauce instead."

Luke made a gagging sound. "Okay, that's not even funny. It's just gross."

"You're right," I agreed, picturing it. "It is."

"So." Luke continued to eat his potato logs but forgot to wipe the ketchup off his chin. "Why the sudden change?"

"What sudden change?" I asked, finding it difficult to keep my eyes from zooming in on the condiment precariously perched on his chin, waiting for it to fall off into his lap at any moment.

"You went from a nasty greeting in the hall to ignoring me to asking me to a dance? I thought Josie turned you against me."

I focused on my turkey sandwich in an attempt to keep from staring at Luke's chin. You'd think I'd be grossed out, but all I could think was that even with ketchup on his chin, Luke still looked pretty hot. "Yeah, well, moving kind of put me in a bad mood. Besides, Josie's over it now," I added, just so he'd know there were no reasons why he shouldn't fall in love with me right then and there.

Luke dipped another potato log in his pool of ketchup, and as he raised it to his mouth, another drop of red landed on his chin. "Do you miss living in Chicago?"

It was a serious question and I wanted to answer him, but all I could do was laugh.

"What's so funny?" he wanted to know.

I pointed to his chin.

"We're not going through this again." This time he reached for my napkin and wiped the condiment off himself. "Maybe next time we get lunch I should order something else. Something that can't drip."

"Next time?" I repeated, just to make sure I heard him right. "Will there be a next time?"

Luke squinted his eyes and pretended to examine me before wiping off the ketchup that still clung to my nose. "We'll see. It depends on what your nose is serving."

I laughed again, and this time he laughed with me.

If you set aside the fact that Luke was way too cocky, that he could be obnoxious, and that he'd cheated on my best friend, he might actually be cute. No, he was definitely cute. And he might actually be *likeable*.

"Okay, I take back what I said." Josie bit her lip. "This is weird."

When Luke dropped me off at the front door, Josie had been waiting for me, pacing back and forth like an expectant father.

Apparently, the parking lot at Sam's hadn't been vacant the entire time—or at least not while Luke and I were eating our lunch inside the steamed-up windows. "I told you it would be. If you hate hearing about it, how do you think I feel doing it?"

"I know. It's that, well, he cheated on me, but I still liked him. I mean, I was planning to sleep with the guy, and now I'm watching one of my best friends hit on him."

"I wasn't hitting on him," I told her for what seemed like the billionth time. "We were just talking."

"Yeah, well, Matt came back from Sam's and he couldn't wait to tell everyone how you and Luke fogged up the car windows."

"If the windows were all fogged up, how did he even know it was me?"

"But it was you," Josie stated matter-of-factly. "So what's your point?"

What *was* my point? "My point is that, yes, I was in the car with Luke, but, no, we were not making out. Look, I was just doing what you guys said I should do. We don't have to go on with this if you don't want to," I offered, almost hoping Josie would take me up on my offer. Okay, I *was* hoping Josie would take me up on my offer.

Josie didn't even hesitate before shaking her head. "We're doing the guide. We have to. But here," she said, taking the brown recycled notebook out of her backpack and holding it out to me.

"You take this. I think you should be writing down everything that happens with Luke. And one more thing—if you really think it's starting to work, I want an apology for what he did to me."

I didn't move to take the notebook from her. "I can stop right now and we can forget about the guide," I offered again, giving her one last chance to put an end to our plan.

"No, I don't want to do that. I want an apology." Josie let out a breath and forced the notebook into my hand. "I'll get over it. I just wish he wasn't so freaking hot."

Yeah, me, too.

chapter ten

I'd promised my mom's friends, the Brocks, that
I'd babysit for their little girl on Saturday night. There was no way
my mother would let me get out of it—being not only an obliga-
tion, but that their reason for needing me in the first place was
that the Brocks were having dinner with my mom.

Before we moved away, I used to babysit for the Brocks about
every other weekend, and more often than not, Lucy or Josie
would come with me. Back then there weren't any other real options for a Friday or Saturday night, except maybe having a sleep-
over and trying out new makeup and stuff like that. It wasn't like I
was making a fortune watching a three-year-old for a few hours,
but I always offered to split the money with them. Lucy always said
no, but sometimes Josie said yes. Now Josie didn't need the money,
and Lucy didn't seem that thrilled with the idea of hanging out

with a six-year-old whose main interests were the new Barbie town house she got for Christmas and the latest *Princess Diaries* movie. Besides, tonight was Curtis Ludlow's party. Sitting around watching TV while a six-year-old sleeps upstairs or going to a party at Curtis Ludlow's house? I couldn't really blame them; I would have made the same choice.

The Brocks' house is down a long wooded driveway and it's pretty secluded. You can't even see it from the street. When you're in an empty house with a six-year-old whose sole means of self-defense is the magic wand she waves around while reciting magic spells, every noise sounds like something worse than it really is. Tree branch scraping against the gutters? Must be somebody trying to get in through a window. Furnace groaning in the basement? Must be someone just waiting for the right time to come upstairs and dismember a little girl and her babysitter. All the noises used to really freak me out, and more than once I'd ended up calling my dad, convinced there was a deranged madman outside the family room trying to jimmy open the sliding glass doors. After those calls, my father would always drive over and reassure me that there wasn't some serial killer hiding in the basement, or an escaped mental patient squatting behind the shower curtain waiting to attack me while I was on the toilet reaching for some Charmin.

Even though one part of me knew I was being paranoid, that there was no way someone was outside plotting how to hide my body in a shallow grave in the woods, there was the other part that had been influenced by way too many Friday nights watching cheesy horror movies on TV with Lucy and Josie. So I usually kept on as many lights as possible without making it too obvious that I was hoping a few hundred-watt bulbs would deter a homicidal killer.

After I tucked Sophie in bed and read her a story, I went back to the family room and flipped on the TV. But I wasn't about to kick back and watch the *E! True Hollywood Story* on the Olsen twins. I had work to do. I had the guide.

I took the brown notebook out of my backpack and prepared to write about turning our lists of tips and suggestions into tangible results. There was only one problem. I've never been someone who bought into that whole diary/journal thing. When I was seven my mom bought me a diary for my birthday and I loved holding the little gold key in my hand and coming up with new hiding places. Of course, I was also so good at hiding the key that eventually even I forgot where it was. But by then it barely mattered. I'd completely lost interest. My entries were always more along the lines of "today I had tuna on wheat for lunch" than hidden yearnings. And even though I tried journaling years later when it seemed everyone was filling blank white pages with poetry and sketches of unicorns, my journal started off with "I think my jeans looked good today" and went downhill from there.

But if the guide was going to be turned into my personal journal for the next few months I had to begin somewhere, and my lunch with Luke in the parking lot at Sam's was as good a place as any to start. Admittedly, there wasn't a ton to write about, but at least I could explain how my attempts to complete step one were progressing. And they were progressing, if I did say so myself. Ever since Sam's, Luke was way more friendly, even waiting for me by our lockers yesterday so we could walk to English class together. He didn't attempt to hold my hand or anything like that, but I didn't take it personally. I couldn't expect Luke to change over night, even if it would make my job a lot easier if he did.

It had been almost three years since I last babysat for the Brocks, and I thought that the strange noises and weird rattling in the basement wouldn't freak me out anymore. And I was right. To a point. I could rationally explain away any creak or squeak in the house, and when I noticed a set of headlights coming up the driveway, instead of freaking out that my killer had borrowed a car, I thought maybe the Brocks had decided to come home early or something. I was even collecting my coat and about to stuff the notebook into my backpack when the doorbell rang. And that's when I knew something wasn't right. Nobody rings their own doorbell.

Instinctively I reached for the phone and then stopped, just like those TV shows where they freeze the action right before cutting to a commercial. This was when I used to call my dad, but my dad wasn't at our house. He was back in Chicago, and that meant I couldn't call him. My mother's Babysitting Etiquette Lesson #4: No long-distance phone calls.

I sat there trying to figure out what to do as the bell continued to ring like bad background music in a horror movie. Wasn't this when you usually see the babysitter get up and go into the kitchen for a butcher knife? That option didn't really seem like an option at all. In those movies the babysitter always ended up with the knife in her back and the telephone cord wrapped around her neck.

So instead of trying to come up with a weapon, I slid off the couch, crouched down, and tiptoed to the front door, careful not to pass by the front window just in case it was really a serial killer, albeit one polite enough to ring the doorbell.

When I reached the front door, I slowly stood up, easing my eye toward the small circular peephole, the entire time hoping the

Brocks just forgot their keys. But when I got there it wasn't Mrs. Brock. Instead, a single large brown eye was staring back at me, and before I could stop myself I let out a noise that was more strangled poodle yelp than scary movie scream.

"It's me," the eye yelled through the door.

This time when I looked through the peephole, the eye had moved back and I could see the head it was attached to.

I unlatched the deadbolt and threw the door open—almost grateful for the familiar face, but also slightly pissed off.

"What are you doing here?" I asked, smoothing some loose hairs back into my ponytail. As if that was the worst of my problems. Who'd notice a few stray hairs when I wasn't exactly dressed to thrill in sweatpants and a ratty long-sleeved Martha's Vineyard T-shirt. And instead of smelling like some fabulous perfume, the only thing I reeked of was ChapStick.

"I was just in the neighborhood," Luke told me, coming in without waiting to be asked. "Your brother told me where you were."

I watched as Luke took off his coat, made his way to the couch, picked up the remote control, and started flipping through the channels like he'd been here a million times. And maybe he had. Who knew which hot high school girls had been babysitting for the Brocks in my absence?

"Look, you can't stay," I warned him, standing in front of the TV to block his view. Had Luke not heard me say that I shouldn't have uninvited guests? Besides, in addition to looking less than stellar, Luke completely caught me off guard. I needed time to psych myself up for my encounters with Luke. I couldn't be expected to just wing it. Especially not when I was wearing TJ's sweatsocks.

"I can't stay?" Luke looked slightly confused. "Why not?"

"You have to go," I repeated. "I'm not supposed to have company."

"Look, there's nothing to worry about. They're not going to come home anytime soon; it's only eight o'clock."

I made a mental note to add this to the list of annoyances: *Do not think that you know better than I do just because you don't like what I know.*

I was about to tell Luke that this was a non-negotiable issue when I saw it. The guide. Luke was sitting about six inches from my backpack and the notebook that contained a two-page description of our lunch at Sam's, ketchup-stained chin and all. And that's when it occurred to me that instead of trying to block the TV with my ass, I should be using this unexpected, and somewhat unwelcome, opportunity to my advantage. The Brocks weren't due home for at least another hour. Instead of arguing, I should be gathering material for the guide. And maybe running upstairs to see if Mrs. Brock had a little makeup I could borrow.

"Okay, but just for a little while." I moved away from the TV, deciding to give Luke a half hour, strictly for the benefit of our little experiment. "So, what are you doing here?"

Luke didn't seem to understand my question. "What do you mean?"

"I mean, why aren't you at Curtis's party with everyone else?"

"You told me you were babysitting."

"I also said I shouldn't have visitors while I was babysitting."

Now Luke looked at me like I was speaking a foreign language. "Yeah? So?"

"Did you not understand that I meant *you* shouldn't come over while I was babysitting?" I repeated, realizing I sounded more than a little testy. I immediately softened the tone of my voice. "No big deal. I guess you just didn't hear me."

"No, I heard you. I just didn't think you were serious."

"Why would I say it if I wasn't serious."

Luke considered this for a minute. "I guess I just thought you were saying that to see if I would come over. When I called your house your brother gave me the address like you were already expecting me or something."

"TJ knows the address because he's been here a million times, not because I told him to send you over."

"So you meant it?" Luke still didn't look like he believed me.

"Yes, I meant it. Why would I say it if I didn't?"

"Because you guys say things like that all the time, and don't mean it."

By "you guys" I assumed he meant "you girls."

I was about to tell him he obviously knew nothing about "us guys," when it dawned on me that while I was having this inane conversation with Luke, the rest of our senior class was at Curtis's party. Which meant that Luke didn't just call my house to talk to me (score one), he'd also ditched Curtis's party to come to the Brocks' and see me (score two). Sure, maybe he thought he had a better chance of getting in my pants in an empty house than at a party, but he was still here. With me. And, from the smell of shaving cream wafting from his direction, he'd shaved. Maybe even showered. So he was trying to impress me. And that meant that my attempt to successfully conclude step one was actually working.

Somehow, I was doing it. And if Luke was on his way to believing that I liked him, if he was on his way to really trusting me, than that meant I should be doing more than blocking the TV so he couldn't watch *Cops*. I should be moving on to step two.

But first things first. I went over to the couch and removed the backpack and notebook from his reach. Now I just had to get them out of the room.

"Do you want something to drink?" I offered, ever the congenial hostess. My mom would be proud. "I think they've got some Sprite in the refrigerator."

Luke nodded. "Sure."

I turned to go into the kitchen and became acutely aware of Luke's eyes following me. All of a sudden I wondered if there was a jiggle scale for rear views, too. Not that my ass was that bad, but gray sweatpants didn't exactly present my assets in the most flattering light. I turned around and faced the TV, pretending to be captivated by a shirtless, handcuffed guy in a trailer park as I walked the rest of the way backward into the kitchen.

The cabinet where the Brocks kept their glasses was empty, and I was about to open the dishwasher to look for a clean glass when I noticed Sophie's macaroni-and-cheese–encrusted My Little Pony cup in the sink. There were probably eight adult-size glasses in the dishwasher without cartoon characters, but I didn't go looking for them. Instead, I washed the remaining chocolate milk out of the plastic cup and filled it with Sprite. Watching Luke Preston drink out of a My Little Pony cup complete with an attached pink Krazy Straw in the shape of a horse's head was just too good an opportunity to pass up. Cool Luke Preston drinking out of a plastic cup with pastel-colored ponies on the side. He'd be mortified. And I'd have my chance to transition to step two by teaching Luke a thing or two about being gracious, even if what he was gracious about was a six-year-old's plastic cup.

I couldn't help grinning as I carried the cup over to Luke.

"Here you go." I handed him the Sprite and waited for his reaction, a snide comment or eye roll that was meant to tell me there was no way Luke Preston was going to drink out of a My Little Pony cup. Then I'd have to explain that this wasn't a restaurant, I wasn't a waitress, and he should just say thank you for the effort and drink the damn Sprite. But Luke didn't say anything. Instead, he just took the cup and didn't seem to care as much as I thought he would. Maybe he was just really thirsty.

So much for Luke's first lesson.

"So, you really didn't want me to come over?" he asked again.

I shook my head. "No, I really didn't want you to come over."

Luke smiled.

"Why do you think that's funny?"

"Because I can't figure you out."

"Am I that perplexing?"

"Maybe."

"Why's that?"

"Because you didn't throw a shit fit when I didn't show up at the dance. And you didn't tell me not to come over tonight just to test whether or not I would."

Maybe the night wasn't a total loss. Maybe I'd be able to teach Luke a few things after all. "Well, first of all, I'd just like to say that, while I didn't throw a fit about you not showing up at the dance, it was still a pretty rude thing to do," I told him, putting step two into action: guide Luke in the right direction. "Why do guys say they're going to do something if they're not? It's just like when a guy says he's going to call and he doesn't. I mean, really, what's the point?"

I hadn't expected Luke to give me an answer, but he offered one anyway. "Because, at the time, we think we will. Or, if I really don't think I'll call, I don't tell you because you'll just get mad."

"Well, it's not like *not* calling makes us any less mad." I sat on the arm of the sofa and attempted to process what Luke was telling me, trying to make logical sense out of something that was completely illogical. "So what you're saying is, you'd rather us get mad later rather than then and there?"

"No, we'd rather you didn't get mad at all. But if you are, I'd rather take my chances."

I crossed my arms over my chest, beginning to wonder who was the teacher and who was the pupil. "That's insane."

"Not any less insane than when you say something you don't mean."

"Like what?"

"I don't know." Luke took a sip of his Sprite while he thought about it. "Like when Josie told me she didn't care if I got her a Christmas present or not."

"How do you know she really *did* care?"

"Because one minute she tells me I don't have to get her anything, and the next minute she's pointing out some necklace in a Tiffany catalog her mom got in the mail."

"Maybe she just liked the necklace," I suggested.

"Please. She expected some huge present but she wouldn't come out and say that. Instead it was like she was testing me to see what I'd do. She may have a ton of money, but I don't. And even if I did, I wouldn't spend it on some useless necklace."

I felt a tinge of disloyalty talking about Josie like this. Even though she had no problem talking about how annoying Luke was, she'd never mentioned how she acted while they were going out. I had Josie's side of the story, and here was an opportunity to hear Luke's. And, despite myself, I wanted to hear it. I wanted to know more about what went wrong with them. Maybe it would help me figure out what went wrong with Sean. "Is that why you sent Josie a breakup email? Because you didn't want to get her a present?"

"She made me feel bad about the present thing, but that's not why. We just weren't having fun anymore."

I was about to tell him that maybe a relationship wasn't about having fun, but I stopped myself. Even I knew that was ridiculous. Besides, instead of debating whether or not Josie expected Luke to drop a significant amount of cash on a present wasn't going to get me where I needed to go. And where I needed to go was on to step two.

If Luke was going to be here with me, I had to make good use of our time. And that meant he was going to go home knowing that 1) you call when you say you're going to call, and 2) you don't rely on AOL to do your dirty work.

"Maybe she was being unreasonable, but you should have told her in person instead of over the Internet."

"Are you kidding me? If I don't want to say I won't call, can you imagine how I feel about breaking up with someone?" Luke grinned and he almost got me to grin, too. Luckily, I caught myself.

"So you took your chances?"

"Exactly."

I had a hard time believing that Luke was anything more than a coward who wanted to take advantage of the fact that Josie was on some Caribbean island while he was back here thinking about all the girls who would be at Owen's party. Besides, in Luke's world, Sean wasn't being a complete dick when he broke up with me the morning I moved. In fact, he was actually quite brave. Luke would probably think Sean deserved some sort of medal of honor for actually showing up and telling me in person. But I knew the truth. Sean was no better than Luke, even if he did get out of bed on a Saturday morning and trek to my house in the freezing cold. With my family waiting in the cab to go catch our flight, there wasn't a whole lot of risk I'd freak out on him then and there. So, in a way, he gets credit for being honest but without the consequences. Quite well-planned, now that I thought about it. So well-planned, in fact, that I had to wonder if Sean knew he wanted to break up with me long before he actually uttered the words.

This conversation was getting me nowhere. Maybe I was trying to move onto step two too quickly. Maybe I had to go back to step one and continue earning his trust.

I moved over onto the couch next to Luke and watched as he continued to flip through the channels. I probably should have asked for the clicker and suggested he give me a turn. But we'd already covered a few corrective issues and I didn't want to overload the guy all in one night. There was probably only so much he could process—especially while concentrating on a hundred-and-nine cable channels.

It didn't take very long before Luke reached for my hand and laced his fingers between mine without ever once taking his eyes off the TV. For some reason I thought his hand would be sweaty or rough or something equally unappetizing. But his skin was warm and surprisingly soft for a guy. Sean would get calluses on his fingertips from holding the football, and his cuticles were always kind of ragged and peeling. It could get quite gross, especially toward the end of the season.

Once he settled on a show, Luke let go of my hand and draped his arm over the back of the couch cushions in a move that was so transparent as to almost be funny. But I didn't say anything, and instead, I let his arm slowly fall down the back of the couch until it was resting on my shoulder. This was step one in action.

"You smell nice," Luke said, his face moving closer to mine.

I knew I was probably the billionth girl Luke had said that to, but still, I sort of wanted to believe him. Maybe he had a thing for ChapStick. "Thanks."

I could feel Luke's warm breath on my neck and all of a sudden it was like the roles were reversed, like I was the one being tested. Here was my chance to close the deal. All I had to do was let Luke kiss me and we'd be on our way. But all I could think about as Luke got closer was the last time I kissed a guy—and it wasn't exactly a pleasant memory. Besides, I'd be kissing someone who used to kiss my best friend. Didn't that qualify as vaguely creepy, even if she supposedly approved?

I knew I should just do it and get it over with. The guy just wanted a kiss, for God's sake, it wasn't like he was asking me to take the SATs for him. Just one little kiss and I'd prove I could get Luke to want me, and prove that I was over Sean. But I couldn't, and as Luke leaned into me, his eyes closed and his lips aiming straight for my mouth, I quickly stood up and jumped up off the couch like he'd zapped me with a Taser.

"You should really get going," I told him, glancing at my watch. "They might come home early and you really shouldn't be here."

Luke sat there for a minute like he was trying to tell if I was playing hard to get or if I was actually serious. I guess he decided I was serious because he finally got up, grabbed his coat from the chair, and walked over to the front door.

I followed him and offered a halfhearted "thanks for coming" before opening the door.

Luke stood there. "Well, thanks for the Sprite. And thanks for letting me stay. It was nice of you."

Without realizing it, Luke had uttered the magic word.

Nice. I'd show him *nice*. Before Luke could turn to leave I reached out, grabbed his coat collar, and pulled him toward me in one full swoop.

It was kind of off center and a little too hard considering I'd practically jerked him through the door, but I'd done it. So what if it wasn't the greatest kiss in the world? It was still a kiss.

"Good night." I started to back away, but before I could reach for the door handle and put a barrier between me and my project, Luke reached for my hand and pulled me into him, even placing his other hand under my chin so I couldn't look away. Instantly his lips were on mine again, but this time I was sure there wouldn't be any visible bruising. This time it was a real kiss. A really nice, soft, *real* kiss.

After what felt like an eternity, or at least two minutes, Luke backed away. "That was better."

"Yeah, it was," I told him, a little out of breath. I put my finger to my lips and touched them, trying to see if they felt different. Different from the lips Sean used to kiss, the lips of someone who would never kiss a guy just because she had a job to do.

Luke laughed at me. "You sound surprised."

"Maybe," I answered. And it was the truth. I had no idea how many girls Luke had kissed or the extent of his long list of female conquests, but he was an amazing kisser. Like the assumed sweaty hands and calluses, I kind of expected him to have chapped lips or something.

"I'll see you on Monday," Luke called out, already heading down the front walk.

"See you on Monday," I called back, although by the time I got the words out he was already in his car with the engine running.

I'd done it. This was the official start of me and Luke. It was proof that nice Emily was truly on the way out and the new Emily was here to stay. And I expected that thought to make me feel pretty good, but instead I couldn't help thinking that I had no idea the new Emily would enjoy kissing Luke so much.

chapter eleven

If we were in a movie, I would have said something like "the eagle has landed" or "mission accomplished." Instead I just said, "I kissed him."

Lucy looked surprised, but Josie looked like she was going to throw up into her vanilla Frappuccino.

"It was nothing big. No tongue even," I lied, trying to soften the blow by breaking off a piece of my blueberry muffin and offering it to her.

Josie sat there, not saying a word. She wouldn't even look at my blueberry peace offering.

"I'm sorry," I apologized. "Really. I thought I was doing what you wanted."

Okay, so I knew it wasn't *exactly* what Josie wanted. What she really wanted was to get back at Luke. It just so happened that the only way to do that was to have her best friend make out with him. Sort of.

I'll never forget how, in eighth grade, Josie was caught shoplifting a pair of sterling silver hoop earrings from The Limited and the security guard pulled Lucy and me into the back room with her. I swear, it was exactly like those interrogation scenes on TV, complete with uncomfortable metal chairs and a one-way mirror spanning the length of one wall (afterward, Lucy kept insisting it was just a regular old mirror, but I swear there were people back there watching our every move). The guard told us he was calling all of our parents, even though Lucy and I hadn't been caught stealing anything (as far as he knew; later I found out that Lucy had a necklace in her shoe). Josie kept pleading with the guy to let Lucy and me go, trying to convince him that we hadn't done anything wrong. And finally he did let us leave, but not before scaring us straight with stories that practically had us convinced shoplifting led to the electric chair. We left Josie in the back room with the security guard while he dialed her parents' phone number, and the two of us got the hell out of there as fast as we could. The thing was, no matter how much trouble Josie was about to get in, instead of trying to save herself, she was more concerned with sticking up for me and Lucy. And now it was my turn to stick up for her, to get back at Luke for hurting her, no matter how hot Luke looked standing in the Brocks' doorway after our kiss. He was the enemy. And I shouldn't enjoy making out with the enemy.

Josie shook her head at me and bit her lip. "Don't be sorry. It has to be done. Right now there are eight-year-old girls who will one day open the time capsule and thank us."

That was true, but until then, Josie was going to have to hear about how I kissed her ex-boyfriend. And I didn't envy her. If I had to listen as my best friend described how she'd kissed Sean, I think

I'd need to be heavily sedated. Not that my kiss with Luke was anything to brag about, at least not the first kiss, but Josie was handling this way better than I ever would.

This morning when Josie called to tell me they were on their way to pick me up and take me to Starbucks, I almost felt queasy at the thought of telling her about my lip lock with her ex-boyfriend. While I completely understood why she loved the idea of the guide (really, what girl wouldn't?), I couldn't quite figure out why she'd want to test it out on Luke. So what if he was the ideal candidate for reform? And even if I succeeded in turning him into perfect boyfriend material, it wasn't like Josie would want him back after what he did to her. So, while in theory I could see why Josie was into the idea of the guide, in actuality I didn't really get it. The guide would only make him better for his next girlfriend, so what was in it for her?

Not that I was about to ask Josie about it. She was willing to offer up Luke for our experiment, so who was I to question her? Besides, I don't handle conflict well. Which is another reason I dreaded telling Josie about kissing Luke. Although she was the one who'd come up with the idea to change Luke in the first place, I was still afraid she'd kill me, even if, personally, I was quite pleased with my progress. And I don't just mean my progress getting Luke to like me.

Last night after Luke left the Brocks' house, I was feeling pretty damn proud of my last-ditch effort to snare an unsuspecting Luke in my web of deceit. "Web of deceit"—that sounded so cool. Sean would never think I was capable of spinning a web of deceit. The only web he would think I'd spin would be nice and cozy, a web where everyone was welcome and refreshments were served— perhaps even a meat-free option for vegetarians and something vegan-friendly.

But I'd done it. I'd lured Luke into stopping by the Brock's house (so what if I didn't *know* I was luring him there, the point was he showed up). I'd even enticed him into attempting to make out with me on their couch (again, so what if I stood up before he managed to succeed). The point is, I was laying my trap. I was lying to Luke and succeeding, a concept that ran contrary to everything I'd ever been taught.

As I stood at the window watching Luke pull down the driveway last night, his headlights illuminating the bare trees until the only evidence the hottest guy in school was ever here at all were the two red taillights fading into the distance, I'd felt the initial shock that came from doing something so completely out of character. Then there was a sort of euphoria I hadn't expected. I felt like all the rules that once applied to me didn't apply anymore. It was like the first time you realize you won't get hit by a car if you cross the street, and then before you know it you're on the other side looking back, wondering why you hadn't tried it sooner.

While I could hold my mother responsible for a lot of things, including my inability to stand in the express checkout line if I had more than ten items, this was definitely something she didn't teach me. How to lie and get away with it. How to fool someone on purpose. How not to care what someone thinks of me. But it was all a means to an end, and I knew even if my mother wouldn't approve of my method, she'd applaud the outcome. When it was all over, Luke would be a better person, and who could argue with that?

"You know what you have to do next, don't you?" Josie asked, picking at the muffin I'd given her and taking a bite.

I shook my head.

"Matt, Owen, and Luke are all going to Killington over spring break with Owen's family. I'll ask my parents if you and Lucy can come up to the ski house with us, and we'll meet them up there."

"But you hate to ski," I pointed out, as if it mattered. In addition to the palatial house in Branford and the four-thousand-square-foot "cottage" on Cape Cod, Josie's family also now owned a slope-side ski chalet in Vermont. Not that she cared. Josie was about as fond of skiing as she was of horses and dogs.

Josie shrugged. "It's for the cause."

"That's a brilliant idea," Lucy agreed, which didn't surprise me. She was the type of skier who actually scanned the trail maps looking for black diamonds.

"Do you think they'll let us come with you?" I asked.

"Come on, we have five bedrooms, a hot tub, and ski-in/ski-out access to Killington Mountain—and my mom can barely snow-plow! She'll be thrilled at least somebody knows what they're doing."

"I'm in." Lucy turned to me. "Do you think your parents will let you go?"

It wasn't my parents I had to convince. It was just my mom, and I couldn't see why she wouldn't let me go away with Josie's family. As long as I brought an appropriate gift for the hostess.

"I don't see why not," I told them. "Count me in, too."

Phase two of our plan was in place and Lucy seemed satisfied. "You want anything? I'm going to get another hot chocolate."

Josie and I shook our heads and watched in silence as Lucy went up to the counter.

I felt like I should say something about Luke, but I didn't know what was appropriate for this situation.

Josie intently stirred her Frappuccino with a straw, not looking up at me. "So, did you think he was good?"

I just about swallowed my tongue. "Excuse me?"

"Did you think he was good?" she repeated.

Was he good? How was I supposed to answer that? *Give the contestant from Heywood and eight for fresh breath, but add that his saliva content could use improvement?*

"Who?" I asked, buying myself time.

Josie rolled her eyes at me.

"You know, it happened so fast I don't even remember." Josie seemed to know I was lying and it occurred to me that maybe her ski trip idea wasn't so great after all. "Are you sure you want to take us skiing?"

"Of course!"

"I meant, are you sure you want to take us up to Killington and meet up with the guys?" She knew I really meant Luke.

"Absolutely." Josie stopped stirring her drink and looked up at me. "I know you're just doing what we asked you to do. It's not your fault."

I knew she meant it, but it didn't really help. "Thanks."

"Don't forget you have to write down what happened in the guide," Josie reminded me, just in case I wasn't fully aware of my pending journalistic duties. "Do you think that Luke can really change?"

I shrugged. "I don't know."

"Do you think he'll ever apologize for the way he broke up with me?" she continued.

"Maybe. I hope so."

Even though my answer wasn't a resounding endorsement of Luke's ability to change, it seemed to make Josie feel better. "Me, too. And who knows, maybe we'll even get back together once he gets his act straightened out."

Josie couldn't be serious. "You'd actually get back together with him after what he did to you?"

"Maybe," she offered. "I mean, if he'd really changed."

I couldn't say I'd be as forgiving as Josie, but then again, who knew what would happen if Sean showed up on my doorstep a changed man. "Well, I promise I'll do my best to help."

Josie smiled at me. "I know you will."

"You know, he didn't even stay at Curtis's that long last night," she added.

Huh? "Wait a minute, Luke went to the party after he came to see me?"

"Yeah. Lucy was a little bummed because Luke showed up and Owen left with him about ten minutes later." Josie nodded her head toward the register, where Lucy was paying for her order. "What do you think is going on with those two?"

"Who?"

"Lucy and Owen."

"Nothing!" Josie had to be kidding. There was no way anything was going on with them. Lucy would pick twenty minutes of wind sprints in the gym over hanging out with a guy. "There's just no way. Besides, she swore them off—not that she needed to. The Lucy I know has no interest in Owen or any other guy, for that matter."

Josie shrugged. "Still, she was pretty bummed when he left last night."

"I didn't know Luke was going to Curtis's party," I admitted, feeling slightly foolish. Of course he went to the party. How could I have been so dense?

Josie laughed. "You didn't expect him to go straight home, crawl into bed, and spend the rest of the night dreaming about you, did you?"

Yeah, I kinda did.

●　　　●　　　●

When they dropped me off at home, I did as I was told (surprise!), only I decided to add my own little twist. I went to my room and took the brown notebook out of my night table drawer and prepared to write about last night. I'd gone from sitting at a Valentine's Day dance waiting for a guy to show up to having him blow off a party so he could see me (at least he blew off the first hour of the party, and that had to count for something, right?). As I started to chronicle our conversation and the kiss—the second one, of course—it became obvious that the Guy Don'ts we'd come up with were really just the beginning. The true benefit of the guide would come from seeing Luke's transformation—from seeing how *I* could transform Luke. It was the difference between the *concept* of changing a person and the reality. The difference between the theoretical and the tangible. The Luke we started out with and the Luke we hoped he'd become.

This was so much more than just The Guy's Guide to Girls or a Handbook for the Clueless. It was documentation, an owner's manual, so to speak. So I took my black permanent Sharpie, crossed out the title Josie had written across the cover of the notebook and wrote in a new title in capital letters, a title that genuinely reflected what was going to be written on the spiral-bound notebook pages. It was no longer just a guide, it was THE BOOK OF LUKE.

As I replaced the cap on the marker and sat there admiring my handiwork, there was a knock at my door. "What are you doing?" my mom asked, coming into my room and taking a seat at the foot of my bed. "Homework?"

"You could say that," I answered.

"Well, you certainly looked like you were concentrating when I came in." She tried to get a glimpse at my work, but I'd turned the notebook over on my bedspread so only the plain brown cardboard backing showed.

"It's just something I'm trying to learn."

"Anything I can help with?" She looked hopeful.

I was about to say no when I decided that maybe she could help me with something after all. "Maybe. I have a question: If one of your readers wrote to you and asked how they could get someone to change undesirable behavior, how would you tell them to do that without making it too obvious?"

My mom let out a long breath and tipped her head to the side, like she does before answering audience questions at her seminars. "I think I know why you're asking me this."

I instantly froze and my fingers gripped the edge of the notebook. "You do?"

"I do. And that's part of the reason I wanted to talk to you."

This was it. This was when she told me that what I was doing was cruel and despicable. That I wasn't just an affront to decent people everywhere, I was a professional liability, as well. Who'd attend seminars and buy books from a woman offering advice even her own child didn't follow? I braced myself and tried to think of an explanation before she even started in on me.

"Just because your dad is a little *confused* at the moment doesn't mean he feels any differently about you. He still loves you."

"Dad?" She thought I was talking about my dad?

"Besides, he misses you terribly and wishes you'd call him and talk to him more often," she continued, like she'd rehearsed this conversation in her head a million times, which she probably had. "In fact, he'd really like you and TJ to go out to Chicago and visit him for spring break."

"No way." I shook my head. "I can't go."

"You can't?" she repeated, folding her hands and placing them on her knees in a gesture that was vintage Jackie O. "And why can't you?"

"Josie invited me to go skiing for a few days." I didn't add that Jackie and Lauren had no idea my dad was still in Chicago, and if I went back they'd inevitably ask why I was visiting a father who was supposed to be in Boston.

"Emily, you can go skiing anytime. Your dad wants to see you. He misses you."

I wanted to point out that if he missed us that much he would have gotten on the plane and come back with us in January. But that would be a smart-ass remark that would only piss off my mother even more, and wouldn't do much to get her to say yes to the ski trip.

"Come on, all we'll do is sit around some corporate apartment all week staring at four white walls with bad art bolted to the wall," I pleaded, hoping to appeal to her sense of appropriate décor—she detested white walls and had no patience for bad reproductions of classic paintings. "Please?"

"Emily, I really wish you wouldn't punish your dad like this." She frowned at me like I was the one being unreasonable. Me!

I remember once hearing that if you try to hold in a sneeze you can rupture a blood vessel in your head and die. Well, I was tired of holding in every inappropriate thought and comment. It was either speak out or wait for that blood vessel to rupture. And, as much as I knew my mom wasn't going to like what I was about to say, I had a feeling she'd like blood splattered on the walls even less.

"I'm punishing *him*?" I practically yelled. "If anyone's doing the punishing, it's Dad."

My mom was silent while she tried to figure out how to respond—either that or she was trying to figure out how her perfect daughter had turned into a raging lunatic in the course of a few short days. "How can you say that?" she asked, her voice even and unemotional. "How can you even say that?"

"How can you *not* say that?" I demanded. "He's punishing all of us! And we didn't even do anything wrong. He's the one who's wrong."

My mom seemed surprised that instead of backing down like I always did, I was actually being disagreeable for once. And that made me feel even bolder.

I stood up, finally ready to say what I'd really been thinking instead of being concerned about hurting people's feelings. "You can pretend that nothing's going on, that things are all hunky-dory around here, but I'm not going to. And I'm not going to visit him in Chicago. He was the one who wanted us to move, and that's what we did. Now I'm not leaving."

For once, my mother didn't have a rational response. She sat there watching me, trying to figure out how to deal with the pissy girl who'd obviously taken up residence in her lovely daughter's body.

"I think you're making a mistake, Emily."

"I'm making a mistake? What about you? You just let him stay there. You didn't even try to get him to come with us."

"This isn't about me, Emily. It's about you and your dad."

"And I'm not going," I reiterated.

"Fine. If you want to tell your dad that you'd prefer to go skiing with your friends instead, go ahead—if you think it's the right thing to do."

I knew her answer meant she thought it was the wrong thing to do, but I didn't care.

"Fine, I'll do that," I said, sounding as snippy and obnoxious as possible.

My mom stood up and glanced around my room, as if she'd just noticed that my room was still in a state of postmove disarray, with boxes to be emptied and clothes to hang up.

"Before you do anything, finish unpacking and bring the empty boxes downstairs when you're done," she told me. "And hang your clothes up first. They're getting wrinkled."

"I will," I answered, but when she left the room, I didn't. Instead I went to the box clearly marked "Emily's Room" and opened the flaps. I buried my hand deep into the cardboard box until I found what I was looking for. The picture of Sean I'd sworn I'd keep packed away.

There he was, his white football pants dirty after a game against Loyola. It was the first game of the season, and Jackie, Lauren, and I had gone to watch from the sidelines. The morning was warm, it was still early September, and when Sean walked back to the locker room after the game I was waiting for him, sunning myself on the bench outside the door. I don't remember what he said to me, or why he decided that it was the right time to kiss me, but I do remember that he tasted salty from sweating, like how my fingers used to taste when I was little and we'd go to the beach on the cape (the fingers never stayed there very long; my mother always reminded me to get them out of my mouth). Later on, after we were officially dating, I learned that he always tasted salty after practice or a game. I always imagined that he'd taste the same way after sex, a slight sheen on his face and neck and an exhausted way about him.

But I didn't take the picture frame out for one last trip down memory lane. No. This time I was putting Sean away for good. This was just one last look. Because that was how I wanted to remember him, grass-stained knees and all, his hair flattened down from his helmet, and those two black half-moons under his eyes to reflect the sun. I didn't want to remember him with a small smattering of cream cheese on the right-hand corner of his mouth, and the L.L.Bean jacket I'd coughed up good library clerking money to buy. I mean, he didn't even offer to give it back. *Hey, thanks for the coat—I'll make sure and wear it when I take out my next girlfriend.* Jerk. Give me the sweaty guy with the helmet hair any day over the guy who stood in my driveway that morning.

Come to think of it, I'm sure he'd take the old Emily over the new Emily, too. He would never think I was capable of manipulating anyone. And he definitely wouldn't believe I could come up with the idea for a guide that was going to shed light on every horrible, terrible thing about the opposite sex—and then tell them how to correct it. Sean would never think I had it in me. But, as I was discovering, he was wrong. And that alone already made me feel like a different person than the person I was in Chicago. That girl was still naïve enough to believe everything always turned out for the best, that being a good person paid off, and love conquered all. Now I knew better. And I wouldn't make the same mistake twice.

chapter twelve

I hated to admit it, but TJ was right. At Heywood, everyone really did know everything. By Monday afternoon the entire school seemed to know that there was something going on between Luke and me, even if no one knew exactly what it was—including me. Guys smiled at me with a new sense of appreciation, like I'd received Luke's seal of approval. The middle schoolers practically genuflected when they passed by my locker on their way to class, as if my status had been elevated from mere senior to *that* senior. Upper-school girls seemed to slow down when they spotted me in the hallway, their eyes watching me with a look that was part reverence and part envy. Sometimes they'd even stop and just stare, waiting for me to be out of earshot before whispering something to their friends. And I had a feeling that what they were whispering was, "There goes Luke Preston's new girlfriend."

All Monday morning I felt invincible. Unbeatable. I felt like I was finally winning.

Only there were still people who didn't seem to believe I *could* win. Not against the venerable Luke Preston.

"What do you think about Luke and Emily?" a faceless voice asked above the water rushing out of the girls' room faucet.

My hand paused on the stall lock, just as I was about to exit. But instead of leaving the beige stall to see who was there, and who she was talking to, I stood still and listened, my ear pressed against the cold metal door.

"I don't know. Maybe Emily doesn't know about Luke. She's been gone a few years, after all," the other voice answered.

I bent down and peeked under the stall at two sets of shoes—one black, one navy blue—and tried to figure out who those feet belonged to. Nobody I instantly recognized, but then again, I wasn't exactly used to scrutinizing the footwear of Heywood's female students.

"I just hope she knows what she's getting herself into," the navy blue feet continued.

Thank God Heywood had paper towel dispensers. If they'd had to use hand dryers I never would have been able to hear what happened next. And what happened next was that those two pairs of feet totally underestimated me.

"She's way too nice for him," the black shoes stated, and then started for the door. "I hope she doesn't get hurt."

The blue shoes followed and the door opened just before she ended the conversation with a small sigh of resignation and a sad, "Me, too."

Oh, poor misinformed girls. They had no idea what I was capable of doing to Luke. And that was going to make it all the more enjoyable.

I walked around Heywood mentally high-fiving Josie and Lucy, sending them secret signals that, yes, Luke had been waiting for me to walk to class with him, and, yes, I'd caught him looking at me from across the science lab. By lunchtime I felt like I should have a large *S* on my chest and a cape around my neck. But who needed to be faster than a speeding bullet or more powerful than a locomotive when you were capable of something even more amazing, something so few could lay claim to—the ability to change the biggest asshole in school. Look, down the hall, in the front seat of Luke's car, it's not Nice Emily offering to scrape the ice off his windshield, it's New Emily—and she kicks ass!

I was on my way to the cafeteria to meet Josie and Lucy and report on my morning encounters with Luke when there he was, standing in the doorway to the cafeteria, waiting for me. At least, it looked like he was waiting for me. Maybe he was just debating whether or not he was in the mood for beef stew.

"Hey," Luke called out when he saw me. And then he did something that I couldn't quite process. I mean, it had only been two days since our kiss, and here he was offering to hold open the door for me? Had Luke gone out and bought one of my mother's books or something?

"Hi," I answered.

He stood there holding the door for me and I knew it was time to jump to step two, offering positive reinforcement for his sudden display of graciousness.

"Thanks for holding the door. I appreciate it."

Luke just shrugged and let the door close behind us. "Hungry?"

I nodded. "Starving."

Over by the lunch line I could see Luke's Lunch Legion waiting for him, watching to see if he was going to stay and eat the food they were about to retrieve for him, or if he'd head out to Sam's.

"I think there are a few people waiting to serve you." I tipped my head in the direction of the four girls and turned to go find Lucy and Josie. "Enjoy your lunch."

"Wait." Luke reached out and grabbed my shoulder. "I'm not much in the mood for stew. Want to go out and get something?"

By "something," I assumed he meant potato logs. It looked like, instead of joining Lucy and Josie, I was in for another working lunch. Maybe this time we could start working on how to keep the ketchup from falling on his chin in the first place instead of discussing how to wipe it off. And another bonus: a turkey sandwich beat beef stew any day.

"Sure. Let me go upstairs and grab my coat."

Luke reached for the door and held it open for me once again, almost as if proving the first time hadn't been a fluke. "I'll go get my car and meet you out front."

I started to leave the cafeteria but couldn't resist taking one more glance over my shoulder at the Lunch Legion. Their eager smiles and hopeful eyes disappeared when they realized Luke and I were leaving. Together. I almost felt sorry for them, just standing there watching us with disappointment written all over their faces.

I said *almost* felt sorry for them, and even that only lasted a second. Because there wasn't any room to feel sorry for anyone when I was feeling so victorious. Besides, someday they'd thank me for this.

• • •

"So, what are you in the mood for?" Luke asked, pulling out of Heywood's driveway.

"Aren't we going to Sam's?" We were already heading in that direction.

"If you want."

"You really like that place, don't you?"

"It's okay. Good potato logs."

"And ketchup," I added, and Luke smiled.

"And good ketchup." He reached over and changed the radio station. "I think half the reason I go there is because I can, you know? Like, finally, after six years of watching seniors leave at lunchtime, it's my turn."

"So, you're the new Billy Stratton?" I asked, thinking that he really was.

"I guess, but without the bong."

"I still can't believe that about him."

"You just don't want to," he told me, and he was right. My beautiful, perfect Billy Stratton wasn't just an introvert who was too sweet to tell the eighth grader lurking outside his economics class to leave him alone. He was just too stoned to notice me in the first place.

"So, Sam's it is?"

"Unless you've got another suggestion. What was your favorite place to eat before you moved away?" Luke asked.

That was easy. "Friendly's."

"Friendly's?" Luke laughed. "You have the best lobster and clam chowder in the entire world at your doorstep and you miss a place with burgers and ice cream?"

"Yeah, you know, there's nothing like a Fribble in Chicago. No regular milkshake even comes close."

"Fribbles are pretty damn good, I'll give you that. What flavor?"

"Chocolate."

"I'm a strawberry Fribble guy myself."

He didn't exactly strike me as a strawberry kind of guy. I would have guessed something more along the lines of butter pecan or pistachio. Those nutty ice creams always sounded like something a guy would order. But pink ice cream? No way.

Luke slowed down and I figured he was preparing to turn right toward Sam's. But instead of turning, all of a sudden he sped up and kept driving straight.

I pointed to the passing street sign. "Hey, you missed the turn."

"We're not going to Sam's."

"We're not?"

Luke shook his head. "Nope. Today we're getting ourselves a couple of Fribbles."

"I used to want to work here," I told Luke after we'd been seated and given the waitress our order.

"Really? Why?"

"Well, there was the idea of free ice cream," I told him, watching the waitress head our way with a completely unbalanced lunch. "Then there was the whole apron thing."

"The apron thing?"

"Yeah. My mom is a big proponent of aprons."

Luke smiled at me, like he was trying to picture me in an apron. I hoped that wasn't all I was wearing.

"So, is it strange coming back here?" Luke asked, attempting to suck his superthick Fribble through a straw. It wasn't working.

I waited for the waitress to place my order of fries on the table before answering. "Sort of." I nodded my head toward our departing waitress. "Did you notice that?" I asked.

Luke leaned over the table and we both answered at that same time. "No more aprons."

"Ah, it's the end of an era." Luke shook his head in mock disappointment. "There goes your dream of free ice cream."

I reached for my fries and popped one in my mouth, burning a layer of skin off my tongue in the process.

"Little hot?" he asked, grinning at me. Under the table I felt his leg press against mine and I quickly moved it away.

"Little," I told him, waving my hand in front of my mouth to cool it off.

Luke stopped sucking on his straw and decided to spoon out the ice cream instead. "So, what do you remember about me?"

Sure. *Enough about you, what do you think of me?* How typical.

I didn't have a whole lot to tell him, at least not what I figured he wanted to hear (*I watched you from afar and imagined one day you'd take me to Friendly's*, instead of, *You had that nasty cowlick and got winded playing badminton in gym*). My memories of Luke just weren't that vivid. He was more like a bit player instead of having a starring role.

"I remember you were friends with Owen, but you didn't say much. Why? What do you remember about me?" If Luke could be vain, so could I. Besides, I really wanted to know.

"Let's see." Luke took a big gulp of his Fribble and ended up with a strawberry mustache.

I probably should have pointed out to Luke that, if he kept a napkin on his lap, it would be easily accessible for the next gulp. It was a prime opportunity to impart a few table manners, but instead I reached for a napkin and handed it to him. There'd be plenty of opportunities to teach Luke about the appropriate placement of napkins, and right now I just wanted to enjoy my chocolate Fribble in a Guy's Guide-free zone.

"I remember that you bent over that Bunsen burner in science class and singed one of your eyebrows off," he told me.

"Okay, I can live without that memory."

"I also remember that you and Lucy and Josie did that dance routine at the talent show," he told me, wiping away the pink mustache.

Was he doing this on purpose? Didn't he have any normal memories of me?

"And I remember you were slightly obsessed with going to Brown."

"You do?"

"Diorama incident in sixth grade. Not to mention that brown felt pennant you had taped up inside your locker."

"You remember that?"

"Are you kidding me? I felt like a total slacker—I could barely figure out where I wanted to go to camp and you'd already decided where you were going to college."

"Yeah, well, things change," I told him and hoped he'd let the subject drop. "Looks like Brown isn't in the cards, after all."

I had no idea why I said that. The last thing I wanted to do was share personal information with Luke. This was a purely professional lunch—I was just doing my job.

It was just that he made it seem so easy. Maybe because he didn't seem to have any preconceived notions of what I'd do or say. Or maybe because I wasn't supposed to give a crap about how he felt about what I did or said.

I caught Luke eyeing my fries. "Mind if I have one?" he asked, his fingers already on their way toward the plate.

"Actually, I do," I told him, reaching for the plate and pulling it toward me and out of neutral territory where he could get the idea that I'd intended to share.

"Really?"

"Really." I nodded, feeling a sense of power that I'd never quite felt before. "I'd prefer if you didn't."

Luke didn't seem mad that I wouldn't share my fries, he seemed slightly confused, if anything. Almost like he couldn't figure out why I'd be so stingy with the fries and at the same time slightly impressed that I admitted I wanted them all to myself.

Before I actually turned Luke down, I'd never realized how, by always being concerned about other people's feelings, by always being so worried about what people would think of me, I'd learned not to say what *I* wanted. Because, let's admit it, if I *really* cared about whether or not Luke liked me, I would have handed him the plate and told him to have at it. The old Emily would have passed the salt and ketchup, even though I hate ketchup on my fries. But that was me. I was always the crossing guard who spent so much time looking out for everyone else that she never sees the Mack truck barreling right toward her until it was too late. Sean was living proof of that.

But what I wanted now were those fries. Every single one of them. They were mine and I wasn't sharing. I'd had an epiphany, and all because of a little plate of fries.

"Yeah," I told Luke. "Really."

He sat back in the booth and went back to stirring his Fribble with a straw.

"You know what else I remember? You were the first girl Owen felt up," he continued. Maybe he was trying to punish me for the french fries.

"He told you that?"

Luke nodded. "Yep."

I was hoping my first Fribble in three years could be enjoyed without having to think about how I'd write about it later in the notebook, but Luke wasn't making it easy. And this was just so glaring, there was no way I could avoid addressing the issue.

I put down the french fry in my hand and prepared to play teacher. "See, that's just wrong. You don't go around telling your friends you felt some girl up."

"Didn't you tell your friends what happened?"

"Well, yeah, but that's different."

"Why is it different?"

"Because when I told Lucy and Josie I didn't do it to be mean. I wasn't bragging."

"How do you know Owen was bragging?"

For some reason, I couldn't help thinking about Luke's jiggle scale. "That's not very nice."

"What I meant is, Owen didn't tell me to be mean, either. And he wasn't bragging. He was just doing the same thing you were doing."

I didn't believe that for a minute. "I seriously doubt that."

Luke shrugged, like it wasn't his job to convince me. Unfortunately, he was right. It was my job to convince *him*.

I pushed my Fribble away. I couldn't drink the thickest milkshake known to mankind and convince Luke at the same time. Something had to give, and unfortunately, it was the Fribble. I always knew this plan would require some sacrifices.

"Luke, it's not the same thing," I started, my voice trying to remain rational, like Mrs. Blackwell discussing the political and moral corruption in *The House of Mirth*. But we were talking about boobs here, my boobs, so I came off sounding less like a removed-

and-unattached teacher imparting knowledge and more like a girl who was still wondering where she ranked on the jiggle scale. "And, in case you haven't figured this out already, most girls don't want to have their boobs or any other body part discussed by a group of guys—especially if one of them has hands-on experience, so to speak."

"Like I said, it wasn't like that." Luke pointed to my Fribble. "It's going to melt."

I had to make this fast. "Do you understand what I'm saying?"

"Yes, Emily. I understand what you're saying. I just don't agree."

I had two choices: I could sit there trying to get through to Luke or I could go back to enjoying my Fribble before it melted. Besides, he'd said he understood, didn't that count for something? Maybe it wasn't exactly step two, but it was like step one and a half.

I reached for my shake, but not before giving Luke one more piece of advice. "You should really try the chocolate next time, it's way better than strawberry."

"I'll remember that."

I hoped he'd remember more than that, but at least it was something.

After consuming enough calories to last the rest of the week, including every single french fry just on principle, Luke and I headed back to school.

Needless to say, the idea of strapping a seat belt across my protruding stomach didn't excite me. Who'd need a seat belt when it felt like I had my very own air bag swelling up inside me as it was? I swear, my stomach couldn't hold one more thing and a seat belt wasn't going to make me feel any better. That's why the first thing I did when I got in the car was recline the seat back.

"A little full?" Luke asked, noticing I kept rubbing my stomach. I'd once read if you rubbed your belly clockwise it aided digestion. Or maybe that was just for colicky babies.

"No, I'm fine," I answered, even though I knew Luke was dying to make a comment about the fries.

"So, have you been by your old house yet?" Luke asked. We were about a mile from where I used to live. Maybe he remembered my address from the Valentine's Day incident, but more likely he remembered that time Owen's mom dropped me off after school.

I shook my head. "No."

"Why not? Aren't you curious?"

"Not really."

"Come on. You have to be a little curious."

"Okay, maybe a little," I admitted. "But not a lot."

"Then why haven't you been by to see it?"

"I just haven't wanted to." I knew that TJ had been by our old house the first week we were back. I could never bring myself to go see it. Partly it just seemed like a waste of time; I mean, it wasn't our house anymore, so why bother? All it would do would remind me that the family who used to live in that house no longer existed. Now we were a family of three living in a different house about five miles away. You know how they say you can never go home again? Well, I wasn't about to try.

"Come on, we'll drive by. It will take five minutes, we won't even be late," Luke assured me, anticipating my first excuse.

"It's okay, we don't have to, really," I objected, but Luke wasn't about to listen.

"No, we're going."

"I really don't want to," I repeated, losing my patience. It was the babysitting scene all over again. Why couldn't he just believe me?

"Sure you do," he insisted, but this time I wasn't just going to repeat myself. This time he was going to listen.

"No, Luke, I don't," I practically yelled. "Why can't you just listen to what I say, okay? I think I know what I want."

He let it drop, but I knew he could tell something wasn't right. It was the way he kept glancing over at me, shifting his eyes off the road to look at my face and try to figure out why I couldn't even drive by a freaking house.

"It's just a house, Emily," he finally said.

"It wasn't just a house. It was my home." For some reason the word choice made a difference.

Luke pulled the car over to the side of the road and put it in park. He flipped off the radio and turned to face me. "What's really going on with you? Nobody's ever cared so much about a house before."

"My dad's still in Chicago," I blurted out, and even as the words were spilling out of my mouth, I couldn't stop them. "He's living in some corporate apartment until he decides what to do. He didn't move back with us—yet," I added at the last minute, as if that one word meant his moving back was an inevitability instead of a huge question mark.

Luke draped his arm around the headrest of his seat, his knee bent and resting against the gear shift. "Why not?"

I fixed my eyes on the glove box, avoiding his gaze. I'd just told Luke Preston the one thing nobody else knew. Not even my best friends. Why was I sitting here in Luke's car spilling my guts like some patient on a therapist's couch? And why did it almost seem easy? "That's the million dollar question, I guess."

"Well, didn't you ask him?"

I shook my head.

"Why not?"

"I don't know. I guess I didn't want to make things worse."

I almost expected Luke to give me some clichéd words of encouragement, to tell me that it will all work out or that my dad still cared about us, blah, blah, blah.

But he didn't. Instead he said, "That's got to suck."

"Yeah, it does."

"Nobody's family is perfect. Hell, anyone with a perfect family is *ab*normal, Emily, not normal."

I wanted to tell him that mine was perfect, or at least it used to be.

"I know that. But this time it's my family that's screwed up."

"So now you can just join the rest of us." Luke smiled and I knew he was trying to get me to smile, too, but I didn't. "I still don't get why you won't go see your house, though."

"Well, first of all, because it isn't even my house anymore. And secondly, it will just prove that everything is different now. I'd rather just remember it the way it was, if that's okay with you."

"Your family isn't a house, Emily."

Did he think I was an idiot? "I know that, Luke."

"Then let's go take a look."

Luke reached for my hand and laid it on his knee, holding it there so I couldn't pull away. "Look, if you don't want to share your fries with me, that's fine. But the least you can do is let me take you to see your old house."

I really was curious, but I was also afraid. What if it looked nothing like the place I remembered? What if the new owners had done something ridiculous, like that house down the street that replaced all their front shrubs with little bonsai trees and white rocks?

Maybe I just wanted Luke off my back, but more likely it was that his thumb was stroking the palm of my hand and I couldn't think straight.

"Fine," I agreed. "Let's go."

"Do you know who lives here now?" Luke asked, slowing down as we approached the house.

I avoided looking for as long as I could, instead focusing on everything but the house—the trees lining the road, the mailboxes, that dumb house with the miniature bonsai trees out front. But once Luke stopped the car I couldn't avoid it any longer. And so I looked straight out my window and there it was. My old house. I'm not sure I would have recognized it if someone had just shown me a picture.

"It was perfect the way it was, why'd they change it?" I asked, even though I didn't expect Luke to have an answer.

"It looks pretty good to me."

It wasn't that it didn't look good. It just wasn't the same exact house I used to live in. They'd painted the gray shingles white and the black shutters were now a dark forest green. They'd cleared away a few trees, and even the trees that remained didn't seem as tall or imposing as I remembered.

"See over there?" I pointed toward the side yard. "There used to be a huge tree right there with a rope swing. Now it's gone."

"Maybe the tree had a disease or something?" he guessed.

"Maybe." I had a hard time believing a tree could come down with an incurable disease in two years. It was fine when we left.

Now, instead of the rope swing, there was a swing set in the backyard, complete with slide and attached tree house, and while we watched, a little girl stuck her head out of the tree house's front door and started climbing down the ladder. She skipped the last three rungs altogether and jumped to the ground, then ran toward the back door.

"Looks like someone doesn't miss the rope swing," Luke observed.

He was right. The little girl probably thought a swing set with a tree house trumped an old rope swing any day. And the house didn't look all that different, if you didn't count the new paint job, which it probably needed. TJ used to try and hit baseballs over the back of the house and more often than not he ended up pounding the balls into the shingles. The curtains in the bedroom on the left even looked a little pink, just like mine used to be.

"I always wanted one of those," I told Luke, pointing to the swing set.

"A slide?" he asked.

"No, a tree house." I turned to face Luke. "Hey, thanks for making me do this. It really wasn't as bad as I thought it would be."

Luke tipped his head to the side and scrutinized me. "I never would have guessed you were a tree house kind of girl."

"And I never would have guessed you were a strawberry Fribble kind of guy," I told him. "See, we both have a lot to learn."

And even before I realized what I had said, I knew I was right. And that scared the crap out of me.

Back in the school parking lot, Luke pulled into the same space we'd left. It was always empty unless Luke was here, almost like everyone knew it was reserved especially for him. Now that we were running late, I was almost thankful for the available spot and short walk up the hill to school.

"So." He turned off the car and sat there dangling the keys from his finger.

"So." I was already going to be late for class, but I didn't make a move to leave. What were a few more minutes? "Can you do me a favor and not tell anyone about my dad."

"Sure, if that's what you want."

"That's what I want," I told him.

Luke leaned over and pulled me toward him. "I had a nice lunch."

"Me, too."

Before I could react, Luke's mouth was on mine, his lips slowly parting until our tongues touched. He tasted vaguely of strawberries and, even though I'm not a huge fan of strawberry Fribbles, I could definitely see becoming a fan of kissing Luke after he'd had one.

"Wait, one more thing," I said as I pulled away from Luke. "Have you ever thought about apologizing to Josie for the way you broke up?"

Luke shook his head. "This is why you stopped kissing me? To ask about Josie?"

No, I stopped kissing you because kissing you makes me feel guilty about Josie. Only I couldn't say that. "It's just that it might be nice if you said you were sorry."

"Look, Em, I sent the e-mail. I probably should have called or told her in person, but it's over. I'm not going to apologize for it three months later, that's ridiculous."

Point taken.

Even though I knew the bell was about ten seconds from ringing, I let Luke tip my head back onto the seat and continue kissing me. It was different from our first kiss in the Brocks' doorway, and not just because this time I wasn't practically knocking his front teeth out. It was different because, with my eyes closed, it didn't feel like I was kissing Luke Preston, Super Prick. It felt like I was just kissing a guy. A guy who was someone I could see calling my boyfriend.

"I should get going." I pulled away and this time instead of swiping my fingers across my lips, I let the feeling of Luke stay there. "I'm already going to be late for history."

"I'll call you tonight," Luke told me before I closed the car door.

And you know what? Even though I knew better, I actually believed him.

chapter thirteen

I really overestimated myself. Or maybe I overestimated Luke. He hadn't said exactly when he'd call me, but
from the time I got home from school, I made sure our phone
was free and I was close enough to hear it ring. But after two
hours with no call, I started to worry.

Six o'clock: nothing. I check to make sure our phone is still
working. It is. I figure maybe Luke meant he'd call me on my cell,
although I hadn't given him the number. Even so, I made sure my
phone was charged and the ringer was on. But still, nothing.

Seven o'clock: Josie calls to see if I've heard from Luke. I have to
tell her no. And then she asks if I'd gotten Luke to apologize to
her, and I have to say no again. Then I start thinking about what a
horrible friend I am, sipping Fribbles with Luke while I was supposed to be making him better for Josie. I suck.

Eight o'clock: I call Lucy to see if maybe I should call Luke instead of waiting for him to call me.

"No way, you can't do that. It would be cheating. Besides, it's not like you really want to talk to him. You just need Luke to call you so we can see if he's learning anything from you."

I knew she was right. Sort of. Luke and I had talked all about calling when you say you're going to call; it was practically the first lesson at the Brocks' house. So, yes, he knew he should call. But there was another reason I kept picking at my cuticles with the kitchen scissors while I watched the phone. A reason so completely insane it made me almost wonder if I wasn't cut out for this after all. Or if I was so weak, I'd let Luke get under my skin when I was supposed to be the one getting under his.

A small part of me really *did* want to talk to Luke. Not a *huge* part, but a part big enough to make me feel like I was losing control over the situation. And if Josie and Lucy knew that, they'd call an end to my little mission ASAP. So I didn't say anything.

And I sat there for another hour.

Nine o'clock: Still no call. That little part of me that actually thought I wanted to talk to him? Well, it's gone. At this point all I could think about was how I wanted to bitch him out tomorrow morning at school, to tell him he was not only obnoxious and full of himself, but that he was unreliable to boot. But somehow I didn't think that he'd find "unreliable" to be some huge put-down (although my mother would rank reliability right up there with excusing yourself from the dinner table as one of the top ten cardinal rules of good manners).

Ten o'clock: No call. Nada. Nothing. Complete silence. After six hours it was time to give up and admit that Luke wasn't going to call.

Before going to bed, I called Lucy and Josie to give them an update. Josie conferenced us all in on her digital phone system. "He didn't call."

"God, he sure isn't making this easy for you."

"I will persevere," I assured them, thinking that I'd been really dumb to let Luke lull me into a false sense of security. Maybe this was what he did with every girl. Damn, he was good. That whole Friendly's thing, it was probably something he did with all his conquests, the only thing that varied was the location—Friendly's, Pizzeria Uno, Burger King. It didn't matter. "Don't worry. There's only going to be one winner when we're done. And that will be me."

"Well, don't forget the other winners," Lucy reminded me. "All the girls who'll have the guide when they open up the time capsule."

"Yeah, sure. I meant them, too."

But I didn't. This wasn't about them. This was between me and Luke. Tomorrow morning I wasn't just going to persevere. I was going to succeed.

I'd let my guard down and Luke had weakened me. And all it took was a freaking Fribble. God, I was easy. No Chinese water torture, no bamboo shoots up my fingernails, just a thick chocolate shake and my resolve took a backseat to my stomach.

I'd let Luke wear me down. And I wasn't letting him do that again.

"I thought you were going to call last night." I was waiting for Luke when he walked through the front door before homeroom.

But instead of feeling ambushed and making a run for the music room, Luke smiled. He smiled! Like a smile was going to get him out of this.

"Yeah, sorry about that. Coach had a meeting for the lacrosse team after school and I ended up getting home later than I thought and I still had to study for the calc test."

It was a completely plausible excuse, but it was still an excuse. There was still plenty of time to pick up the phone and make a call. There was still plenty of time to call *me*.

But I couldn't point that out. I didn't tell him that I'd sat by the phone waiting for it to ring. Because that was what he probably expected. Luke probably thought every girl would wait by the phone hoping he'd call. So, instead, I did the opposite.

I changed my tactic. "It's no big deal." I actually managed to sound like I meant it.

Luke turned to me, looking more than a little skeptical. "It's no big deal?"

I almost got the feeling he was testing me to see if I'd flip out, like he expected. Like most girls would. He was probably waiting for me to bring up our conversation at the Brock's, but I wasn't going to do that. I wouldn't give him the satisfaction of turning me into a bundle of insecurities like he expected.

If he could lull me into a false sense of security, then I could do the same thing to him.

"Don't worry about it," I repeated, trying to make it look like I was smiling instead of gritting my teeth. "Like I said, it's no big deal."

"No big deal, my ass," Josie spat when I told her about his lame excuse. We were hanging out in the dark room during lunch, one of the few places we could talk without worrying about someone hearing us. Lucy and I watched as Josie dipped rubber-tipped tongs into a tray of liquid and swished it around until a black-and-white image started to appear. "Are we kidding ourselves thinking we can change him?" She looked up at me and the red light gave her hair an orange glow.

"I don't think so. There are times I actually believe he's getting better." I thought about our lunch at Friendly's and how Luke had taken me to my old house. He'd displayed such promise, so much, in fact, that I'd believed him when he said he'd call. It was the relationship equivalent of getting sucker punched.

"Well, he sure had me convinced—and so did you. Check these out," Josie told us, reaching over into a pile of glossy photo paper and spreading out a handful of black-and-white pictures like she was dealing a hand of cards. "You actually look like you're enjoying yourself!"

I reached for one of the five-by-seven glossy photos and almost stopped breathing when I realized what I had in my hand. They were pictures all right, but they weren't just random snapshots of arbitrary subjects. They were pictures of me making out with Luke in the front seat of his car.

This time *I'd* been ambushed.

Lucy looked over my shoulder. "Wow, you really do look like you're having fun." She patted me on the back, impressed. "You're pretty good at this."

"How'd you even know I was there?" Josie lifted a fully developed photograph out of the tray and hung it on the clothesline strung across the room. "I tried to make sure Luke didn't see me, but then when I saw you lean over and kiss him, I knew you knew I was there."

"Yeah, well, I figured as long as we had an audience . . ." I let my voice trail off because I didn't know what else to say. That I'd had no idea she was there? That I hadn't kissed Luke to show her our plan was working, I'd kissed him because—I couldn't even think it. The idea was too mortifying. "Why didn't you tell me you were going to check in on us?"

"I didn't plan it, or anything. I just went down to my car to get my camera and I saw you two sitting there in his front seat. Until I saw you I hadn't even thought about it, but then it made perfect sense. I think your idea is brilliant!"

My idea? What idea? To make out with Luke and confirm that he's a great kisser? "You do?"

"Yeah, including photos in the guide will prove it works."

"That *is* a good idea," Lucy agreed. "Boy, you're really getting into this guide thing, aren't you?"

I shrugged, not feeling like I was getting into the guide so much as I was getting into the subject matter.

Lucy sorted through the stack of photos—me and Luke close up, farther away, moving together, kissing, and then pulling apart. She handed the stack to me and I quickly sorted through each sheet. It was like one of those flip books; if I went through the pictures fast enough it almost became a movie, only it had gone from a romantic comedy to a horror flick.

Look at me! Lucy was right. I *did* look like I was having fun. And why? Because I was! I was a traitor to my own cause.

Could we look any more oblivious in the pictures? I mean, Josie couldn't have been more than ten feet away snapping away on her camera and we didn't even notice her. She was a good photographer, but it wasn't like Josie was a seasoned paparazzo or anything. At the very least we should have seen her when we came up for air.

"When I was in the girls' room yesterday I overheard two girls talking about me and Luke," I told them.

Josie and Lucy looked over at me. "What'd they say? Do they know what we're up to?"

"Quite the opposite," I answered. "They said they were afraid I was going to get hurt. Like Luke would break my heart or something."

"That's crazy." Josie frowned. "Besides, if that was really the case, why would Lucy and I let you do this? We're your best friends, we wouldn't let that happen."

"Yeah," Lucy agreed. "We'd never knowingly let you get your feelings crushed."

I pulled out the last photograph. It was a close-up of Luke and me just after we pulled away from our kiss. Luke looked so genuine. Not like someone who was playing a game with me. Then again, I was looking pretty genuine, too. And I was supposed to be playing a game. Only now I didn't know what I was doing.

"I know you wouldn't." I turned the entire stack of pictures facedown and placed them on the counter. "That's what friends are for, right?"

Lucy and Josie nodded. "Right."

I stayed clear of Luke for the rest of the day, not because I was giving up, but because I felt like I'd given up any leverage I'd gained over him. I'd let down my guard and in that moment given Luke the upper hand. I needed to get it back, and I thought that, maybe, giving myself a little distance from him would give me that. If nothing else, it would give me a little perspective. Because, if anything, my perspective was definitely becoming skewed.

Luke must have noticed I was avoiding him (perhaps because every time I spotted him I ducked behind some unsuspecting underclassman and attempted to morph into a shadow), because after the last bell he was waiting for me. And, because he stood directly in front of my locker, it wasn't like I could pretend I didn't see him. Or leave school without coming face-to-face with the situation.

"Hey, can I talk to you for a minute?" he asked.

Lucy shut her locker and waited to see what I would say. I waved her away. "You go ahead, I'll meet you in the parking lot."

Lucy took off and left me standing there with Luke.

"So you really don't care that I didn't call?" he asked.

I shook my head and pretended to organize my books. "Not really."

"I know I told you I would, but it was late and I had six chapters to catch up on for the calc exam."

"I understand." I thought he'd take his get-out-of-jail-free card and run. Instead he stood there and held my locker door open while I put on my coat. I tossed my backpack over my shoulder and prepared to leave. "Really. I do."

"I know I should have called," he repeated. "It's just . . ."

"I know. The test."

"And the lacrosse meeting, don't forget that," Luke added, as if he was pleading his case before a judge and wanted to make sure I weighed every piece of evidence.

"How could I forget?" I answered. He really did seem sincere. Even repentant. Besides, wasn't I really the one who should be apologizing? For lying to him this entire time. For letting him pay for my Fribble and fries when I had ulterior motives?

It wasn't that I felt sorry for Luke—I'm not *that* much of a softy. I just felt something, even if I wasn't sure what it was.

"Okay," I gave in.

Luke smiled and let go of my locker door.

"Can you do me a favor, though? In the future, don't make promises you can't keep."

"Promise." Luke held up two fingers like he was making some sort of Boy Scout oath. Come to think of it, I'm pretty sure in sixth grade he went to some sort of Boy Scout training camp where he learned how to tie knots—something I only remember because he'd tied Lucy's sneakers together while demonstrating some nautical knot and she ended up having to play soccer barefoot that day. "Hey, I hear you're going up to Josie's house for winter break."

"Yeah. That's the rumor." I started to walk away and Luke fell into step next to me.

"I'm going to be up there with Owen and Matt. We'll have to make sure we meet up, do a few runs together."

"We could do that," I told him, feeling the upper hand shift in my favor. "I better go meet Lucy, she's waiting for me."

"Okay." Luke turned to go, but then stopped and looked back at me. "You know, you're different from Josie."

"Oh yeah, how's that?" I asked, enjoying my regained position of power. I was waiting for Luke to tell me that I was a sparkling conversationalist, that I was an amazing kisser, and that he found me fascinating.

Instead, he grinned and told me, "You're taller."

And as much as I wanted to tell him he was an asshole, I couldn't help but laugh. And neither could he.

chapter fourteen

How do you sum up four days of skiing with a guy who looked better in ski pants than I did, a gondola ride that had me making out at an elevation of 3,840 feet, two hours in a hot tub that left me with pruned fingers, sore lips, and an untied bikini top, and a huge slope-side log cabin that had me sharing a bedroom with two friends who thought I was hating every minute of it?

I had no idea. But that was my job.

When Mrs. Holden dropped me off at home after our three-hour ride back from Vermont, the house was dark and it was obvious nobody was around to greet me. TJ wasn't coming back from Chicago until tomorrow night, and my mom had probably gone over to the Brocks' house or to the movies.

"Do you want to come back with us and have dinner?" Mrs.

Holden offered, obviously feeling bad for the forgotten latchkey kid getting out of her backseat.

"Thanks, but I'll be okay. My mom will probably be home soon and I'm tired."

As I was about to close the car door, Josie grabbed my arm. "Don't go to bed without writing in the notebook first," she whispered. "We don't want you to forget any of the details."

The details. How could I forget the details when they were all I kept thinking about? How Luke reached around my waist to keep me from falling when our gondola jerked forward unexpectedly. How he offered to carry my skies over to the racks when I told him my arms were tired. The look he gave me before we said good night at Josie's house. No, there was no risk of me forgetting the details. It was the big picture I had trouble with. Because in the big picture, things were going according to plan. Luke was becoming perfect boyfriend material and he had no idea that I was the one manipulating him like a seasoned puppeteer. He was Pinocchio to my Gepetto.

So when I got up to my room and pulled the notebook out of my desk drawer, I didn't know what to write. It wasn't that I'd need to lie to prove that everything was working out the way we wanted, because the truth was, it couldn't be going better. The problem was, if I wrote about what really happened, if I didn't leave out the details, it wouldn't be the story Josie and Lucy—and every other girl reading the guide—was expecting. They say the devil is in the details, and in my case that was certainly true.

Because the details were fast becoming the most interesting part about Luke and me.

I'd taken a shower, done a load of laundry, and spent a half hour sitting on my bed trying to forget the fact that I dreaded picking up that damn notebook. Finally, after staring at the empty page for twenty minutes, I started writing.

Here's what I wrote:

Friday Night—Arrived at Josie's house. Luke called my cell phone (has memorized number, good sign) and made plans to meet me at the mountain in the morning. 'A' for effort and planning. Project Luke progressing nicely. Interested to see if he can pull off four days of this.

Here's what I *didn't* write:

The week before winter break officially started, I'd undergone meticulous preparation, including a deep-conditioning treatment (to avoid aforementioned static cling and flyaways), a deep-cleansing mud mask (to eliminate aforementioned blackheads on chin), a double application of Crest Whitestrips, and a generous daily slathering of Neutrogena self-tanning mousse. Gave Luke a Post-it with my cell phone number on it. Figured it would stick to the inside of his coat pocket and he couldn't forget it.

Here's what I wrote:

Saturday Morning—Luke waiting for me by the lift ticket line (keeping promises as promised, our boy is learning!). He looked good in navy blue ski pants, red jacket, and mirrored sunglasses. Owen asked Luke where he was planning to ski, and before answering Luke looked at me. Told him to go ahead and ski Skye Peak with his friends. Made plans to meet us for lunch at K-1 lodge before heading over to the lift.

Here's what I *didn't* write:

Josie was color coordinated from the tips of her purple Rossig-
nols to the fuzzy lavender headband covering her ears. If she
looked like the perfect snow bunny, my black puffy ski pants and
rental skis made me look like fashion roadkill. Seeing my reflection in Luke's mirrored sunglasses didn't do much to help my ego.
Nor did the fact that Luke was obviously an amazing skier and I
was trying to remember what I learned in ski school when I was
six. The idea of resorting to the snowplow in front of Luke was
about as appealing as being carried down the mountain on a
stretcher if I attempted to join him on the black diamonds. It
seemed safer to just meet him for lunch, where I knew I couldn't
hurt myself and end up in the first aid station.

Here's what I wrote:

> Saturday Afternoon—Luke met me at K-1 lodge for lunch,
> saved table with enough seats for all of us (thinking of
> others, chalk one up for the boy). Offered to carry my
> cafeteria tray and even put extra ketchup packets on the
> table for everyone's use. Forgot the napkins and straws.
> Will work on that. Made plans to meet back at the
> lodge at end of day. Showed up on time. 'A' for punctu-
> ality.

Here's what I *didn't* write:

Extra ketchup packets! I knew nobody else got it, but I did. It
was Luke's little way of paying homage to our inside joke. And I
thought it was cute. After that I even offered him a few of my
french fries. I figured he'd earned them.

•   •   •

By three o'clock, when the guys were supposed to meet us at the lodge, Josie, Lucy, and I had already been sitting around for a half hour, our boots unbuckled and our coats off, ready to call it quits.

"I think I have frostbite. Remind me again why my mom insists we come up here?" Josie asked, rubbing her toes.

"Perhaps it has something to do with that sweet little chalet you have on the mountain?" I suggested, even though the chalet was anything but little.

"I think she does it to torture me." Josie wiggled her toes at us, trying to get the blood going again.

"Hey, who wants to make one last run?" Luke asked, coming toward us with Matt and Owen trailing behind.

Nobody volunteered.

"Come on, anybody?" Luke tried again.

Owen pulled out the chair next to Lucy and sat down. Matt was already taking off his coat.

My thighs were burning, my lips were chapped, and the only run I wanted to make was to the cafeteria line to get a cup of hot chocolate with whipped cream.

"I'll go," I offered halfheartedly, hoping Luke would see it was just the two of us and decide to call it a day.

Instead he reached for my hand and pulled me up off my seat. "Come on."

"Can I run to the bathroom first?" I asked, thinking perhaps I should try to shake out my hat head or, at the very least, blow my running nose.

"We don't have time if we're going to catch the last gondola."

Josie and Lucy watched for my answer, probably thinking my bathroom request was precipitated by a full bladder when it was really a result of my desire to look hot for Luke. "Okay," I told Luke. "Let's go."

The lift line was empty, so we had our very own gondola to the top of the mountain. I fished around in my coat pocket for the tube of Burt's Bees lip balm I'd made a point to remember.

"Want some?" I held the tube out for Luke.

He shook his head. "That's okay."

"You're a really good skier. I guess you've been skiing a long time."

"Don't you remember that ski trip our freshman year?"

I vaguely remembered a day trip we all took to Jiminy Peak. "I guess so. Why?"

"You don't remember how I could barely stop and went plowing into Mr. Wesley, who went plowing into Nurse Kelly, who went plowing into the entire ski lift line and proceeded to knock everyone down like dominoes?"

"Come on, I think I would have remembered that."

"Nah, you probably wouldn't. You were going out with Owen."

"So?"

"So? So I wasn't exactly on your radar then. Remember?"

The funny thing is, he was right. I could remember Owen exactly, including the navy blue ski jacket he wore, with the red piping down the sides, and how his goggles left an impression in his hair. But Luke bowling over an entire lift line? Not one bit.

"All set?" I asked, holding on to the metal handrail to keep from being jostled around as the gondola made its way into the lift shed.

Luke stood up next to me. "Almost," he told me, before leaning over and kissing me. "I decided I needed some of your lip stuff after all."

• • •

Here's what I wrote:

> Saturday Night—Luke, Owen, and Matt show up at Josie's.
> Five minutes late. Luke says his watch is slow. Decide to
> believe him but tell him to get new battery when he gets
> home.

Here's what I *didn't* write:
Two words—hot tub.

I'd made it through a day of skiing without causing any serious
damage, unless you counted the blister on my pinkie toe, a little
windburn and sunburn on my cheeks, and what felt like a bruise
along the entire right side of my leg. But skiing was nothing compared to the test waiting for me that night. A test that included a
hundred and sixty jets with wave-massage motion, contoured seating, and minimal skin coverage.

Underneath my jeans and top I had on my favorite bikini—
favorite because it made me look like I had bigger boobs than I
did without making me look like I'd stuffed a roll of Bounty in
the cups. The plan was for Josie and Lucy to take Matt and Owen
downstairs to the game room so Luke and I could be alone on the
deck. Alone and half-naked, that is. Because essentially that's what
hanging out in a hot tub meant. I'd never seen Luke without his
shirt off (unless you counted our trip to Block Island freshman
year, which I didn't). But I knew he was going to look good. And
so I wanted to look better than good. I wanted to look killer. I
knew the whole point was to not really care what Luke thought of
me, but somewhere along the way that had changed. It was
Stephanie Potter syndrome all over again. I could see caring from
an objective "Is our plan working?" point of view, but this was different. I didn't know if it started when he took me to Friendly's or

when he helped me up after my wipeout on our last run down the mountain, but I cared. Probably more than I should have. Make that *definitely* more than I should have.

Josie's parents were gone by 6:30, and around 7:00 the doorbell rang and Owen, Luke, and Matt stood outside on the front steps, waiting for us to answer the door.

"Ready?" Lucy and Josie looked at me and waited for my answer.

I took a deep breath, adjusted my bikini top, and nodded. "Ready."

"Wow, this place is huge." Owen craned his neck as he followed the wall of windows up toward the roofline and the second-floor loft.

"The pool table's downstairs," Lucy told him. "And there's air hockey, too."

"Cool, show me the way." Owen followed Lucy down the hallway and she seemed more than eager to lead the way. She probably couldn't wait to kick his ass at air hockey—which I knew she would.

It took less than ten minutes for the six of us to pair off, and before you could say "take off your clothes and climb into six hundred gallons of bubbling water," Luke and I were in the hot tub.

I don't care how much self-tanner you slather on your body for a week, when it's twenty degrees outside and you skin is sprouting goose bumps from every pore, it's not a tan you're thinking about. You're just hoping you make it into the water before the guy you're with notices you look like something that belongs in the Butterball aisle—or the fact that your nipples are standing at attention.

"Cold?" Luke asked, as if he hadn't noticed my nipples poking through my bathing suit top.

I slipped down into the water and sat across from him on the bench. "A little bit."

"My legs are killing me." He made a point of rubbing his thighs, which only reminded me that there was more skin in the hot tub than bathing suit. "That was fun today."

"Obviously you're not counting my thoroughly humiliating wreck at the end of the day."

"Actually, that was the most fun part." Luke slid toward me. "You looked cute all covered in snow."

I hadn't been just covered in snow; I'd lost my hat and one ski about halfway up the run. My goggles were only covering one eye and I had enough snow up my back to make a decent-size snowman.

"Thanks, but it was way too painful to be cute."

Luke slipped his hand under mine and he laced our fingers together. I wondered if it was a move he'd perfected with other girls. Maybe even in other hot tubs. I tried not to think about how good he looked or how I wanted to reach out and touch him, and instead tried to see the situation for what it was. Just another phase in the plan.

Only it didn't feel like a phase. Or even like just part of a plan. It felt right. Absolutely one hundred percent perfect.

"Look at all the stars." I tipped my head back and rested it against the edge of the hot tub. "Is that bright one there the North Star?"

Luke rested his head next to mine. "Well, I'd say yes if it wasn't for the blinking blue light and the fact that it probably has a Delta logo on its side."

I watched my North Star moving away and saw that he was right. "Plane, star, what's the difference?"

"For our purposes, not much." Luke turned his head toward me and placed a kiss on my nose.

"You missed," I joked. "My lips are a little lower."

"Then let me try again."

This time he found his target just right.

"Can I ask you a question?" I asked.

Luke reached over and wiped a few droplets of water from my cheek. "Sure."

How was it possible that the guy sitting next to me was the same person who devised a scale that measured the buoyancy of a girl's breasts? Maybe Josie and Lucy were mistaken. Maybe the jiggle scale was something else entirely.

"What's with the jiggle scale?"

Luke smiled. "What do you mean, what's with it?"

"I mean, it's kind of obnoxious."

"It was just a joke, Emily. As in ha-ha funny."

"Well, it's not very funny. Would you like us to go around rating you guys?"

"You already do," he told me.

"We do not."

"Really? Then what do you call it when you comment on how some guy's ass looks in a pair of soccer shorts?"

He had me there. "An observation," I suggested. "At least we're not rating you."

"So, we're obnoxious because we do the same exact thing you do, but we just happened to come up with a name for it?"

I knew I'd sound ridiculous if I said yes. Besides, he had a point.

"Do you still use it? The scale?" I asked.

Luke shook his head. "The scale has been retired."

I wanted to believe him, and not just because I wanted Luke to be better than the creator of the jiggle scale. I was almost hoping that, after me, he didn't even notice anyone else's jiggling anymore. "Good."

I don't know if it was the sound of the bubbling water, the feel of Luke's warm skin pressed against mine, or the way he slid his hand lightly down my side until it rested on my waist, but I couldn't think of the last time I felt like this. Like I was exactly where I wanted to be with exactly the right person.

I tried to remember how Sean kissed, but all I could recall was how the last time I'd kissed him he'd tasted like a sesame bagel with a hint of garlic. And that thought alone made me lean into Luke and kiss him again. Because it was so much better.

And then I didn't just not think of Sean, I didn't think *period*.

This is what I wrote:

> Tuesday Night—Home. All in all, a productive four days. Luke seems well on his way to improving. April deadline seems possible for an entirely new-and-improved Luke Preston.

But this is what I *didn't* write:

My hand reached around Luke's neck and rested on the wet curls of hair clinging to his skin. I was all too aware that the only things between us were a Victoria's Secret Miracle Bra bikini and Luke's nylon swim trunks. And when you think about it, those aren't exactly hard barriers to overcome. If you wanted to.

Luke's fingers wandered up my back until they reached the thin string of my bikini top. I know I probably should have stopped him. I probably should have been thinking about the jiggle meter and how he'd no doubt tell Owen and Matt what we were about to do. But I wasn't. All I was thinking was that I didn't want him to stop.

And that wasn't just *not* part of the plan. It was downright dangerous.

chapter fifteen

The Monday after spring break, Lucy started lacrosse practice and Josie was busy working on the yearbook. Thank God. It saved me from having to come up with ways to avoid them. The last thing I wanted to do was spend another afternoon with Josie and Lucy talking about the guide. Or what I wrote in the guide. Or how Luke was changing because of the guide.

It was bad enough feeling guilty about my feelings for Luke. I practically couldn't look Josie or Lucy in the eye for fear they'd see that all my talk about how everything was going according to plan was complete crap. Every time I had to replay another one of our conversations or recount what happened when Luke and I went to lunch, I managed to avoid their gazes. Because they knew me too well. And they'd be able to tell that something wasn't right. That something was going horribly wrong. And I had to do something about it.

"Hey, Josie." I pushed back the heavy black plastic curtain to the photo lab and stepped into the darkened room. Somehow, the idea of not being able to completely see the look on Josie's face made what I was about to try and do a little easier.

"Look at this." Josie held up a piece of eight-by-ten paper still dripping with developer fluid. "What do you think?"

"What is it?" I asked, tipping my head to the side as I tried to figure out what it was. In the red glow of the only lightbulb dangling from the ceiling, it didn't look like anything I recognized.

"That tree out by the parking lot," she told me, and I knew exactly the tree she was talking about. The trunk had to be at least five feet around and it's been hovering over Heywood since the day the school opened. "It's a close-up of the trunk—see that's the bark curling up and that mark, there, is where Billy Stratton ran into it with his car that time."

As soon as Josie said that, I saw the tree through the ragged furrows and wrinkles. I don't know how I could have missed it. I'd seen that tree almost every day since sixth grade. The tree was even part of the Heywood Academy crest.

"That's really cool."

"Thanks."

"So, I was thinking about it," I said, "and maybe getting back together with Luke isn't such a great idea. I mean, what if his change is just temporary and he really isn't that different after all?"

"Well, we'll just have to see what happens." Josie flipped the light switch on and the sudden burst of white nearly blinded me. I rubbed my eyes and tried to get my bearings straight, which, given that I was about to try and convince my best friend that she didn't want anything to do with Luke, wasn't easy.

"I'm just saying, it's not like you really liked him, you know?"

Josie stopped organizing the bottles of chemicals and turned to me. "How can you say that?"

"Because it's not like you ever really like any guy you go out with," I explained, not that Josie needed an explanation. Everyone knew Josie wasn't the type to fall head over heels for a guy. "You date them for a little while and then move on."

"Maybe I used to," she agreed. "But Luke was different. I really liked him."

Not exactly the response I was expecting. Or the response I wanted.

There could only be one explanation for Josie's fixation on Luke—his status as the hottest guy in school. There was no other reason Josie would want Luke any more than she's wanted the twenty guys she's gone through since seventh grade.

"There are plenty of other guys who'd go out with you in a heartbeat," I reminded her. "You don't really need Luke, do you? Especially after what he did to you."

Josie went back to cleaning up. "You're right, I don't need the old Luke, but it looks like Luke will be new and improved after you're done with him. And that's a Luke I'd like to have another shot with, but I appreciate what you're trying to do. It's sweet of you."

Funny, I'd never use "sweet" to describe what I was doing. "It is?"

"Yeah, I know you just don't want me to get hurt again. But who says I will? Who says Luke and I can't end up even better than before?"

For the first time it occurred to me that the Luke Josie was waiting for was a lot like the Luke we knew in eighth grade. The Luke who sent me the valentine and candy.

"Maybe you won't like the new Luke, either," I suggested. "It's not as if you liked him before he became the guy everyone wanted."

"Maybe I was too busy lusting after Billy Stratton to notice Luke back then." Josie shook her head and laughed at me. "Is it so hard to believe that I could really like him? You're talking about *eighth grade,* Em. We're totally different people now."

There was no convincing her. And that meant that I'd have to figure out another way to get out of this. Only at that moment, the single other option I could think of didn't seem like an option at all.

While I missed hanging out with them after school, I was grateful that my two friends had more going on in their lives than a freaking recycled notebook. Unfortunately, I didn't.

Coming in midyear, I had no club. No sports team. Not even an invitation to help out with the set design for the drama club's spring production—and they *always* needed warm bodies as Heywood wasn't exactly known for its theatrical prowess. In any case, it was my last semester of high school, my last two-and-a-half months at Heywood, and I had nothing to do. But I had plenty to think about.

Mostly I thought about one of two things (three, if you counted the increasingly inspired ways I'd managed to avoid more than a three-minute phone call with my father). I thought about the college acceptances that would be arriving in my mailbox in about four weeks (I say "acceptances" because I couldn't even fathom the idea that they'd be college rejections—although, with the way my luck had been going, I probably should have considered the possibility). And I thought about Luke. Way more than I should have.

My birthday is April first, April Fool's Day. In the past this usually meant that my dad would say to me, "What? Today's your birthday?" and act like he totally forgot. Which he never did, but he just liked yelling "April Fool's!" before handing over my gift.

So when the phone rang before I even had a chance to brush my teeth, I figured it was my dad calling to wish me a happy birthday. And when my mom called my name and I went to the phone, I knew that before he got to happy birthday, he'd go through the whole April Fool's thing. But I was wrong.

"Happy birthday," he said, instead, cutting right to the punch line. "I can't believe my little girl is eighteen."

"I know, me neither," I answered, wondering why this year he'd left out his running joke.

"Big plans today?"

"Not really, just school."

"Well, I'm sure your mom will make it special."

"Probably."

There was an awkward silence and I realized how little my dad knew about what was going on in my life. I'd hardly spoken to him, *really* spoken to him, since before Christmas.

"I miss you, Emily." He paused, almost as if he was waiting for me to say something. My dad spoke the words slowly, as if he'd been practicing them for a while, trying to get them right. There was no mistaking the tone in his voice. And the sadness almost made me forget I was mad at him. I almost forgot he was the person who stayed behind in Chicago, the one who let us leave without him, and instead remembered he was my dad.

"I've got to go," he told me, his voice back to normal again. "I really wish I was there to give you a birthday kiss."

He hung up before I had a chance to say, "Me, too."

"I feel it's my duty to warn you. Josie and Lucy decorated your locker with balloons and streamers." Luke was waiting for me in the parking lot when I got to school that morning. There was no present hiding behind his back or even a card in his hand. But it didn't bother me, even though I knew it should. Even though I knew that Josie and Lucy would wish me a happy birthday and immediately ask if Luke got me a present. But it was only eight o'clock in the morning and I already had what I wanted. Luke.

"So, what's your family have planned for your birthday?"

"Nothing special. My mom will probably get a devil's food cake with buttercream icing from the bakery and we'll call it a day."

"Then I guess it's my job to do something really good." Luke fell into step beside me and we walked up to school. "Tell you what, meet me outside before lacrosse practice. I have a little birthday surprise for you."

Despite myself, I perked up. "A surprise?"

"Well, yeah. You didn't think I'd forget your birthday, did you?" Luke stopped when we reached the front door. "If you don't mind, I'll leave you here. I think Josie and Lucy wanted to surprise you."

I left Luke and walked down the hall, where, as promised, six purple and pink balloons were taped to the front of my locker, along with a cardboard cutout-letter sign spelling the words HAPPY BIRTHDAY.

"Surprise!" they both yelled when they saw me.

"Oh my God," I cried, pretending to be completely shocked. I even covered my mouth as if I couldn't believe they'd gone to all that trouble. And the thing is, they couldn't even tell I was faking it. I guess I'd become so good at hiding my real feelings they couldn't even tell the difference anymore.

Needless to say, I could think of nothing but my little birthday surprise for the rest of the day.

"I hope it's something good." Josie seemed more excited about my surprise than I was. "This is the big test, right?"

I couldn't tell Josie that it was a gift, not a test. Or that it didn't matter what he got me. And the reason I couldn't tell her that was simple and complex and totally beyond distressing: Somewhere along the way, Luke had become more like my boyfriend and less like a project.

I hated the idea that my birthday gift from Luke had become some sort of gauge of my progress, a way to see if I was succeeding at changing him. And I hated that Josie still saw this whole thing as an opportunity to get back together with Luke. But what made me hate myself was that I didn't want that to happen.

"I'm taking this as a good sign. As long as it's better than what Luke got me for Christmas, I'll be psyched."

"What'd he get you?" I asked.

"Nothing. So what do you think it is?" Josie wanted to know.

"I have no idea," I admitted.

"Well, if it's good then we can pretty much assume he's changed for the better, right?" Josie looked to me for an answer.

So I just said, "Right." Because I couldn't say anything else.

After the last bell, Josie and Lucy wished me luck and I headed down to the parking lot with a mixed sense of apprehension and anticipation. Luke was leaning against his car, already in his shorts and lacrosse gear. I wanted to believe he was as good a person as I thought. I wanted to believe it so badly. Regardless of what present he got me, I knew he wasn't as bad as Josie and Lucy made him out to be. Or even as bad as *I* made him out to be.

"Hey, birthday girl," Luke called out when he saw me walking toward him.

Despite myself, my heart jumped.

He patted the backpack sitting on the hood of his car. "Are you ready? Because I think you're going to really like this."

"I'm ready," I told him.

Luke reached into his backpack and pulled out my present. It wasn't wrapped in fancy paper with ribbons and bows, and when Luke handed it to me I couldn't come up with any words, not one single thing. Not even a thank you.

"Happy birthday, Emily," Luke said.

I held it in my hands and didn't know what to say.

"Well, what do you think?" Luke asked, a huge grin on his face. "Honestly. You can tell me the truth."

Staring down at my hands, I didn't know what I thought. Honestly. And the truth was, I wasn't sure if I'd succeeded with flying colors or failed miserably.

chapter sixteen

Lucy and Josie were waiting for me at Starbucks as planned. I'd had two hours to try and figure out what to make of my gift and how I'd pitch it to them. And it hadn't been easy. I knew what they'd think. And I couldn't blame them. Two months ago I would have been thinking the same thing.

Josie had her face in this month's *Cosmo,* but as soon as she heard the door open she glanced up at me and looked relieved. "We thought you'd never get here. I'm on my fourth vanilla Frappuccino."

"Sorry, I had some stuff I had to take care of."

"So, how'd it go?"

I slipped the tickets out of my pocket and fanned them out on the table.

Josie grabbed one of the tickets and held it up for inspection.

"A basketball game? It's your birthday and he gets you tickets to a basketball game?"

"Not just any game," I clarified, already feeling defensive. "A Celtics-Bulls game."

Lucy took the ticket from Josie's hand. "Oh my God, this is bad. He's never going to change—although it should be a great game. These tickets aren't easy to come by."

I silently thanked Lucy for her knowledge of all things sports.

"You know," I said as I pulled out a chair and sat down, "I was thinking about this on the way over, and maybe he has changed."

"He got you basketball tickets, Emily. That would be like you getting him a gift certificate to Sephora."

"Maybe not," I continued, ready to change her mind. "Yes, they're basketball tickets. But he specifically got tickets for Saturday's game against the Bulls—the Chicago Bulls, see?"

Josie shook her head. "Not really."

"He had a choice between Knicks tickets on Friday—and they're in first place—or Bulls tickets. He picked the Bulls because he knew I missed Chicago."

Josie nodded as if she was starting to understand. "Ah, I see where you're going with this."

"I think Emily may be right," Lucy agreed. "It really did require some forethought."

"Will he be picking you up in a limo or anything? Taking you out to dinner beforehand at some fabulous Boston restaurant?" Josie wanted to know.

"I don't think so," I conceded, sensing that even if Josie understood that Luke had put considerable thought into my present, without a lobster dinner it really didn't count for much. "We'll probably have hot dogs at the game or something."

Josie pondered this for a minute. "Well, he may not be one

hundred percent better, but at least it sounds like he's making progress. Job well done."

Her accolade did not make me feel any better. In fact, I felt worse.

The night of my birthday, Luke picked me up at seven o'clock. We had forty-five minutes alone in the car and I wanted to savor every second. So what if there was no long black limo waiting for me in my driveway, no bouquet of red roses, or a lobster dinner? And it didn't even matter that it was raining and the traffic was horrible and when we got to the tollbooth we got in the fast lane by mistake even though we didn't have a pass, because it just gave us more time to talk. We covered everything from the college letters that were a mere two weeks away (Tufts was Luke's first choice) to graduation and what we'd do once school let out. We pretty much talked about everything except the topic that loomed over my head like that huge weight that falls from the sky and lands on some unsuspecting cartoon character—the time capsule and my contribution to it.

"My uncle has a house in Falmouth," Luke told me, taking my hand and laying it on his thigh. I could feel his muscle contract every time he moved his foot over the break. And each time he slowed down to change lanes or accelerated to pass a car, the only thing I could think was, *You've got to love a guy who runs a mile each day in lacrosse practice.* And then I'd think, *Did I just think that?* Because I most certainly could not love the guy next to me who runs a mile each day in lacrosse practice. Because that would be just about the worst thing ever. Worse than getting deferred from Brown. Even worse than having Sean break up with me. It would be a mistake I wasn't sure I could recover from—betraying my best friend.

I would have proved that I was no better than anyone else, no better than an admissions officer who says one thing but means another, or an ex-boyfriend who does what's convenient for him regardless of how it makes someone else feel, or a father who lets his family leave because he's thinking of no one but himself.

Luke squeezed my hand. "I was thinking that it might be fun to head down to the cape for a weekend."

He may not have come right out and said it, but there was no mistaking what Luke meant. He meant that he thought it might be fun if *we* headed down to the cape for a weekend. Together. As a couple. And even though I knew I was supposed to be thinking about *me* versus *him*, and how all of this was going to end the day I put the guide into the time capsule, I wasn't. All I could think about was *us*.

Well, it wasn't *all* I could think about. Luke didn't come out and say it, and there was no sidelong glance that would even make me think he was implying it, but there was something else that immediately popped into my mind: sex. Sex with Luke.

Not because there would be a romantic sunset along a stretch of deserted beach, or some canopied bed in a quaint cottage. Not because it fulfilled some notion of how my first time should be, or because it was exactly like I'd always imagined it would be. But because it was Luke. Because somehow I knew it would feel right, even if sleeping with the guy my best friend wanted was all wrong.

"Are we going to be late?" I asked when we finally pulled into the parking garage just after eight o'clock.

"We'll be okay," Luke told me. "But we're going to have to make a run for it."

"Do you have an umbrella?"

Luke held out his empty arms and looked at them. "Does it look like I have an umbrella?"

It had been so long since I cared about teaching Luke any lessons, I almost didn't even realize that this was my chance to give him a tip. "Maybe you should carry one in your car, just for situations like this," I told him, but my heart wasn't really in it. In fact, the idea of running through the rain with Luke almost sounded like fun.

"I'll remember that. But for now, this will have to do." He handed me his coat and pointed to my head. Even I had to admit—it was way more thoughtful than an umbrella.

"What about you?" I asked, ducking under the jacket.

"A little rain never killed me before. Just run fast."

He grabbed my hand and the two of us made a sprint for the Fleet Center.

We managed to make it to our seats just before tip-off. And they were great seats.

"How'd you get so lucky?" I asked, still shaking the rain off. It wasn't the most attractive look, but at least I'd managed to cover my face with the coat so my makeup wouldn't run. My water-logged shoes were in much worse shape.

"My dad's company has season tickets," he explained and I instantly deflated.

Was it really possible that, despite my insistence that the tickets were a good thing, Josie and Lucy were right? Was it possible that two tickets to a Celtics-Bulls game didn't mean he'd thought long and hard about how we should celebrate my eighteenth birthday, that he'd gone to great lengths to secure tickets to an otherwise sold-out game? It just meant his dad handed him some spare tickets?

"Oh." I tried not to sound as disappointed as I felt.

"You have no idea what I had to go through to get these tickets," he went on, not even appearing to notice I'd slumped down into my seat and was pressing the heel of my shoe against the chair in front of me so hard it was trickling water onto the concrete floor. "A guy my dad works with was supposed to have them tonight. I had to promise to walk the guy's dog when he goes away for a week this summer and mow his lawn the entire month of June."

"Oh." I perked right up, leaking shoes and all. "Really?"

Luke smiled at me. "Yeah. Really. So you better know how to work a lawn mower, because I'm not doing it by myself. The guy owns like three acres."

I smiled back and reached for his hand. "You mow, I'll supervise."

"Oh, you'll do more than that. Ever used a weed whacker?" Luke grinned and squeezed my hand.

"No, but I'm a quick study," I assured him and squeezed back.

"So, what do you think? Pretty cool, huh?" Luke pointed down at the floor, where a slew of players in green and red jerseys were running down the court. "I was almost afraid you'd wear a Bulls T-shirt or something tonight. I know how you Chicago fans are."

"What? And get us killed? I know better. My dad took me and TJ to a few Celtics games before we moved."

"Is he still a Celtics fan or did moving to Chicago change him?"

What an interesting way to pose a seemingly innocuous question. Did moving to Chicago change my dad? Only if you counted that it made him not want to live with us anymore.

I let go of Luke's hand and stared at the green lines outlining the parquet floor. "I'm not sure my dad's ever going to move back with us," I answered.

He reached for my hand again and lightly stroked my skin in circular motions, like he was tracing my name in script or something. "You really think he'd stay there?"

I shrugged. "Who knows."

"Don't let it bum you out. Maybe you'll wake up one morning and there he'll be, in your kitchen cooking eggs and bacon, or something. Things change, you know. I mean, look at us." Luke glanced down at our intertwined fingers and for a second I felt a stab of guilt, or maybe it was just my stomach grumbling—I *was* starving. "Freshman year you would never have come to a game with me and you would never have held my hand."

"Sure I would," I told him, not all that convinced it was the truth.

Luke frowned, like he knew I was kidding myself. "Owen, sure. Maybe even Matt LeFarge or Curtis. But not me."

I didn't bother trying to deny it. He was right. Freshman year I wouldn't have been with Luke. Would I even have been so willing to make him my project if he was still the quiet, slightly pudgy kid with the braces and cowlick? Could I really be that shallow?

I must have looked worried, because Luke reached over and put his hand under my chin, forcing me to face him. "I'm glad you're here with me now."

"Me, too," I told him, feeling only slightly less guilty.

"Are you hungry?" Luke asked.

"Famished," I told him, and placed an order for one hot dog.

With Luke gone to get the food, I actually started paying attention to what was happening on the court, and by the time he got back I was so into the game, I didn't even notice him standing there holding a cardboard carton with our dinner inside. But I did notice something. The Jumbotron suspended from the center of the ceiling, a huge video screen that showed instant replays, the score, and even a few announcements. HAPPY ANNIVERSARY, SCOTT flashed one message. WELCOME NEWTON CLASS OF '86 read another. I figured it was only a matter of time until I noticed a message especially for me, some grand gesture orchestrated by Luke.

"Are you in the market for a new investment advisor?" Luke asked, pointing to the Fidelity ad lit up next to the instant replay screen.

I took my eyes off the Jumbotron just long enough for Luke to pass me our dinner.

"No, just checking it out," I explained.

"Must be really interesting, you seemed pretty captivated by it."

"No, not really," I mumbled, and then sheepishly added, "I thought maybe you would have had them put up a birthday message on the sign, or something."

"Up there?" Luke pointed to the huge screen where an instant replay of a three-point shot was playing.

"Yeah." Now I felt ridiculous.

"Do you have any idea how much these seats cost?" He held up his dinner. "And this hot dog? This Coke?"

I looked down at the cardboard carton in my lap. "No."

"Obviously." Luke shook his head at me and reached for his hot dog.

"I'm sorry. I love my hot dog. See." I took a bite and rubbed my stomach with my free hand. "Mm, delicious."

"It better be." He still didn't look at me. "Eat up, you need all the energy you can get. I don't know if I have enough money left over to get the car out of the parking garage, so we may be walking home."

"I can use the exercise," I joked, but Luke didn't laugh.

We sat there in silence while everyone around us yelled and cheered and clapped. I attempted to eat the barely warm hot dog that probably cost Luke eight dollars, but I didn't feel all that hungry anymore. I just felt ungrateful. I felt like a total bitch, which, a few months ago would have made me happy, but now only made me feel lower than low.

"I'm sorry," I told Luke, but my apology was drowned out by an eruption of applause as the Celtics scored a basket. For the second time that night, my timing sucked.

Luke turned to me. "What?"

I took a breath and this time made sure he heard me. "I said, I'm sorry."

Luke accepted my apology and the rest of the game we held hands and watched the Celtics beat the Bulls 92–81. Even though he'd said it was okay and told me to forget about it, I couldn't. And that's why when we reached the parking garage I decided to do something I knew was so anti-guide, so completely un-handbook, I knew there was no way I could ever tell Josie and Lucy. But I also knew there was no way I couldn't do it.

"Here." I took a twenty-dollar bill out of my purse and held it up. "Let me pay for the parking. It will be my treat."

"But it's your birthday," Luke objected, not accepting my peace offering.

"I know. Think of this as my way of saying thanks."

Luke eyed the money. "I'm going to accept your offer, you know. I've already spent close to a hundred bucks tonight."

"I know. I want to pay for it. Really." Even as I said it, I knew Josie and Lucy would kill me. I was supposed to be teaching Luke how to be a better boyfriend and here I was offering to pay for part of our date. My birthday date.

"Okay, as long as you mean it." Luke still didn't look convinced.

I stuffed the twenty-dollar bill into his hand. "I mean it."

"Thanks." He smiled and a small shiver crawled down my spine.

I loved making him smile. "No, thank you, Luke."

"Happy birthday, Emily." Luke leaned in and kissed me, and I wrapped my arms around his neck and kissed him back. It wasn't the kiss of someone pretending to like a guy or the kiss of someone who was just doing what she had to prove her point. It was a real kiss, the kind you give a real boyfriend.

chapter seventeen

Even though it was almost midnight when I got home, the light was still on in the family room. I thought it had to be my mom, who was addicted to old classics and had been known to stay up way into the wee hours for an Audrey Hepburn movie, but when I peeked in on my way upstairs it wasn't my mom. It was TJ, who was probably waiting up for me so he could hear about the game.

"The Celtics won," I told him as I walked toward the couch, where he was lounging with his feet propped up on a pillow. My mom had to be asleep. There was no way he'd do that if she was around to see him.

But when TJ heard me he didn't sit up and ask me where our seats were or if I got to see any players up close. Instead he held something up in the air where I could see it—a brown notebook. "What's this?"

"Nothing," I snapped, rushing over to him and grabbing for the notebook in a way that completely contradicted my claim that that it was nothing.

TJ jumped up and held the book over his head as he read the title I'd written across the cover in black marker. "The Book of Luke," TJ recited. "At first I thought you'd gone all religious on us, but this isn't exactly very Christian."

"Give that to me," I demanded, but, because TJ was now about four inches taller than me, he didn't exactly look threatened. He actually seemed to enjoy having me hop up like some trained dog reaching for a treat. "I swear if you don't give me that, you'll regret it."

"Oh yeah? What are you going to do? Write me a guide on how to be a better brother? The Book of TJ?" he teased, making fun of me.

"I'm serious, TJ. Give it to me now," I demanded, trying to keep my cool. The last thing I needed was TJ telling everyone about the guide. Or Luke finding out. I couldn't have Luke find out. Not yet. Eventually he'd have to, when we put the guide into the time capsule, but not yet. I wasn't ready for it to end. I had two more weeks with Luke, and I wanted every minute.

"Give it to me, or I swear I'll go wake Mom up right now and tell her you went through my stuff." It was pretty lame threatening to tell on him, but I was feeling that desperate. And I knew it would work. If there was anything that bothered my mother as much as bad manners, it was not respecting someone's privacy.

TJ watched me to see just how serious I was.

"Fine, here." He unceremoniously lowered his hand just close enough for me to reach the spiral metal spine. "So, what is it?" he asked.

"Didn't you read it?"

TJ shrugged. "Maybe. Parts of it. It looks like it's a bitch session for you and your friends."

"It's a project for the senior time capsule. And it's not a bitch session. It's a guide."

"Like a how-to book?"

Maybe he hadn't read it after all. "Yeah. Kind of like a how-to book."

"Then what's Luke have to do with this? What are you doing, testing out your lame theories on him?"

There was no maybe about it. TJ had definitely read the notebook. He knew what I was up to—or, at least, what I was *supposed* to be up to. And now it was time for some serious damage control. But first I had to figure out how to play this. I could make grand accusations and threats and put him on the defensive, but that wouldn't exactly achieve my desired outcome, which was for TJ to forget he'd ever laid eyes on the guide. Or I could let him be the good guy. I thought I'd try the second route first.

"Look, it's just some stupid school project. When you're a senior, you'll have to do one, too. It doesn't mean anything."

But TJ wasn't going to back down. He had the upper hand and he knew it. "If it doesn't mean anything, why are you freaking out over it?"

"Don't be an asshole, TJ."

"Me?" He laughed like he'd heard a joke. "Me? Are you serious?"

TJ reached for the remote control and turned off the TV. "Funny how you're writing a notebook filled with crap, and playing some sort of game with Luke, but *I'm* the asshole."

He turned to walk out of the room, flipped off the light switch, and called over his shoulder to me. "And not every guy is an asshole, Emily. Maybe *you* are."

I heard his footsteps climbing the stairs, but I didn't attempt to defend myself. Instead, I just stood there in the dark, clutching the notebook under my arm, wondering how the hell I was going to get myself out of this.

chapter eighteen

Monday morning I hid out in the girls' bathroom as long as I could in hopes that Josie and Lucy would give up and head to first period without me. There was no way I could face them. There was no way I could tell them about my birthday date with Luke. I may have thought I'd be good at this pretending thing, but I was horrible.

I knew I had to come clean, only I wasn't ready to do it. I needed some time to figure out what I was going to say. And what I was going to do if Josie and Lucy didn't understand.

At 8:11, I slowly opened the bathroom door and peeked down the hall. Most people had already headed to class. The coast looked pretty clear—or at least as clear as it was going to get without showing up late for first period.

I ventured out into the hall and practically ran toward my locker. Of course, the minute I turned the corner, I was dead.

"Where have you been?" Josie demanded. "We've been waiting to hear all about your date."

Lucy was practically jumping up and down trying to get my backpack away from me. She tore the zipper open, took out my books, and threw the empty backpack to Josie, who opened my locker and tossed it in. "Quick, we're probably going to be late as it is."

"Oh, what do you care, you've already been accepted to Duke," Josie said.

"Wait a minute." I slipped out of my coat and turned to Lucy. "You heard from Duke."

"Yeah." Lucy almost looked embarrassed. "Mr. Wesley pulled me into his office this morning. The soccer coach called him over the weekend. Owen is taking me to Sam's for lunch to celebrate."

"That's great." I gave Lucy a hug, but it wasn't exactly enthusiastic. Not that I wasn't happy for her, I was. It's just that the timing was all wrong. Everything was happening way too fast. If Duke had already decided to accept Lucy, then that meant I'd be hearing from colleges soon. And if decision letters were on their way that meant it was getting closer to April 15. And April 15 was one month before graduation. And one month before graduation was when the senior class buried the time capsule.

"So?" Lucy and Josie were still waiting for me to tell them about my birthday date with Luke.

"It was fun."

"Fun?" Josie sat on the radiator and threw her hands in the air like I was exhausting her.

"Yeah. Fun."

"Well, I think your 'fun' is almost over because I think you've done your job."

I finished stuffing my coat in my locker and then turned to face them. "Yeah, about that," I started, but Josie cut me off before I could finish.

"I bet Luke's on the verge of apologizing to me."

"You do?" How was I supposed to tell her that Luke had no intention of apologizing to her?

"Yeah." Josie smiled at me. "I can't believe it, but it worked. The guide totally worked, and we have you to thank for that."

Me. Yes, I was the one to thank for all of this. I had no one to blame but myself.

Lucy agreed. "You know, I'm glad the guide worked, but I'm also glad this is all over. Even if Luke needed to learn a few lessons, maybe not every guy is a jerk."

"Well, it doesn't matter anymore, because I think it's time for the big breakup," Josie continued. "Then I can be there to console Luke and everything will be great."

"So, when are you going to do it?" Lucy asked.

"Maybe you should do it sooner rather than later," Josie suggested. "No reason to keep hanging out with Luke if the guide's done."

It was too late. There was no way to get out of this now. There was no way I could tell them how I really felt about Luke. As much as I wish I could fix everything, there was no way around it—this was the beginning of the end for Luke and me.

"Fine!" I practically yelled. "I'll take care of it."

Josie and Lucy looked at each other.

"Now I've got to get to class." I grabbed my books out of Lucy's arms. "I'll see you later."

I bolted down the hall and into the stairwell without even

looking back. I didn't have to see them to know exactly what Lucy and Josie were doing—staring at me and asking themselves, *What the hell is her problem?*

I didn't eat lunch. Don't get me wrong, I was starving, but I couldn't face Lucy and Josie. I couldn't go through another round of twenty questions about Luke and the guide. For the life of me, I couldn't figure out how it had come to this. How did I go from hiding out by the bathroom because I was afraid my two former best friends wouldn't like me when I moved back, to hiding out *in* the bathroom because they *did* like me and actually wanted to talk? Only now I had another big problem. And his name was Luke.

I started looking forward to the end of the day more than the mornings. I arrived right before first bell and spent every lunch period in the library studying. I'm sure Lucy and Josie just thought I was stressing out about where I'd get in to college (probably because that's what I told them). And while, yes, the idea of finally finding out where I'd be spending the next four years of my life was slightly stressful, lying to my two best friends was turning me into a basket case. Luckily, with Lucy at lacrosse practice and Josie in the yearbook office laying out her photos, the 3:05 bell had become my salvation.

"Come on, I'm taking you somewhere." Luke came up behind me and took me by the arm, pushing me out Heywood's double front doors and onto the school's front walk.

"I can't," I told him, even though there was nothing I wanted to do more than just escape with Luke. "I'm going home. Besides, don't you have lacrosse practice?"

He loosened his grip and let his fingers fall down my arm until he reached my hand. "Not today."

"Where are we going?" I asked.

"To check out Tufts' lacrosse practice."

"Why?"

"There are two reasons, really. First of all, I've been accepted."

"No way!" I stopped walking. "Why didn't you tell me?"

"I haven't told anyone yet. You're the first person who knows, besides my parents."

I didn't know what to say. Luke hadn't told Matt or Owen or even Coach Walton. He'd told me. Before everyone else. What was I supposed to say to that?

"It's not *official*," he went on. "I haven't gotten the letter yet or anything, but the Tufts lacrosse coach called and so it's pretty much a done deal."

"Well, congratulations, that's great news." For some reason, I resisted hugging him, maybe because I knew this was the beginning of the end.

"Thanks."

"But why don't you bring Matt or Owen or someone who'd actually care about watching their practice?" I suggested, already trying to distance myself from him.

"Because that brings me to the second reason I wanted to drive all the way to Medford to check out the lacrosse team."

"And what's that?"

"Because I wanted to be with you."

The team was already practicing on a field that was more mud than grass thanks to Saturday night's rain. Luke parked the car and opened his door to get out.

"I'll wait here," I offered. I may have agreed to go with Luke, but there was no way I could stand on the sidelines and pretend everything was normal between us. I couldn't fake being happy that he'd gotten into his first choice school when I knew that in less than ten days *we* would no longer exist. The only proof we'd ever existed at all would be placed in the time capsule for the class of 2016. And I'd be left with nothing.

"No way, you're coming with me," Luke insisted.

"I'm not going with you." I pointed to the windshield, where dollops of water slid down the glass. "It's drizzling. Besides, it's muddy and I'll ruin my shoes."

"Come on, it's not that bad. Look." Luke reached under the driver's seat and pulled out a black Totes umbrella. "I'll even let you use my umbrella, if you'd like."

His umbrella. Luke Preston was driving around with an umbrella under the front seat of his car. And it was all because of me.

Luke came over to my side of the car and opened my door. "I know it seems like we've been hanging out in the rain a lot lately," he observed, holding the umbrella over me as I stepped out of the car, "but if you come with me, I promise this will be the last time."

The last time. Just hearing him say the words made me want to jump out of the car and throw my arms around him.

"Okay," I agreed, a lump growing in my throat. "One last time."

I took Luke's hand and we headed down to the field.

I know nothing about lacrosse, and dating Luke (or pretending to date Luke or whatever) hadn't changed that. Add to my lack of knowledge the fact that everyone had on the same jerseys so I couldn't tell who was supposed to be doing what, and that those jerseys were coated in mud so I couldn't tell who was who anyway, and it looked like wrestling with sticks to me. But Luke was digging it big-time.

"I can't believe next year I'll be out there," he mused, his eyes following the ball from stick to stick.

"So you're going to say yes?"

"Hell yeah. I don't even care if anyplace else accepts me."

"I should have such problems." Even though I thought he'd been concentrating on the scrimmage, Luke turned to me.

"What are you talking about? You're totally getting in everywhere."

"One word: Brown."

"Oh, who cares about Brown." He waved away the word like a pesky mosquito.

"I do." Or, I used to. I didn't nearly care as much as I did a few months ago.

"No you don't," he disagreed.

I kicked a glob of mud and watched it splatter on Luke's pants. "How can you say that? Of course I want to go to Brown."

"Oh, because Providence is so great?"

"No."

"Then why?"

I couldn't tell Luke the real reason, and not just because it would sound utterly insane if I said it out loud.

"Brown is a good school," I told him.

"And so is every other school you applied to," he replied. And he was right, of course. "So what's the real reason?"

Here's where I cringed. "Everyone expects me to go there. I've been talking about going there ever since I can remember. If I don't go, what will everyone think?"

"You applied to Brown because that's what everyone expected you to do?"

It sounded even worse when Luke said it.

I nodded. Barely. It was kind of a cross between a nod and single chin bob.

"Okay, I know it's dumb. Let's forget about it."

"So if Brown accepts you, you're going to go there just because you think it's what everyone expects? You know, Emily, sometimes I think you care way too much what other people think of you."

If he only knew. If Luke thought I wanted to go to Brown to make my mom happy, what would he say if he knew that the only reason I'd started hanging out with him in the first place was to make Josie and Lucy happy?

"Well, maybe you don't care enough," I replied.

"What's that supposed to mean?" he asked.

"I mean that, from what I've heard, you haven't exactly been the nicest person in the world."

"Why? Because I broke up with Josie? Because people offered to bring me my lunch and I accepted? At least I don't do things just because I think it's what people want me to do. Maybe you should think about what *you* want for once."

"It's not that easy." I hated talking about this. If I actually took Luke's advice, then I'd tell Lucy and Josie that I was done with the guide. I'd tell them that I wasn't faking it with Luke. And I'd have to tell Luke that it had all started out as a plan designed to teach him a lesson.

"Actually, it is. So, if you didn't care what anyone thought, would you still go to Brown?" he asked.

I thought about Luke's question—*really* thought about it—before answering. In January, I would have immediately said yes. "No, probably not."

"Good." Luke nudged me. "You're shivering. Come on, I'll race you back to the car."

It was just a nudge, but still, I almost took a header right there in the mud. "No way. It's too slippery. I'll kill myself."

"Then you better get going." Luke started to make a break for it, but I grabbed for his sweatshirt and caught his sleeve.

"No you don't," I yelled and tried to pull him behind me so I could get a head start. Of course, Luke had some pounds and inches on me, so even though I'd intended to keep him from going anywhere, all I succeeded in doing was latching on to a guy who was used to running in the mud with a lacrosse stick.

My foot slipped out from under me and I went down, my ass landing smack-dab in the center of a huge puddle.

"Hey, I'm sorry," Luke apologized and reached out a hand for me to take hold of. "I didn't mean for you to fall."

If I was going down, I wasn't going down alone. I reached for his hand and acted like I was about to help myself up, but instead of standing, I yanked his arm and watched him tumble down next to me, where he landed with a splash.

"That wasn't very nice," he said and laughed, wiping splattered mud from his face.

"Whoever said I was nice?" I asked, throwing a handful of mud at him.

Luke held his hands up to shield his face. "Not me."

Then, before I could say "mud in my underwear," Luke had me pinned down in the puddle, his knees sinking in the mud on either side of my hips.

The ground was freezing, and I could feel my hair grow heavy as it soaked up the grimy water. But that was pleasant compared to the cold ooze seeping into my shirt. Still, I didn't move. Instead, I closed my eyes and focused on Luke's warm breath on my neck as he leaned down and whispered in my ear. "So, you want to play dirty, huh?"

I didn't know if he was trying to be funny or if he was challenging me to try and break free. Before I had a chance to figure it out, his lips were making their way from my mud-caked ear to my mouth.

As our lips parted and our tongues mingled with gritty grains of dirt, my head sunk farther into the mud. And, still, I didn't stop.

Just when it occurred to me that there may be worms about to use my ear canal as a direct entrance to my brain, Luke pulled away. I opened my eyes, but he didn't get off me. Instead, he kept his face a few inches from my own, the cloudy gray sky acting as a backdrop.

"You know, I wasn't exactly being honest with you."

He wasn't being honest with *me*? "About what?"

"When you mentioned the Valentine's Day chocolates. I do remember sending them."

"You do?"

Luke nodded and splattered a new layer of mud drops on my face.

"So, why'd you send them?" I asked, curious to finally hear the answer to a six-year-old mystery.

"It wasn't anything in particular, I don't think."

"So it wasn't my rockin' sixth-grade bod?" I joked.

"Unfortunately, no." Luke moved off me and lay on his side. "I just kind of liked you."

"You liked me? How could you like me, you hardly knew me?"

"True, but you were nice."

There it was again. The four-letter word that got me into this mess in the first place. Only when Luke said it, it didn't seem so bad. In fact, it sounded pretty good.

"Besides, you hardly knew me a few months ago, but you liked me." Luke waited for an answer, but what was I supposed to say to that? *Um, Luke, about that liking you part, see, it was really just a game so I could write a handbook about changing you . . .*

Luke reached for a strand of my hair and used it to write something in mud on my face. "Now what are we going to do?"

"I suppose we should go back to your car and try to figure out a way to get home without completely destroying your upholstery."

This time when Luke extended a hand and offered to help me up, I let him.

"So did you like the chocolates?" he asked, leading the way up the hill.

I could have told him the truth. I could have said that I gave the gross flavors to my mom and wished that they came from Carl Mattingly. But I lied. Not because I'd become so good at it, but because I didn't want to hurt his feelings.

"I loved them."

When we reached the car, Luke pointed to the backpack I'd tossed on the backseat.

"Do you have a notebook in there?" he asked. "Maybe we could rip out a few sheets of paper to sit on?"

I had two notebooks in my backpack—my five-section notebook with all my class notes and a brown notebook that I couldn't let Luke see.

Here was my chance to get rid of the guide once and for all. I could tell Lucy and Josie it fell out of the car into the mud. I could tell them the pages got soaked through and all my notes weren't even readable anymore. There was no way we could re-create three months' worth of work in two weeks, so we'd have to come up with something else to put in the time capsule. All of a sudden, a CD and this month's *People* magazine didn't sound so bad.

I wanted to, I really did. But I couldn't. Josie trusted me. And I'd let her, believing that there was no way something like this would happen. Believing that I was better than all the guys who did stupid things. Better than the people who'd hurt me.

"Why don't we take the floor mats up and put those on the seats instead?" I suggested.

Luke thought it was a good idea, and the whole ride home, as I sat on a rubber floor mat, I could practically hear the brown notebook on the backseat screaming to me, telling me that even though I'd just done what it would take to keep my friends, I'd also just blown my chance to keep Luke.

chapter nineteen

"What happened to you?" TJ stopped talking and held the cordless phone against his chest. "You're a mess."

"I got caught in the rain."

I thought TJ would go back to talking to his friend and I could go upstairs and get cleaned up before my mother realized I'd just tracked muddy footprints across the kitchen floor. Instead, TJ held the phone out and waited for me to take it.

"Here. It's Sean."

I stood there in the kitchen, my bare feet on the cold tile floor, and stopped in my muddy tracks. Sean. Sean was on the phone. A few months ago I would have killed for this moment. I would have been dancing little muddy toe marks all over the kitchen floor if Sean had called to talk to me.

"Well, are you going to take it or what?" TJ asked.

I reached for the receiver, not even bothering to wipe my hands off first.

"Hello?"

I don't know which surprised me most, that Sean was on the phone or that he was coming to Boston or that he wanted to see me when he was here. And it didn't really matter which surprised me most, because what really threw me was how my stomach flipped over as soon as I took the phone and heard his voice.

"I'm coming out to visit," Sean told me, although I knew he meant he was coming to visit the Boston College campus, and not visit me specifically. "Can you come into the city and meet me?"

There was no "I'm sorry," or apology for the three months I never heard a word from him. Just an invitation to meet him in Boston. And I didn't know what to say. Three months ago I thought I knew what I'd say. I'd wanted to tell him to go fuck himself. I wanted to tell him that I was going out with the hottest guy at Heywood, even if that didn't exactly explain the entire situation. I wanted to remind him that we weren't just no longer going out, we were no longer friends. But I didn't. Despite myself, a part of me still wanted to see Sean. I wanted him to see me. The last time we were together he left me in tears, my eyes red and puffy. That wasn't the way I wanted to be remembered.

"When?" I asked, turning my back toward TJ, who'd decided to camp out on the kitchen counter and listen to our conversation.

"This weekend. I get in Friday night."

"Nothing like waiting until the last minute to call me," I couldn't help remarking, even though I knew I sounded like a bitch. I think after what he did to me, I was entitled to at least one bitchy remark.

"I know. I wasn't sure you wanted to hear from me."

"You were right."

"So you don't want to see me?"

I hesitated, but it was more for effect than because I was actually considering my options. "No, I'll see you."

Even with my back turned, I could feel TJ raising his eyebrows at me.

"Are you coming alone?" I asked.

"My dad's coming with me, but he was going to meet a friend for lunch on Saturday. You want to meet somewhere and grab a bite to eat?"

"How about Fanueil Hall at noon?"

Sean told me that would work and then asked me one last question before hanging up. "Are you seeing anyone in particular?"

"You mean, do I have a boyfriend?" I clarified.

"Well, yeah."

I immediately thought of Luke. But even if I felt like Luke was my boyfriend, even if I wanted him to stay my boyfriend, in a few days it would all be over. The moment I put the guide into the time capsule, Luke and I would be history. "No," I finally answered. "I don't have a boyfriend."

"You don't have a boyfriend?" TJ repeated after I'd put the receiver down. Of course he'd been listening the entire time, even though he was pretending to read the back of a box of Shredded Wheat. "If you're telling Sean that you don't have a boyfriend, why does the entire school think you're going out with Luke Preston?"

I attempted to wipe my muddy fingerprints from the phone, but all I managed to do was turn the dishtowel a dingy gray. "Look, you wouldn't understand."

Actually, TJ would understand perfectly. I'd been playing a

game with Luke, a game that was turning out to be way more hurtful than any game he'd played before. The jiggle scale paled by comparison.

Obviously, I couldn't tell TJ what I was doing, and part of the reason was that even I wasn't sure what I was thinking when I told Sean I'd meet him in Boston. It wasn't like I was still pining away for Sean. But it wasn't like I still hated him, either. At least not as much as I used to. Three months later it was what it was. We broke up and it sucked. Maybe I hoped that seeing Sean would somehow make me care less about Luke. Or maybe I wanted to prove to Sean that I was over him. But most likely I didn't tell Sean about Luke because I was preparing myself for what it was going to be like from here on in. *Life after Luke.*

Besides, I knew Lucy and Josie would say I was crazy not to go, so I couldn't say no. Saying no would mean I had a reason, and that only reason would be Luke. And he wasn't supposed to be a reason not to see my ex-boyfriend. He was supposed to just be my project.

"No, I understand," TJ answered. "I understand perfectly. I just heard you tell Sean you didn't have a boyfriend, which makes me wonder why Luke Preston took you to a Celtics game for your birthday. I guess I just didn't realize you were such a big basketball fan."

"The Celtics used a two-one-two zone defense tonight," I proceeded to tell him. "And the Lakers couldn't move the ball around the perimeter."

It was something Luke said while we watched the game, and even though TJ and I both knew I was full of crap, at least it got me out of the kitchen without having to answer any more questions.

·　　·　　·

"Hey, Mom?" I knocked on her office door. "Can I take the car into the city on Saturday?"

She looked up from her laptop, where I could tell she was working on notes for an upcoming seminar. "Sure. What do you need it for?"

"Sean's coming into town and he called to see if I wanted to meet him for lunch."

There was no mistaking the look on my mother's face. "Are you sure you want to do that?"

I nodded. "Yeah."

She waved me in and pointed to the armchair facing her desk. "Come sit down."

I pulled my robe around me (I'd showered first—I wasn't dumb enough to ask my mom while looking like I'd just crawled out of a mud bog) and went in.

"What's going on with you?"

"What do you mean?" From the tone of her voice I knew exactly what she meant: *What the hell is going on with you, alien who's taken up residence in my daughter's body?*

"What I mean is, I thought you were going out with Luke?"

I shrugged.

"So he won't mind that you're meeting your ex-boyfriend for lunch?"

"What he doesn't know won't hurt him," I told her, quickly realizing it was the wrong answer.

"Really? I seriously doubt you'd feel the same way if it was Luke meeting his ex-girlfriend for lunch."

I didn't bother telling her that Luke's ex-girlfriend was one of the main reasons I was even going to lunch.

"Is that it?" I asked, standing up. "I need to go dry my hair."

"You know, Emily, eventually it's all going to catch up with you—the not talking to your father, lying to Luke about meeting Sean in the city. Sometimes it's best to just tell someone the truth, even if it seems easier to ignore it."

"Can I go now?" I could already tell my bangs were drying in some funky S-shaped curl against my forehead.

"Think about what I said," she added. "Denying something won't make it go away."

This from a woman who won't even acknowledge that her husband is living in Chicago. If I was the Queen of Denial, then my mom ruled the kingdom.

I knew I should have wasted no time calling Jackie and Lauren in Chicago to tell them about Sean. Maybe four months ago I would have been on the phone gloating, relishing the idea that Sean wanted to have lunch with me instead of hanging around a college campus checking out the co-ed scenery. Only now that I was over Sean, I didn't feel like I had much to brag about. Unless you counted the fact that I'd tricked Luke Preston into falling for me even though he was nothing more than an assignment to be completed. And considering how that was working out for me, I wasn't about to call Lauren and Jackie to brag about that, either.

"I think you should wear jeans," Lucy suggested when I told her and Josie I was meeting Sean in the city on Saturday. "That way it doesn't look like you tried too hard."

"Come over here before you leave and I'll do your makeup." For her birthday last year, Josie's mom had given her a consultation with Newbury Street's most sought-after makeup artist, and now she had more tubes and tubs and pencils than a department store makeup counter.

"And I'll do your hair," Lucy added.

So much for not trying too hard.

That's how, on Saturday morning at ten o'clock, I ended up in Josie's palatial bathroom with a towel draped over my shirt and a hot curling iron perched precariously close to my ear.

"Hey, be careful with that," I warned, pulling my head away from Lucy's grasp. "You're going to burn me."

"I'm just going to give you a little wave. I'm not going to burn you."

Of course, that's exactly what she did. "Ouch, that hurt." I jumped up, pushing Josie's hand away from my lips in the process, which resulted in a slash of brownish pink lip gloss across my cheek.

"I said don't move," Josie scolded.

"Well, I said don't burn me." I rubbed the sore spot on my neck. "Can you get me some ice or something?"

Josie went into her room and returned with a bottle of Evian. "No ice. Will Evian do?"

Lucy took the bottle and held it up to the hot spot below my ear. "I'm so sorry. I didn't mean to do that."

I knew it was an accident. I also knew that I was going to have one hell of a burn mark. "How bad does it look?"

Lucy removed the Evian bottle and took a look. "It's not so bad."

Josie leaned in for closer inspection. "With a little foundation we should be able to cover it up."

I turned toward the mirror to take a look. "Oh my God." I gasped. "It looks like I have a big red hickey."

"It won't once it scabs over," Lucy offered, trying to help. "Then it will look sort of like a rug burn."

"I don't want a rug burn on my neck any more than I want a hickey," I practically yelled. "I'm going to see Sean in two hours and I'm going to look ridiculous."

"Go in my closet and grab a T-shirt so we don't get powder all over your top." Josie reached for a vinyl pouch filled with makeup brushes of varying sizes and shapes. "This is going to require some work."

I got up and went over to Josie's walk-in closet. "What's this?" I asked, holding up a Hawaiian-print button-down shirt that looked way too big to be Josie's.

"Don't ask. That's the shirt I got Luke in the Bahamas."

I rubbed the silky material between my fingers and thought about how good Luke would look in it. "You're saving it?" I hung the shirt back up and grabbed a blue Heywood Academy T-shirt off one of the shelves.

"I was thinking that if our plan works and Luke and I get back together, I still might give it to him."

"And if the plan doesn't work? If he hasn't changed for good, what then?" I asked, hopeful Josie would say something like, "No big deal, never really liked the guy anyway." While she was at it, it would also be nice if she added, "And I'd totally understand if you fell for Luke; as a matter of fact, I'd love nothing more than if you and Luke ended up happily ever after."

But Josie wasn't going to cooperate. Instead, she said, "Maybe I'll make it into a voodoo doll and stick it with pins."

I tried to laugh. Really, I did. Only I couldn't find the humor in our situation. The only thing I could do was tell them the truth. I could tell them right now and get it over with.

"If you need extra pins, I'm sure Emily's got some left over from her Sean doll, right?" Lucy laughed and nudged me.

"I'm sure I won't be needing any. Em's done a great job with Luke, right, Em?" Josie looked at me hopefully.

"Right," I agreed, and returned to my seat at the bathroom counter.

I was wrong. I couldn't come clean. The only thing I could do was sit down and let them do my makeup. "So, how are you going to hide the huge scald mark on my neck?"

"Don't worry about it. We're going to make you beautiful."

"Half my head is wavy and my neck is seared, how are you going to do that?"

"Don't you worry," Josie assured me, dabbing a brush in a pot of concealer. "Just leave that to us."

Thirty minutes later I was ready to go. The mark on my neck was camouflaged and, after finally giving in and letting Lucy work on the other half of my head, I looked pretty decent. No, I looked better than decent. I looked good enough to make Sean regret that he ever let me go.

chapter twenty

drove around for a half hour before finally giving in and parking in a garage. I didn't want to spend the twelve bucks, but I was already late. As I ran down the steps of the parking garage, my cell phone rang. I grabbed the phone out of my purse and glanced at the screen. Sean's name and number appeared on the display, reminding me that he was still programmed into my phone.

I flipped the phone open and started speaking even before he had a chance to say hello. "I'm almost there. I'm crossing State Street right now."

"I almost thought you decided not to come. You're never late."

He was right. Whenever he'd come to pick me up, I was always ready. I was always on time. Punctuality was a given in our household. Even my period always arrived on time.

"Yeah, well, things change."

I was fifteen minutes late, but I did show up, and there he was, sitting on a bench, waiting. Wearing the same coat he had on when he said he wanted to break up with me.

In the movies this is where either the girl goes running to her guy and he embraces her and spins her around, legs flying in the air, or there's a moment when both people realize that that old spark isn't there. That meeting was probably a huge mistake and they would have been better off imagining meeting up one last time instead of actually attempting to do so.

In our case, neither of those happened. Instead of running into Sean's open arms, I walked over to him just fast enough to show I wasn't afraid to see him, but slow enough to demonstrate I wasn't in a rush. The entire time I walked toward him, Sean sat there watching me, a little grin on his lips. And even though I'd promised myself I wouldn't let him get to me, he got to me.

When I reached the bench he finally stood up. "Long time no see."

Not exactly eloquent, but it would do. "You could say that."

I didn't know if I should hug him or shake his hand or what. How did you act in front of someone you once thought you loved, someone you thought would love you a hell of a lot longer than he did?

"What are you in the mood for?" he asked, leading me toward Quincy Marketplace. "They've got anything you could ever want to eat."

"Pizza," I told him, noticing how the field coat had become worn in around the elbows.

After we ordered slices at Pizzeria Regina, we found a table and sat down.

"You look tan. Did you go somewhere?"

"I went skiing for spring break."

"Who'd you go with?"

"My friends Josie and Lucy. Josie has a house in Killington." Sean had given me my opening, the perfect opportunity to say I'd gone skiing with Luke. I don't know why I didn't just tell him. That was the point of all this in the first place, right? To show Sean I could land the hottest guy in school. To prove that I wasn't going to sit around and bemoan the fact that Sean unceremoniously dumped me.

But I didn't mention Luke. Not because I wanted Sean to think that I was still waiting for him or that, if he went to Boston College and I stayed around here, too, we might start seeing each other again. I didn't tell Sean because I had to stop thinking that Luke was really my boyfriend.

"Don't you want to get that?" Sean asked, pointing to my ringing purse.

Instead of answering, I reached for my phone and pushed the off button without even glancing at the screen. I didn't want to know who was calling. I wanted to ask Sean the question. Actually, I wanted to ask him two questions.

"Why'd you never let me have the last slice of pizza?"

Sean looked at me. "What?"

"Whenever we ordered pizza you'd always take the last slice."

"I guess because you never said you wanted it," he explained. "I wouldn't have cared if you had it, you just never asked."

I never asked. Was it really that simple?

Sean held out his slice for me. "Why? Do you want this one?"

I shook my head and prepared to ask question number two, which I was sure wouldn't have anywhere near as simple an answer. "Why'd you break up with me?"

Sean stopped midbite, his pizza flopping in the air as he tried to figure out if he should answer or finish taking a bite. He decided to take a bite. Probably needed the extra time to come up with a good answer.

I waited while he finished chewing, and then waited while he wiped the corners of his mouth with a napkin.

"Well?"

He shrugged. "I broke up with you because I knew you wouldn't break up with me."

Of all the answers! "Of course I wouldn't break up with you," I told him, my voice rising loud enough to get some disturbing looks from the couple at the next table. "I liked you, why would I break up with you?"

"Because you were moving. Because we wouldn't be seeing each other."

"We could have seen each other plenty, if you wanted to. The fact was, you didn't want to."

"When?" he asked.

"When what?"

"When would we have seen each other? We have different school breaks, neither of us is exactly putting up the dough to fly back and forth. It wouldn't have worked, and you're crazy if you think it would have."

"*I'm* crazy? I wasn't the one who waited until the morning—*the morning*," I repeated, for emphasis, "I was leaving for Boston. That's not just crazy, Sean, that's downright shitty."

So much for a nice lunch. So much for acting like I was over him.

But I was. And even if I was yelling at Sean, it was more out of frustration than anger. Because if Sean wasn't the bad guy, if he wasn't the one to blame for how things ended up between us, then who was?

"I'm sorry," he apologized. "I know it wasn't probably the best way to do it, but I didn't know what else to do. Would you rather I let you leave and we acted like nothing would change?"

"Maybe." My voice sounded more sulky than I'd intended. "Would that have been the worst thing in the world?"

"It would have been if you actually believed it was true."

"You let me give you this coat for Christmas, for God's sake." I touched the sleeve of his coat, almost expecting to feel the same electrical current that used to pulse through me whenever I touched Sean. But there wasn't. I didn't feel anything at all. "Why didn't you at least tell me before I went out and bought you a present?"

"Because I wanted us to keep having fun right up until you left. If I'd said anything earlier you just would have been miserable and we wouldn't have hung out. We had fun over Christmas break, if you remember."

"Of course I remember, that's why I was so pissed."

"Don't act like you really believed it would have worked out with you living all the way in Boston. You know you'd be lying. I was just being honest with you."

He was being honest with me. Funny how that worked out. Sean was honest with me and ended up breaking my heart. I was lying to Luke every single day and in the end my heart would still end up broken.

Sean pointed to my neck. "So, where'd you get the hickey?"

"It's not a hickey. I burned myself with a curling iron."

"Then why'd you try to cover it up?"

I felt the spot on my neck and then inspected the smudge of foundation on my fingertips. "I lied. I do have a boyfriend."

"Who is he?"

"This guy in my class. His name is Luke."

"How long have you been seeing him?"

"Since February."

"It sure didn't take you very long to get over me."

I didn't bother correcting him. I didn't bother pointing out that, until I actually saw him today, I didn't think I was over him, at least not completely. A big part of me didn't even want to be over him. Because if I was, then maybe it meant Sean was right when he said we couldn't last after I moved away. Which meant he did the right thing when he broke up with me.

"Yeah, well, I guess you were right after all."

Sean laughed. "You know, I was kind of hoping I was wrong."

Yeah, me, too. In fact, I'd been counting on it.

chapter twenty-one

"Luke called looking for you," TJ shouted when he heard the kitchen door open.

I found him in the family room playing with his Xbox. "What'd you tell him?"

"Nothing. I just said you weren't home. I told him to try your cell phone."

I hoped that was all TJ told him. Even though I hadn't *technically* done anything wrong—I mean, *technically*, Luke wasn't really my boyfriend. *Technically*, I was just pretending to be his girlfriend while I tried to prove the guide worked. And even if Luke *was* my boyfriend, *technically* it wasn't like I'd cheated on him by going to see Sean. So, if I hadn't done anything wrong, why did I feel so guilty?

"And, while I was playing answering service, Josie called, too,"

TJ added. "She wants you to go over to her house when you get home."

I had two choices. I could call Josie or Luke. I could call Josie and continue lying about how I felt about Luke, or I could call Luke and lie about where I'd been all day. And lie about who I was with. And lie and lie and lie.

You'd think that after so many years of holding in the truth (*no, of course I don't mind if you cut in line ahead of me; I'm not hungry, you have the last slice of pizza; sure, Dad, it's okay that you want to stay in Chicago for a while even though your family is moving to Boston*) I'd be used to it. You'd think I'd be able to continue ignoring how I really felt and just let the lies roll off my tongue. The only problem: It was exhausting. And the pressure was getting to me.

Never in a million years would I have predicted I'd turn into the kind of girl who'd call a guy over her friend. In eighth grade Mandy Pinta was like that when she went out with Ricky Barnett, and Josie, Lucy, and I always swore that friends came first. But we also swore that we'd never lie to one another or keep secrets, and look how that turned out.

I picked up the phone and dialed Luke's number.

"Where were you all day?" Luke immediately wanted to know. "I tried calling your cell."

"Yeah, my battery was dead." Lie.

He believed me, of course. Why wouldn't he? "There's not much going on tonight, you want to do something?"

You know what I felt like doing? I felt like telling Luke the truth. I wanted to tell him that the only reason I ever started hanging out with him was to prove I could make him better. I wanted him to know that, even though he'd started out as a project, it wasn't like that anymore. And I even wanted to tell him that

I'd gone to see Sean today, and that seeing Sean just reminded me how much I wanted to be with Luke. I didn't want to be with my ex-boyfriend, I wanted to be with my *real* boyfriend.

So, did I say it? Did I suck it up and take my mom's advice to stop ignoring how I really felt? Did I just finally get it all out in the open?

Of course not. Because then I'd have to admit the ugly truth—I was someone who'd fallen in love with her best friend's ex-boyfriend. I was someone who'd knowingly *continued* to fall in love with her best friend's ex-boyfriend even after she knew said best friend wanted to get back together with him.

And I'd have to admit something else, too. I'd have to tell Luke that he'd started out as a way to prove myself. He'd been nothing more than a flaw that I was determined to correct.

Only now I had the flaw that needed to be corrected. But I wanted one more night with Luke. Just one more night. I mean, I'd already made a complete mess of things, what was one more night? One more amazing, fantastic night. A night to remember long after this is all over.

"Yeah, I'd like that," I told him. "I'd really like to see you."

"You know what? I missed you today." Luke waited for me to say something back. And for the first time during our entire conversation, I told him the truth.

"Me, too," I whispered. "I missed you, too."

chapter twenty-two

Luke's parents were out to dinner in the city. The same city in which I'd just had lunch with Sean. It was like the universe was trying to tell me something. And I wasn't going to listen.

Somewhere between leaving a message on Josie's voice mail and driving to Luke's house, I'd decided to forget what everyone else wanted me to do, and just do what *I* wanted me to do. Maybe, somewhere deep down, I knew this was the last time we'd be together. Our last time and our first time all at once. I found myself wondering if they'd almost cancel each other out. And I hoped they wouldn't.

Sitting on the couch watching a movie with Luke, it was exactly where I wanted to be. It didn't matter that he didn't offer to get me a drink or that he hogged the remote control. Unfortunately, what mattered the most to me was exactly what I wouldn't be able to have.

"Do you want to go upstairs?" I asked, my voice sounding a little like I'd just run a marathon.

Luke muted the TV and turned to me. "Why, do you?"

I nodded. "Yeah, I do."

Luke took my hand and led me upstairs, not even bothering to turn off the TV.

When we lay down on Luke's bed, he didn't start unbuttoning my shirt or try to unzip my pants. Instead, we just lay there together, my head resting against his shoulder.

"What's with the glow-in-the-dark stars?" I asked, pointing to the ceiling.

"Leftovers from years ago. I went through a phase where I was all into space and planets and that stuff. I always forget they're up there until I go to bed, and then I don't feel like taking them down."

It wasn't the perfect beach scene I once envisioned. There were no waves lapping at our feet, no sunset or shooting stars. Just glow-in-the-dark planets stuck to the ceiling above us. It wasn't how I'd always pictured it, but for some reason it still felt perfect.

I just had one more thing to do. It wouldn't change what was about to happen, but I owed it to Josie. "Can you do me a favor?" I asked.

Luke stopped running has hands across my stomach. "Sure."

"Can you apologize to Josie?"

Luke hesitated before answering. "Yeah, I can do that. For you."

I rolled on my side and faced Luke.

"Do you have something?" I whispered.

Luke propped himself up on his elbows and smiled, like he was getting ready to make fun of me. "*Something*? Like a can opener or a bag of frozen peas?"

Despite myself, he got me to laugh. "You know what I mean."

"Yeah." Luke closed his eyes and kissed my neck. "I know what you mean."

I could tell Luke had had sex before, who knows, maybe even with the sophomore from St. Michael's on New Year's Eve. But, as he looked down at me, his eyes barely an inch from my own, I knew I was different. And I swear, right before I closed my eyes, Luke muttered something that sounded an awful lot like "I love you." And then I heard myself muttering, "Me, too."

Three months ago if somebody had told me I'd be lying in bed with Luke, I probably would have assumed I was doing it to prove I was over Sean. But that's not why I was here right now. It wasn't why I wished I never had to leave and that Friday would never come. I slept with Luke because I wanted to. I slept with Luke because—I can't even believe I'm saying this—I slept with Luke because I really believed I loved him.

chapter twenty-three

When I opened my eyes the next morning, for one brief moment, one tiny tick of the second hand, it seemed like any other Sunday. I could hear my mom in the kitchen and smell the scrambled eggs she was whipping up for breakfast. I even placed a hand on my stomach and considered heading downstairs for some eggs myself. And then it hit me. The night before.

Less than twelve hours ago I'd been lying in Luke's bed, lying naked while he curled his body around me to keep warm. Less than twelve hours ago I could almost still convince myself that this was still a game. Or maybe I'd just convinced myself that the game didn't matter. I couldn't tell anymore. All I knew, lying there in my own bed with the covers pulled up to my chin while the smell of eggs wafted under my bedroom door, was that less than twelve hours ago I'd been the happiest I'd been in a long time. And now I was going to have to pay the price.

Last night in bed with Luke, I wasn't thinking that he was the originator of the jiggle scale or that he'd e-mailed my best friend to break up with her or that he was making out with a St. Michael's sophomore while his girlfriend was planning how to give him the shirt she bought for him in the Bahamas. Instead, I was thinking about the guy who bought me a hot dog at the Celtics game and then wrote "happy birthday" in ketchup before handing it over to me. I thought about the only person who volunteered to take me to see my old house and how he'd gone out of his way to put an umbrella in his car, even though he couldn't care less if he got wet. And now he was the first guy I'd slept with. And now that I'd done it, losing my virginity didn't seem nearly as frightening as the idea of losing Luke.

I pulled the covers over my head and tried to hide, and not just because the eggs were making my empty stomach growl. I hoped that a down comforter and a cotton sheet with pale yellow pin-stripes could make it all go away. But there was no hiding from the truth. And the truth was, in five days I was supposed to put the completed guide into the time capsule and act like I'd finished my assignment, like the last three months had never happened. Only something *had* happened. Everything happened. And in five days I'd have to make a choice to either lose my best friends or lose Luke. Because there was no way Josie and Lucy would understand about me and Luke, and there was no way to tell them I'd slept with Luke because I loved him without making them feel betrayed. And the minute I put the guide in the time capsule, Luke would find out it had all just been part of some grand plan.

I'd never intended for Luke to actually become my boyfriend— a real boyfriend. Even now, looking back, I can honestly say that.

There was always a part of me that thought he was cute—I mean, I'm not blind—but I swear I never thought this would happen. I never thought I could fall for Luke and lose my friends in the process. He was just some guy I was supposed to reform.

"Get up, Dad's on the phone." TJ threw open my door without even knocking.

I peeked out from under the sheet. "Tell him I'm sleeping."

TJ put the phone up to his ear. "She says to tell you she's sleeping."

Why did I even think TJ would cover for me?

"He says he'd like to talk to you."

"Tell him I'll call him later."

I grabbed my pillow and buried my face in it while TJ relayed my message.

"You could have at least pretended I was really sleeping, you know," I told TJ, lifting the pillow after I heard him say good-bye and press the off button.

"I'm not going to lie for you."

"I wasn't asking you to lie for me," I told him, even though I was.

"Right." TJ turned to leave, but then stopped and ripped the pillow off my head. "I don't know why you think you have to keep punishing Dad—like it's not enough you wouldn't go to Chicago over spring break to see him."

"I'm not punishing him." I grabbed for the pillow and took it back.

"It's not like you're making the situation better for any of us, Emily. Maybe you should think about somebody besides yourself for once."

"Just get out," I ordered, and TJ did just that. I didn't need to listen to him telling me how I should or shouldn't treat my dad.

What did TJ know? In the grand scheme of things, TJ was the least of my problems.

Monday morning I couldn't bear the idea of facing Lucy or Josie. I was so afraid they'd be able to tell something was different. Not that I believed all that crap about a woman glowing after she's had sex or anything—I wasn't afraid they'd be able to tell I was different *physically*. No, I was afraid they'd take one look at my face and know that I wasn't pretending anymore. That I really did fall for Luke. Failing to write the guide was one thing, but falling in love and sleeping with your best friend's ex-boyfriend was an entirely different story.

So there was no way I could go to school and face them. Or Luke, for that matter. I felt like I was drowning in the Bermuda triangle, flailing between my two best friends who thought I was just pretending to be Luke's girlfriend to prove the guide worked, and the guy I'd fallen for, the guy I'd slept with, even though our entire relationship was based on a lie.

Instead of getting up when my alarm clock went off at seven o'clock, I reached over, smacked the off button, and burrowed under my comforter.

"You're going to be late," my mom reminded me, poking her head into my room.

I didn't even attempt to fake a scratchy voice or stuffy nose. I figured the look on my face would pretty much sum up how I felt. "I'm not feeling well. Can I stay home?"

My mom came over to my bed and laid a hand across my forehead. "You don't feel warm."

"It's my stomach," I told her, and I wasn't even lying. It *was* my stomach. I felt absolutely sick to my stomach about everything. I just wished I'd never agreed to test the guide. I wish we'd never come up with the idea for the guide at all. I'd set out to change Luke and instead I'd changed everything.

"Okay, you can stay home." My mom smoothed her hand across my bed, attempting to eliminate the creases I'd created overnight. "I'll go and get you some ginger ale to settle your stomach."

I was pretty sure a glass of ginger ale wouldn't settle anything, but at least I didn't have to go to school.

My mom returned with the glass of ginger ale and some toast. "I thought this might help," she offered, placing the plate on my night table. "You just get some rest and I'll check on you in a little while."

I gave her a weak smile, which was about the only kind of smile I could muster. "Thanks."

After she left I eyed the whole wheat toast and debated whether or not I should even try to take a bite. But I didn't have any appetite.

So instead of taking the toast I opened my night table drawer and reached for the brown notebook I'd stuffed in the back. I opened the cardboard cover and read the first page: *The Guy's Guide Tip #1: Forget everything you thought you knew about girls. You don't know anything.*

The first tip had been my idea. The *whole* guide had been my idea, my attempt to prove I didn't have to be the nice girl everyone expected me to be. And I'd succeeded. Only instead of just being *not-nice,* I was also now *not-happy.* If it wasn't happening to me, I'd almost point out how ironic that was. Only it *was* me, and it didn't feel ironic. It just felt horrible.

I laid the notebook on my lap and flipped through the pages we'd filled in, reliving the last three months. At the bottom of the pages I'd written notes about my dates and conversations with Luke, providing color commentary to go along with our tips and don'ts. I read each page, trying to pinpoint exactly when Luke stopped feeling like a project and started feeling like a boyfriend. But I couldn't identify exactly when it happened, I only knew it did. I continued reading and stopped when I reached the photos I'd glued to the back of some of the pages. There was me and Luke in the parking lot, the two of us in the hot tub at Josie's ski house, Luke and me walking together in the hall. Anyone looking at those pictures would have thought we were like any other couple. They never would have guessed it was my attempt to show guys how to be better people, better boyfriends. Looking at those pictures Luke didn't look like the horrible guy I thought he was at the start of all this. And that made me feel even lower. I was the lowest of the low. I was worse than all of them. Because I was the one who didn't care about anyone else's feelings. I went out of my way to be mean. I did it on purpose, and I knew better.

I was still in my pajamas at two o'clock when my mom came into my room waving five envelopes in the air. At that point, I'd almost convinced myself that as long as I stayed in my pajamas I wouldn't have to deal with what was waiting for me at school. I could spend the last month of school in bed pretending I had mono or something, using my yellow pinstriped sheets to shield me from the outside world.

"Delivery for Emily Abbott," she called out, coming over to the side of my bed and motioning for me to make room so she could sit down.

I scooted over and sat up. "Are those what I think they are?"

My mom handed me the envelopes. "Only if you think they're letters from Smith, Swarthmore, Amherst, Bowdoin, and Northwestern."

Just when I thought things couldn't get any worse, the U.S. Postal Service proved me wrong.

I held the envelopes in my hands but didn't make a move to open them.

"Go ahead," my mom urged, nudging me. "Let's see what they say."

This wasn't how I pictured finding out, with bed head and morning breath, even though it was well into the afternoon.

"Come on, what are you waiting for?" my mom wanted to know. "Open them."

So that's what I did. One by one I slid my finger under the sealed flaps and ripped them open. And each time my mom kissed me and offered her congratulations.

"What's wrong?" she asked, taking the letters and rereading them for herself. "You should be happy."

"I know. I am." In fact, I sounded about as happy as if I'd been accepted to dog-grooming school.

"Why don't you shower and get dressed and later we'll go out for dinner. Anywhere you want. We need to celebrate."

"I don't feel much like celebrating."

She laid her arm around my shoulder and pulled me in close. "Okay, you rest and we can celebrate tomorrow night when you're feeling better."

I knew I should have been ecstatic about my acceptances. I'd gotten exactly what I wanted, and now I'd have to choose. I had to make a choice. Another choice. And I knew what that would have to be.

I knew I had to break up with Luke, but there was no way I could walk into school tomorrow and face him. And there was no way I could call him and hear his voice and still go through with it.

So I did something I never thought I'd do, something that was so pitiful I couldn't even believe I'd actually view it as a viable option.

I slid out of bed, went over to my desk, and sat down at my computer. Before I could chicken out, I forced my fingers to start tapping the keyboard, and in less time than it had taken me to change Luke, the send button was pressed and it was over. I'd sent Luke an e-mail that said I wanted to break up.

And that night, for the first time in almost three months, I didn't call Luke. And he didn't call me.

chapter twenty-four

I'd been back at school for less than six minutes
and already I was under assault.

"We heard you broke up with him, by e-mail no less." Josie
smiled. "Nice touch."

"So, it's over? The guide works?" Lucy and Josie waited for my
answer. "In three days we have to put it in the time capsule and
we need an answer."

"I think so. I really think Luke's changed."

"That's amazing." Josie hugged me. "See, I knew you could do
it. He'll probably be apologizing to me any day now."

"Probably," I told her.

"I bet you're glad the experiment is finally over."

"I still can't believe you got Luke to really fall for you." Josie
smiled and it was obvious she was proud of me.

All day Tuesday, I avoided Luke as best I could, and it seemed to be working. If I saw him coming down the hall, I'd duck into the nearest doorway (which is how I ended up in the first-floor janitor's closet for fifteen minutes while Luke and his lacrosse friends stood outside talking about the upcoming game against Country Day School). I ate in the cafeteria with Lucy and Josie, and he never showed up. I figured he was probably at Sam's eating his potato logs, dripping ketchup all over himself without anyone there to help clean it up. At least I didn't have to watch the Lunch Legion cater to him. I just couldn't have handled watching that.

Any time we couldn't avoid each other, like in English class, I knew Luke was shooting me dirty looks, even if I never actually met his eyes long enough to prove it. I could just feel him watching me from the last row, like there was an accusing finger pointing at my back—*That's the bitch who broke up with me in an e-mail—even after she told me it was wrong.*

"Man, he's pissed at you," Lucy told me after one particularly nasty look. "Job well done."

"Yeah, well, at least it's over."

"And Luke changed," Josie reminded us. "And that was the point, right?"

"Right," I agreed, even though I didn't agree anymore. That may have started out as the point, but once Luke stood me up at the dance there had been another point. To prove that nice girls didn't have to finish last. To prove that I had it in me to act just as detached and cruel as all the guys we hated. All along I'd almost believed the test was to see if I could change Luke. But now I realized the real test was whether or not I could change. And I'd done it. I'd proved I could be just as much of a jerk as the guys.

"Do you want to do something after school?" Lucy asked.

"Maybe go through the guide one more time before Friday's unveiling? I could meet you after practice."

Josie shook her head. "Can't."

"What, hot date?" Lucy joked.

"Riding practice." Josie rolled her eyes. "Maybe tomorrow?"

"Maybe," I told her, knowing perfectly well I had no intention of reading the guide ever again.

On Friday at two o'clock the entire school was on its way to the gym to watch our senior class place objects in the time capsule—which wasn't so much a capsule as a blue plastic Rubbermaid storage container with a snap-on lid.

Heywood liked to make a big deal about the last all-school assembly, and, because everyone got to skip last period, we always looked forward to it, if only because it meant we missed biology lab. But this year I wasn't looking forward to it. I was dreading it.

Lucy, Josie, and I had made plans to meet in front of the girls' locker room so we could all walk into the gym together. A united front.

I waited by the water fountain with the guide, and I knew the moment I saw them coming toward me that I couldn't do it. I couldn't do it to Luke.

"I can't do this," I announced when they reached.

"What do you mean, you can't do this?" Josie asked. "You already did it. The guide works."

"I meant I can't put the guide in the capsule." This wasn't about choosing between my best friends and a guy. It was about doing what's right. And being honest. And, honestly, there was nothing to be gained by putting the guide in the capsule. And humiliating Luke in front of the whole school was nothing to be proud of.

"Sure you can." Josie reached for the brown notebook I was carrying facedown against my hip, but I pulled away.

"No, I can't," I repeated before blurting out the four words I was sure were going to change everything. "I slept with him."

Lucy stepped back from me, bumping into the garbage can and knocking it over. "You slept with who?"

I held my breath for a second before answering. "Luke."

A group of middle school girls came around the corner on their way to the gym, thank God. I only wished they could stay there, a buffer between me and Josie.

"You did *what*?!" Josie screamed as they passed us. Her voice was loud enough, and their fear of seniors big enough, that they scrambled into the gym as fast as their legs would carry them.

"I'm sorry, I didn't mean for it to happen," I gushed, hoping Josie would understand. "It just happened."

Josie looked perfectly white, which was quite a task considering she'd been using a new bronzer her mother got from her makeup artist. She wrapped her arms around her waist and doubled over. "I think I'm going to be sick."

Lucy rested her hands on Josie's shoulders and led her to the water fountain, where she rubbed Josie's back while Josie leaned over the sink and splashed cold water on her face.

Lucy moved aside as more students headed to the gym. "Please tell us you're kidding."

I shook my head.

"Then please tell us that you sacrificed your body for the sake of the project."

"When?" Josie asked through the drops of water.

"Saturday night," I answered, my voice wobbly.

"What the hell were you thinking?" Josie shrieked. "You said you hated him. You said he needed to be reformed. You were supposed to be making him a better boyfriend for me!"

It wasn't until she stopped yelling at me that I noticed a group of sophomore guys—a group that included my brother—watching the entire scene from the entrance to the gym.

Lucy shook her head, confused. "Wait a minute—this just happened? Saturday night?"

"I'm so sorry," I told them in a voice so meek it almost sounded like I was whispering. There was nothing else I could say, nothing left for me to do.

I set the overturned garbage can upright and tossed the notebook into it, watching as it landed between two Gatorade bottles and a wad of paper towels.

Lucy continued rubbing Josie's back and I knew right then and there, as her hand circled Josie's shoulder blades, that I'd lost her. Lucy was on Josie's side.

"How could you do this to her?" Lucy asked. "How could you lie to us all along?"

I shook my head. "I don't know. I didn't mean to."

"How could you do this to me?" Josie yelled. "He was my boyfriend! And you decided to screw him?"

I glanced over at TJ, who, from the way he uncomfortably looked down at his shoes, had obviously heard that last piece of information.

"I didn't mean—" I started to answer, but Josie wouldn't let me.

"Forget it," she snapped, and then pushed open the door to the girls' locker room and disappeared. "I'm out of here."

Lucy didn't move. She didn't yell at me or say it would all be okay. And I knew it wouldn't.

"Remember when Josie was caught shoplifting those earrings? She knew I had that necklace in my sneakers. She saw me drop it in there. And you know what? She didn't say a word to that security guard, even though she could have. She got in trouble all by herself, and she didn't have to." Lucy let out a long breath and shook her head at me before starting for the door after Josie. "I feel like I don't even know you anymore, Emily. When you said you were done being nice, you weren't kidding. There is nothing nice about screwing over your best friend."

Then Lucy was gone and I was left standing alone.

"Can we have the senior class down on the floor?" Mr. Wesley asked into the microphone set up in the center of the basketball court.

Everyone sitting on the front row of the bleachers rose up and walked to center court. Lucy and Josie were sitting as far away from me as possible. Only Luke outdid them in the Emily avoidance department—he hadn't even bothered to show up.

"This is it," Mandy Pinta whispered, and nudged me closer to the Rubbermaid container.

Josie and Lucy made sure they were nowhere near me as the senior class made a semicircle around the time capsule and one by one Mr. Wesley called people up to place their contribution inside.

Miranda, Elinor, and Carrie went first, and we watched as they put a *People* magazine and tube of MAC Pink Poodle lip gloss into the capsule.

When Mr. Wesley called out our names, I walked up to the time capsule like a prisoner walking to the electric chair. I didn't look to my left or right, I just kept my eyes on that Rubbermaid container as if it were the most important thing in the world. I didn't have to look up to know that Lucy and Josie were watching me.

"We don't have anything," I told Mr. Wesley.

"Didn't you know you were supposed to contribute something?" he asked me, obviously annoyed.

"We couldn't come up with anything," I offered and then stepped back into the group, where I just wanted to disappear.

After a few more useless contributions, Mr. Wesley reached for the plastic lid, ready to seal up the container for the next ten years. "Well, that does it."

"Wait!" Luke stepped forward from out of nowhere, his right arm bent behind his back so we couldn't see what he was holding. "There's one more thing."

He smirked at our class, but I could swear that smirk was meant just for me.

Luke made his way over to the Rubbermaid container and then turned to face the bleachers. And that's when I saw it. A brown spiral notebook with marker across the front.

Luke looked right at me as he held the notebook up for everyone to see.

"I have something here I thought you'd all find interesting. It's a little book written by our very own Emily Abbott." Luke paused and flipped through the notebook pages. "Emily thought it would be fun to write a book about how horrible I am—how horrible all guys are. I guess she thinks she's so perfect, she can impart her infinite wisdom to the rest of us."

I stood frozen. It could only go downhill from here.

"This is Emily's contribution to the time capsule," Luke continued, but at that point the room went blurry and his voice started to sound like he was speaking into a tunnel.

There was no way this was happening. There was no way Luke got his hands on a notebook I'd thrown in the garbage.

And that's when I saw the familiar face standing beside the

bleachers watching me. And I knew. It was the only explanation that made any of this make sense. I'd been ratted out by my very own brother. TJ had watched me toss the notebook in the garbage can and then he'd taken it out and given it to Luke!

There was only one problem with my conspiracy theory—TJ looked as horrified as I felt by Luke's revelation. He didn't exactly seem thrilled with the idea of being related to me at the moment. And I couldn't blame him.

I glanced across the semicircle of seniors and caught the eye of the girl standing directly across from me. Josie was watching me with eyes so hard and cold I swear she never even blinked, not once. And those eyes told me everything I needed to know.

My best friend had given Luke the guide.

Mandy stood in the stall doorway watching me wipe my mouth with toilet paper.

"Are you okay?" she asked.

I nodded my head, which was still reeling from the scene in the gym.

Mr. Wesley had refused to let Luke put the guide in the capsule but at that point it didn't matter. Everyone knew. And before I could be further humiliated in front of the entire school, before Luke could continue his litany of sarcastic observations on the life of Emily Abbott, I had ran to the girls' locker room to hide.

"Wow, Emily, I can't believe you did that!" Mandy held up her hand and waited for me to high-five her. "Way to go!"

Like everything else, there were two sides to this situation—the people who applauded me, and the people who thought I sucked. I kind of sided with the latter.

I could barely manage a meek "Thanks."

"Don't listen to what Luke said, a lot of us think what you did was great. Long overdue, in my opinion." Mandy handed me a wet paper towel and waited for me to leave the safety of my stall. "All the guys think you're a bitch, of course, but so what? Right?"

"I just can't believe this," I repeated for what must have been the hundredth time. "How could this have happened?"

I had to get out of there. I had to go home and as far away from Heywood as possible. "I'm leaving."

Mandy moved aside but grabbed my arm before I made it to the door. "I wouldn't go out there if I were you—too many angry guys with a few choice words to say to you."

"Damn," I muttered, and this time when I walked into the stall I locked it behind me.

All I could think about was Luke and Saturday night. How could he have done this to me after Saturday night? A wave of nausea was making its way back into my throat.

"Emily?" Mandy rapped lightly on the door. "I know this might not be the best timing, but do you have a copy of the guide I could read?"

I flushed the toilet so I wouldn't have to listen to her anymore.

chapter twenty-five

"How could you do that to me?" I screamed. Finding Luke hadn't been that difficult. It was the Friday before a Saturday-morning lacrosse game. He didn't have practice, so I figured he'd just gone home. And that's exactly where I found him, sitting in his kitchen eating a frozen pizza. Of course, I had to wait almost two hours for the school to clear out before venturing from my stall.

"How could *I* do that to *you*?" Luke laughed at me and reached for another slice. "Who are you kidding, Emily? I didn't do anything to you that you didn't do to me first."

I smacked my head with the palm of my hand—a little to hard. "I'm such an idiot. Here I actually thought you'd changed."

"Well, if anyone changed, it was you, Em. Who would have guessed that 'the girl most likely to be nice' could be such a bitch?"

263

"Look who's talking?! You purposely humiliated me in front of the entire school! Here I thought you were acting differently because you'd changed, and you were still a jerk all along."

"I didn't act differently because I'd changed, Emily. I changed because you acted differently."

I felt like I was listening to Luke recite a tongue twister—Peter Piper picked a peck of pickled peppers.

"And what is that supposed to mean? You changed because I acted differently?"

"What I mean is that I thought you weren't playing the usual games with me. You didn't tell me it was okay if I didn't call and then get pissed when I didn't. You didn't say one thing and then do another."

"That's because I was trying to train you," I yelled before realizing what I'd said.

"Train me." Luke laughed again, as if this whole situation amused him—or was so completely unbelievable he just couldn't figure out how else to react. "Like a dog? Was that the idea? You thought you could get me to sit and obey and all you had to do was reward me with *sex*?"

Even after the single syllable word rang in my ears, I couldn't believe he'd said it.

"I cannot believe you just said that to me." The lump growing in my throat didn't allow it to come out as anything louder than a whisper.

"So, was it rewarding, Emily? I'm assuming after seeing your ex-boyfriend last weekend you had something to compare it to."

I must have looked shocked, because Luke seemed pleased. "Josie told me about that, too."

I managed to recover long enough to answer. "I did not sleep with my ex-boyfriend, Luke."

"Really? Then why didn't you tell me you were going to see him? Why did you lie to me?"

God, Josie had told him everything. And now that Luke was giving me a replay of what I'd said and done, I couldn't exactly deny any of it. Everything he was saying was true.

Luke shook his head and made a *tsk-tsk* sound, feigning disappointment, but it came out sounding more sarcastic than truly disappointed. "Here I'd thought you were someone who didn't play games and it turns out the whole thing was one big game for you."

"I threw the guide out," I reminded him. "Doesn't that count for something? I wasn't even going to put it in the capsule."

"Oh, gee, thanks, Emily. That really makes up for the three months you lied to me." Luke finished off his pizza and pushed back his chair to get up. "You know, Em, if you just needed to sleep with me to prove that you have the awe-inspiring ability to change another person, I wish you would have told me. I would have screwed you a hell of a lot sooner."

"How can you even talk to me like that?" I tried not to blink, but the tears filling my eyes made that difficult. "How can you be so mean?"

"Me? You need to take a look in the mirror, Emily. And then ask yourself the same question."

chapter twenty-six

TJ looked up from the Game Boy he held in one hand, and the bag of Doritos he held in the other. "Tough day?"

I flopped down on the couch next to him. "What do you think?"

The only sound in the room was the crunch of Doritos and some engine-revving noises coming from the Game Boy as TJ considered his answer.

"I think the mighty Emily has fallen," he finally told me, licking orange dust from his fingers. "And finally, for the first time, she has nobody to blame but herself."

"Gee, thanks for all your support, TJ." I reached for a pillow and hugged it to my chest. "You really know how to make a girl feel better."

"Look, I read what you wrote about Luke in the notebook. So, why do you care what he thinks of you?"

"Because I . . ." I stopped before the words came out, before I told TJ why I cared what Luke thought of me. Or that I cared what he thought of me at all. At this point there was no explanation that would make sense. "Because he said those things about me in front of the entire school."

"Yeah, I guess there is the whole public humiliation thing." TJ nodded, obviously seeing my point. "Still, if you don't care what Luke thinks, it really shouldn't matter, right?"

"Right," I agreed. Only that was the problem. I did care what Luke thought. And it really did matter.

Even though TJ went out with his friends that night, I stayed in. As if I had any choice. With my two best friends convinced I was a complete backstabber, and my onetime pseudo boyfriend no longer talking to me because I was a complete liar, going out wasn't exactly an option. Not that I really wanted to.

"How was your day?" my mom asked, coming over to my bed and sitting down.

I looked up and she got her answer.

"What's wrong?"

I lost my two best friends. I lost my boyfriend who wasn't supposed to really be my boyfriend. Not to mention my virginity—which of course, I wasn't about to mention. I wanted sympathy, and telling my mother that I'd had sex with Luke surely wasn't the best way to go about that.

"Nothing," I answered, but as soon as she laid a hand on my head and started stroking my hair, I lost it. I felt my chest caving in, like my lungs were collapsing. I started gasping for breath, and as soon as I opened my mouth the tears started. Full, round drops landed on my comforter like water balloons and then seemed to explode before they seeped into the cotton.

My mom didn't say anything; instead, she crawled into bed next to me and pulled my head to her chest. She continued to stroke my hair and make a *shh* noise, like she was trying to get a baby to go to sleep.

It could have been a few minutes or a few hours, I really didn't know. Eventually all I had left in me was a few jagged breaths and the sniffles. My tears dried up and the only thing remaining in me was an empty hole. As I rested my head against my mom's chest, I could hear her heart beating against my ear. For some reason I started counting the beats, maybe because I was sure my own heart would fail at any moment.

Finally, she pulled away and turned my head to face her. "Tell me what happened."

So I did. I told her about the guide and how I wanted to change Luke. I told her I'd really started to have feelings for Luke, real feelings. And I told her about Josie.

"None of that sounds like the Emily I know," she concluded, trying to understand my mishmash of names and events.

"That was the whole point."

"What was the whole point?" Now she looked completely confused. "To manipulate Luke? To deceive him? To hurt Josie?"

When she put it that way, it sounded even worse. "No, the point was to not be nice."

"Well, you achieved that, I think."

"I was tired of being nice. Look what it got me—Sean bailed on me and I didn't even do anything wrong."

"No, you didn't do anything wrong, but you did move away," she reminded me.

"So, that's just an excuse. Besides, I was tired of being nice. All it does is get you hurt. You teach people how to be nice for a living and look what happened to you!" As soon as the words were out, I regretted them.

She pulled away, like she'd been slapped. "And what exactly do you think happened to me?"

"It's pretty obvious, isn't it? Dad isn't here."

"Your dad didn't not move with us because I was too nice, Emily."

"Well, being nice certainly didn't do you any good."

"Look, he's a forty-seven-year-old man who needed some time to figure out what he wants. I'm not going to force him to do what I want just because it would be easier for me. You can't force people to do what you want them to do, Emily. People don't change unless they want to."

"Lucy said I was the one who changed. She said the person she remembered would never screw over a friend."

"The Emily I know wouldn't do that, either. But she would fall for someone she thought was a good person."

"I'm not sure he really was a good person—when he and Josie were going out, he broke up with her in an e-mail."

I knew she'd agree. Last year my mom launched an entire series of seminars about the Web—she called it "Netiquette."

"Yeah, that's probably not the best idea." She gave me a lopsided frown.

I nodded, but didn't tell her that it was also the same way I'd broken up with Luke. I looked bad enough as it was.

"Still, one mistake doesn't mean he's a horrible person, does it?" my mom asked, clearly implying that I'd made a mistake and still wasn't a horrible person.

"Luke made more than one mistake," I pointed out, and that's when I told her about how Luke got up in front of the whole school and lambasted me.

"Well, you can't really blame him, can you?" she asked, her voice still soft.

Of course I could! What was she talking about?

"But he is to blame," I insisted. "He was horrible."

"So were you," she reminded me.

"But he was horrible before. I just wanted to prove I could make him better."

"Really? What you did was pretty thoughtless and kind of mean, and I know that's not like you. So it seems to me that you're the one who should have acted better."

Her answer sounded eerily similar to Lucy's.

"I'm sorry this happened, Emily, but I really don't know what else to tell you."

My mother had six books under her belt, years worth of columns, seminars that toured across the country, and she couldn't come up with one piece of advice?

"If somebody wrote to you and asked what she should do in this situation, what would you tell her?" I asked.

My mom tipped her head to the side and considered my question. "I guess I'd tell her that being nice doesn't get you hurt. Being human is what gets you hurt, and you can't exactly help that."

I knew she wouldn't give me the answer I was looking for, which was that the situation called for a nicely written apology note to make it all better.

"Hey, why don't you go take a hot shower," she suggested before patting my leg and standing up to leave. "Maybe it will make you feel a little better."

I seriously doubted that good personal hygiene would make my situation any better, but it was about the only option I had.

An hour later I was clean, shampooed, and smelling like freesia bath gel, but no less depressed. I figured as long as I was going to be miserable I may as well be well fed. But on my way downstairs I noticed the faint, fuzzy light of the TV coming from my mom's room. I stopped and knocked on her door.

"Come on in," she told me.

"I was going to get myself something to eat, do you want anything?"

She shook her head no and patted the empty spot next to her. "I'm just watching a movie. You can watch with me, if you'd like."

Watch a movie or attack a pint of Ben & Jerry's? While the Ben & Jerry's would taste awfully good going down, I knew I'd hate myself tomorrow. Besides, we probably only had sorbet anyway. I crawled onto the bed and staked out the vacant spot my dad once occupied.

"What are you watching?" I asked.

She didn't answer right away, and when she did there was an ironic grin on her face. "*My Fair Lady.*"

"How appropriate."

"I promise it's just a coincidence."

I knew it was, it's not like my mother has control over the televised programming of cable stations, but it was still impeccable timing. A commercial had just ended, so we both stopped talking and lay there quietly while we watched Professor Henry Higgins try to turn Eliza Doolittle into someone better, even if there was really nothing wrong with her to begin with. She just didn't fit his view of what a woman should be like.

My mom never said a word, but I knew what she was thinking: that I was Henry Higgins without the accent. And Luke was Eliza Doolittle without the flower cart and corset.

When the movie was over, neither of us made an attempt to move.

"I'm so cozy," I told her, burying myself even deeper under the comforter. It smelled like fabric softener, and I couldn't help but wonder what my father's new bed smelled like. There was no way it smelled this good.

"You know, I went by the old house," I told her, leaving out the part about Luke taking me there. "Remember that huge tree where Dad hung the rope swing? The one in the side yard?"

"I sure do. I remember when your dad hung it up there. He almost killed himself."

"They took down the tree. It's gone."

"The Dutch elm disease probably finally got it. We should have cut it down years ago, but you guys loved that swing, so we kept it up."

"So you knew it was sick?"

"Yeah. For a while. I kept telling your dad to take it down but he refused. He said you and TJ enjoyed it too much to cut it down."

"So he kept it up for me?"

She nodded.

"Then why isn't he here?" I asked. "Why'd he stay in Chicago?"

My mom turned on her side and faced me. "I think that's something you should ask him."

I shrugged. "At least you could have told him it wasn't okay for him to stay."

"You know, Emily, I'm not perfect. Your dad isn't perfect. Nobody is." My mom reached for the remote control and turned off the TV. "Do you have any plans for tomorrow?"

I shook my head. "Nope."

"Why don't you come into the city with me and after my seminar we can go out for lunch or something?"

I knew she just felt sorry for me, but so did I. "Sure."

My mom smiled. "So, here we are."

"What's going to happen to us?" I asked her, not really knowing if I wanted an honest answer.

"I think we'll make it," she assured me. "Good things happen to good people, right?"

I nodded into the pillow, hoping that old saying still applied to me.

chapter twenty-seven

My mom used to take me to the Park Plaza Hotel when I was little. We'd go there for afternoon tea in Swan's Café so she could observe lapses in etiquette for future article and book ideas. I used to love dressing up like a "lady," as my mom called it, and sitting behind the gilded railing overlooking the lobby. With the starched table linens and fine china, I couldn't help but feel like I was supposed to sit perfectly still, my shoulders thrown back. Even now, I immediately sat up a little straighter, aware of my shoulders and chin (imagine a piece of string running up your spine through your head and into the sky, and then imagine pulling the string until you're sitting absolutely straight—weird, I know, but it works).

I used to pretend I was a princess, although without the fabulous wardrobe and prince standing below my window calling my name. But right now there definitely wasn't a prince who wanted to be within one hundred miles of me.

On the ride into the city I kept thinking about what my mom said last night, how she'd never even told my dad that she didn't want him to stay behind while we moved.

"Don't you want Dad to come home?" I asked.

"Of course I do," she answered.

"So why don't you call him and tell him that."

"It's a little more complicated than that, Em," she told me. "One phone call isn't going to make everything all better."

Even though she didn't give me a reason, I knew why. She was afraid of looking foolish or seeming desperate or, even worse, hearing the answer she didn't want to hear.

"It can't hurt," I encouraged. "Just tell him how you really feel. What's the worst thing that can happen? He's already not here."

My mom didn't answer right away. "I'll think about it."

While I was dispensing some well-earned advice to my mom, I figured I may as well take it myself.

I held on to the door's armrest and prepared for my mother's reaction. "I don't think I want to go to Brown." There, I'd said it.

"Did you get in?" she asked, as if she'd missed something.

"No, the letter hasn't arrived yet. But even if I do, I don't want to go."

She flipped on her blinker and changed lanes. "Okay."

Wait a minute, did she really just say okay? "Okay? Didn't you want me to go to Brown?"

"I want you to go where you want to go. I thought you wanted to go to Brown, so I was all for it. Where are you thinking of now?"

Her reaction threw me for such a loop I wasn't prepared to answer. "Maybe Smith. I don't really know, I thought I'd wait and see before I decided."

"That's probably a good idea. Whatever you choose, I'm sure it will be the right decision."

"What about you?" I asked.

"What about me?"

"Have you made a decision about calling Dad?"

She glanced over at me and smiled. "Emily."

"Okay, you don't have to tell me now," I assured her. "But whatever you choose, I'm sure it will be the right decision."

After the seminar and lunch, Mom dropped me off at home and went to the grocery store to do some shopping.

"Isn't there anything to eat around here?" TJ asked, opening and shutting kitchen cabinet doors. "I'm starving."

"Mom just went to the store."

"Why don't you just call Luke?" TJ asked, peering into the near-empty refrigerator.

"Just call him?" I repeated, expecting TJ to turn around and provide a more detailed explanation for this bizarre suggestion. "You mean, just pick up the phone and say, 'hey, what's up,' like nothing's happened?"

TJ nodded, still looking into the refrigerator and not at me, and reached for a carton of lemonade. "That's what I said. I know you think he's a dick, but last night I ran into Luke at the movies and he wasn't looking all that happy. He even asked me how you were doing."

"He did?" A slew of emotions swirled through me. Relief. Excitement. Confusion. But the one that I clung to the hardest was hope.

God, I hoped TJ wasn't mistaken. "Are you sure?"

TJ rolled his eyes at me. "I think I can remember a conversation

I had less than twenty-four hours ago, Emily. Just because I'm not on the honor roll doesn't mean I'm an idiot."

"I never said you were an idiot," I replied, to which TJ just rolled his eyes again and started drinking out of the lemonade carton. "So, what did you tell him?"

"I told him the truth." He stood there gulping down the last of the lemonade while I waited for his answer. Finally he put down the carton and wiped his mouth with the sleeve of his shirt. "Look, I'm not the bad guy here. You're angry at Dad, you're angry at Sean, you make a freaking guide outlining in detail everything that's wrong with the male species. Why can't you just admit you were wrong?"

"I was the one who threw away the guide," I reminded him, sounding more defensive than I'd intended.

"Why can't you just admit that there doesn't always have to be somebody to blame? That sometimes it's not as easy as picking who's right and who's wrong?"

"I don't do that."

TJ just rolled his eyes at me, as if to say, "Yeah, right."

chapter twenty-eight

"What are you doing here?" I stopped in the kitchen doorway and thought maybe I was seeing things. It was Sunday morning and there was my father standing at the kitchen counter with a package of Thomas' English muffins in one hand and a jar of jelly in the other.

"I got in late last night. I didn't want to wake you or your brother up. Do you want an English muffin?" my dad asked, pushing down the toaster knob. "I'm making one for your mom."

The father who had been absent for four months was now offering to make me breakfast. "Sure."

"Eggs, too?"

"Why not?" I nodded, not exactly sure what was going on. "I think I'm going to go upstairs and get dressed. I'll be right back."

I went upstairs, but I didn't get dressed. I went to find my mom.

"What's Dad doing here?"

"Moving in." My mom continued making her bed, as if she wasn't the least bit surprised that my father was in our kitchen wielding a spatula and toasting English muffins.

"And how did this happen?" I asked.

"Why don't you ask him?" she suggested and I headed downstairs to do just that.

"So, your mom tells me you've had quite a week."

I took a bite of my English muffin and nodded. I made sure to lean over my plate so the grape jelly didn't land in my lap, and I couldn't help thinking of Josie.

"I'm not sure I'm done being mad at you." I glanced down the hall, looking for my dad's suitcase.

"The rest of my stuff is being shipped," he told me. "And I know you're angry with me."

I took a deep breath and forged on. "Why didn't you move with us? Why did you decide to come home now?"

He put down the paper and looked up at me. "I'm more than willing to tell you, Emily. I only wish you'd given me a chance to explain."

I put down my juice and waited. "I'm listening now."

"I don't know if this is going to make any sense to you, but things change, people change, and sometimes that's hard. You're about to go off to college, and TJ will be gone, too, in a couple of years. Your mom and I thought a change of scenery would be good, but when it came time to move, I think we both realized that it wasn't where we lived that made a difference. It wouldn't change the fact that things were going to be different no matter where we were."

"And?"

"And I guess I'm sorry that I didn't explain that sooner. When your mom told me to stay in Chicago and figure things out, I just—"

I cut him off before he could finish. "*Mom* told you to stay in Chicago?"

"Well, yeah," he admitted. "She thought that maybe some time apart would make things clearer."

One thing was definitely clearer. "So Mom's to blame for all this?"

"Nobody's to blame, Em. There doesn't have to always be a finger pointed. Sometimes life is like that."

Sounded eerily like he was telling me that "shit happens."

I took a sip of my juice and considered what he'd just told me. "Well, I guess I'm sorry I didn't give you the chance to explain."

"Now it's your turn," he told me.

"My turn?"

"Your mom told me what's going on with Lucy and Josie. Any chance you can talk to them? Explain what happened?"

"I don't know," I told him, even though what I was thinking was, *Probably not*. "I blew it. They hate me, Luke hates me. They'll probably never forgive me."

"Well, why don't you go see Lucy and give it a shot? It can't hurt, right? It sure beats sitting around here wondering."

Still, wondering if my friends would ever forgive me was way better than learning for a fact that they wouldn't.

"I don't know."

"Sometimes you just have to take a chance and hope that people will make the right decision—Mom did and look what happened." He held up his English muffin. "You get my famous English muffin and eggs and you didn't even have to ask."

I reluctantly nodded. "I guess so."

"There's no guessing about it. Go." He pointed to the door. "Go tell them exactly how you feel."

He was right, I knew he was. This wasn't just going to blow over, and I wasn't willing to give up on my best friends just because they seemed ready to give up on me.

I pushed my chair back and stood up. "I'll give it a shot."

My dad smiled. "Good."

Before I turned to leave, I grabbed my remaining English muffin to take with me. "And Dad? Thanks for not cutting down the tree."

My dad tipped his head to the right like he didn't quite understand what I was saying, but I guess he wasn't willing to question a thank you from someone who'd been holding a grudge against him for months. "You're welcome, Emily."

"What are you doing here?" I stared at the guy who answered the door, thoroughly confused. "Where's Lucy?"

Owen stared back at me. "We were just hanging out. She asked me to get the door."

"Who is it?" I heard Lucy call from down the hall before she poked her head around the door to see who Owen was talking to. "Oh."

Sometimes events conspire to make a person feel like she's just had enough. First the Luke thing, then Josie, my dad shows up, and now Lucy and Owen.

Looking at Lucy standing there next to Owen, it was almost like seeing her for the first time. Really seeing her, not the girl who'd been my best friend in sixth grade, but the girl who was my best friend now—at least I hoped she still was. And by seeing Lucy, I saw all of us—the three of us. Lucy wasn't just the girl who was going to Duke on a soccer scholarship, Josie wasn't just the girl who carelessly went through guys, and I wasn't just the girl who was nicer than everyone else. Lucy liked Owen, Josie had really cared for Luke, and I was the girl who was capable of hurting her best friends.

"I wanted to talk to you," I told her. "I didn't know you'd have company."

Lucy stood there deciding what to do. "Do you want to come in?" she finally asked.

Lucy led us into the family room. "So, what did you want to talk about?"

I didn't answer. Instead, I glanced at Owen.

"Whatever you have to say you can say in front of him," she told me, crossing her arms over her chest like she was preparing for a fight. "He knows what happened."

Obviously.

"I just wanted to say I'm sorry," I apologized. "I never meant to hurt you or Josie."

Lucy thought this over before responding. "What I don't get is why you just didn't tell us you really liked Luke."

"I don't know. I guess I was afraid you'd be mad at me."

Lucy grimaced. "Well, it seems that happened anyway, doesn't it?"

"I guess so."

She dropped her arms to her sides and I took that as a sign that she was softening.

"I never would have lied to you if I thought it would turn out like this," I continued.

"How did you think it would turn out?" she asked.

"I don't know, just not like this."

Lucy bit her lip. "You know, we probably would have understood. I just wish you'd been honest with us, Em."

"Me, too," I conceded. "Believe me. If I could do it all over again, it would all be different."

"You really need to talk to Josie," Lucy told me. "You meant a lot more to her than Luke ever did, you know."

I hoped that was true.

We all stood there silently for a few minutes, and I could tell that Owen wished he could disappear. I knew exactly how he felt.

"Well," I began, not sure what I should say, "I guess I should get going."

"I'll walk you to the door," Owen offered, following me out of the room.

"Is Luke still pissed at me?" I asked him, not sure I wanted to know the answer.

Owen nodded and opened the front door for me. "What you did was shitty," he said. "Luke didn't deserve it."

"I know, Owen. I messed up. I know."

"Well, I hope Josie understands because I don't think Luke ever will."

I started to walk out the door, but Owen called me back. "And Emily?"

I stopped and turned around. "Yeah?"

"Luke apologized to Josie, just like you asked him to."

Lucy was just the first stop, sort of a warm-up on my groveling road show. Only it didn't occur to me until I was face-to-face with the script *H* on the Holden's black gate that I'd actually have to be *let in* to see Josie. Thankfully, once I announced myself, Mrs. Holden buzzed me in. Either those meditation classes were making her incredibly Zen or Josie hadn't told her what happened.

"What are you doing down here?" I asked when I found Josie in the stable with Ginger and Pinecone.

Josie whipped around to face me. "Who let you in?"

"Your mom."

She turned her back to me and continued brushing Ginger. Or maybe it was Pinecone, I couldn't tell the difference. "I thought the gate was supposed to keep out the undesirables."

Josie obviously wasn't planning to make this easy for me.

I decided to just get it over with before she had a chance to set off that CIA-endorsed security system and have me taken away in handcuffs for trespassing or something.

"Josie, I'm so sorry." I stepped toward her, but she backed away.

"Is that supposed to make it better?"

"I know it doesn't make it any better, but I mean it. I really am sorry. I made a huge mistake."

"You let me go on and on about how maybe Luke and I would get back together, and the entire time you knew that wasn't going to happen. How do you think that makes me feel?"

"Horrible."

"Good guess." Josie put down the brush. "You made me feel like an idiot, like my feelings didn't matter."

"They matter, Josie. Of course they matter," I told her.

"Do you know what makes this so bad?"

I shook my head, even though I had a feeling I knew.

"Luke was just a guy, Emily. But you were my best friend. I expected more from you. You should have told me as soon as you knew, or at least tried to stop."

"I never did it to hurt you, Josie."

"I don't know that I believe you, Emily. You were so hell-bent on not being the nice girl, you forgot that she was the person we liked. She was my best friend. I don't even know the girl who slept with Luke."

"It was me," I blurted out, and then quickly added, "I mean,

I'm the same person I was, Josie. I'm still your best friend. That hasn't changed."

"And what about Luke?"

"Look, I never meant for this to happen. I never intended to really like Luke."

"So, you really do like him?"

I nodded.

"A lot?"

"Yeah, a lot," I admitted, practically closing my eyes as I waited for Josie to start yelling at me.

Instead, she just asked, "Are you in love with him?"

I didn't say anything.

"I guess I have my answer."

"How I feel about Luke has nothing to do with you."

"It has everything to do with me, Emily. It's almost like you didn't want to believe me when I told you maybe Luke and I should get back together. Like you couldn't believe that I'd actually like someone for real."

"I didn't plan to hurt you, Josie."

"I want to believe you, Emily. I really do."

"Then believe me."

"Did you know that Luke apologized to me for the whole e-mail episode?" she asked.

I nodded.

"I'm assuming you had something to do with that?" Josie absent-mindedly stroked Ginger's—or Pinecone's—mane.

I nodded again and hoped I was right. "I thought you didn't like the horses."

"They're not so bad, I guess. But I'm still never going to be some superstar equestrian like my mom wants."

"That's okay," I told her, thinking that I was never going

to be the type of person who could hurt her friends and not care.

"I was afraid of losing you and Lucy if I told you the truth," I admitted. "I was afraid you'd hate me."

"I don't hate you, Emily." She actually seemed like she meant it. "I could never hate you."

I so wanted to believe her.

Josie shook her head at me. "I'm just not sure I can forget what you did."

"I'm not asking you to forget, just maybe forgive."

"Here." Josie tossed me another brush. "I could use some help."

"Is this Pinecone or Ginger?" I asked, rubbing the brush against the horse's neck in the same circular motion as Josie.

"You know what?" she confided, and for the first time since I arrived she cracked a small smile. "I have no idea."

> **The Guy's Guide Tip #105:**
> We're not perfect. If we can admit it,
> why can't you?

chapter twenty-nine

"Josie called while you were out," my mom told me when I came through the kitchen door.

"But I was just at her house." It didn't make any sense for Josie to call me fifteen minutes after I left her.

My mom shrugged. "She just said that you should go to Friendly's. Somebody's there waiting for you."

"Who?" I asked.

"I think his name was Eliza Doolittle."

I found Luke in a booth toward the back of the restaurant, sitting all by himself. He didn't notice me at first, and when I sat down across from him, he looked so startled I almost wondered if Josie hadn't told him I was coming.

"Why are you here?" I asked, sliding along the vinyl seat.

"You tell me. Josie called and told me to meet you here. She said you had something to say to me."

I did? I guess I did.

"I'm sorry."

Before Luke could say anything, a waitress appeared at our table. "Are you ready to order now?"

I watched Luke before I answered. There was no way I was going to order something before I knew if he planned on staying. But then I changed my mind. I wasn't going to wait for Luke's response to gauge what I should say. I already knew what I wanted.

"I'll have a strawberry Fribble, please," I ordered.

Luke hesitated and I found myself crossing my fingers for good luck. "I guess I'll have a Fribble, too. Strawberry."

Once the waitress collected our menus, we were alone again. Unfortunately, it was going to take more than an extrathick milkshake to make Luke forget about everything that had happened.

"I never meant for the guide to go as far as it did," I tried to explain. "It wasn't supposed to turn out like this."

Luke shook his head and tore the corner off the paper napkin sitting in front of him. "How was it supposed to turn out, Emily? Because as far as I can tell, you had plenty of chances to end this long before it got this far. But you didn't."

"If I'd told you about the guide you would have hated me."

He continued tearing the napkin into pieces until there was nothing left except a pile of odd little shapes.

Finally, he looked up at me. "And how would that have been different from the way I feel now?" he asked.

"You don't hate me," I told him, and hoped I'd be able to convince him it was true. "You can't just hate me overnight."

"I don't know what to believe anymore. I don't know when you're telling me the truth or when you're just pretending."

"I'm not pretending, I swear." My voice cracked and I could feel a lump growing inside my throat. I swallowed hard and hoped it would dissolve. "I couldn't fake the way I feel about you."

Luke silently considered my answer, but he wasn't offering any immediate forgiveness. And so I watched as he reached for the napkin dispenser, pulled another white sheet, and added to the growing mound in front of him.

"Did you really think I was so bad that you had to change me?" he asked.

I shrugged. "I didn't even really know you," I admitted. "I guess I wanted to think so."

And that was the truth. It was so much easier to believe that Luke was some bad guy who needed to learn how to be good. Or to think of my dad as the one who was wrong. Or even to look at Sean and see somebody who'd intentionally hurt me. It was so much simpler than trying to understand that sometimes people do things and say things and make decisions that aren't always right—just like I did with Luke. It doesn't necessarily make them bad. It just makes them human.

"They're hiring, you know." Luke pointed to a red sign hanging in the front window. "Maybe they'd let you bring your own apron."

"Maybe." I tried not to smile, but it didn't work.

"Why didn't you just tell Lucy and Josie about us? Or tell them that you didn't want to do the guide anymore?"

"I don't know," I told him, hating my answer even before I said it out loud. "I guess because I didn't want to admit I'd made a mistake."

"Is that what I was, a mistake?" he asked.

I shook my head and wanted so badly to take his hand, only I was afraid he wouldn't let me. "I made a lot of mistakes—lying to you and then lying to Josie and Lucy. But how I feel about you isn't one of them."

Luke reached for the salt shaker and held it in his hand while he thought. "You know why I sent you that valentine in sixth grade?"

"Because your mom made you?"

"No," he answered, and then broke out into a grin. "Well, maybe a little. But I could have sent it to anyone. I sent it to you because I thought you were nice."

"I was. I still am."

Luke sat back against his seat as the waitress placed our Fribbles on the table. "Anything else?" she asked, laying down two straws.

"How about an order of fries," I suggested.

She started to write on her pad of paper and then stopped. "Just one?"

"Yeah," I told her. "We're going to share."

Luke smiled and bumped knees with me under the table. Instead of moving my leg, instead of saying "excuse me" and politely giving Luke room, I kept it there pressed against him. And instead of feeling wrong, it felt absolutely right.

I'll never have any idea why Luke and I ended up together. We probably seemed like two of the most unlikely people to wind up making sense. Even now, looking back at how Josie and Lucy and I had changed, how our friendship would be different but not necessarily worse, I had a feeling we'd be all right. I guess relationships are just funny like that. It's impossible to figure out why some work out and others don't. Why someone can be so imperfect and still be the perfect person for you. Maybe, in the end, it's not about changing the person you care about. Maybe it's about learning what you can live with. Or maybe it's really about learning what you can't live without.

In ten years the Heywood Academy class of 1016 will open our time capsule and find some crusty old lip gloss, a few discolored magazines, and other remnants of our senior year. They'll think they know all about us—what we liked and disliked and what we thought was important. But they'll never know how over the course of four months so much happened and yet we all managed to survive—me, Lucy, Josie, Sean, TJ, my mom and dad, even Luke. They'll have no idea that I'd left behind a boyfriend and two best friends and come close to losing two friends and a boyfriend. They'll have no clue that hiding how you really feel and trying to make everyone happy doesn't make you nice, it just makes you a liar.

They'll never know why there's nothing in the capsule from three girls on the senior class list, and probably just think that someone made a mistake.

And I did. I made several, actually. But you know what? Sitting there with Luke sipping my strawberry Fribble, I wouldn't change a thing.